Sarah's Return

by

Jonas Saul

PUBLISHED BY:
Imagine Press Inc.
Ebook ISBN: 978-1-927404-52-2
Paperback ISBN: 978-1-998047-66-6
Hardcover ISBN: 978-1-998047-67-3

Sarah's Return

The Sarah Roberts Series

Dark Visions (One)
The Warning (Two)
The Crypt (Three)
The Hostage (Four)
The Victim (Five)
The Enigma (Six)
The Vigilante (Seven)
The Rogue (Eight)
Killing Sarah (Nine)
The Antagonist (Ten)
The Redeemed (Eleven)
The Haunted (Twelve)
The Unlucky (Thirteen)
The Abandoned (Fourteen)
The Cartel (Fifteen)
Losing Sarah (Sixteen)
The Pact (Seventeen)
The Terror (Eighteen)
The Chase (Nineteen)
The Betrayal (Twenty)
Sarah's Return (Twenty-One)
The Hunt (Twenty-Two)
The Delivery (Twenty-Three)
The Trap (Twenty-Four)
The Ultimatum (Twenty-Five)
The Depraved (Twenty-Six)
The Condemned (Twenty-Seven)
Payback (Twenty-Eight)
The Unknown (Twenty-Nine)
Wrath (Thirty)
The Damned (Thirty-One)

The Game (Thirty-Two)
The Decoy (Thirty-Three)
The Disappearance (Thirty-Four)
The Whole Truth (Thirty-Five)
Alex (Thirty-Six)
Parkman (Thirty-Seven)
Darwin (Thirty-Eight)
Aaron (Thirty-Nine)
Remains To Be Seen (Forty)

The Jake Wood Novels

The Immortal Gene (Book One)
The Immortal Target (Book Two)

Standalone Novels

'Til Death Do Us Part
The Drowning
The Woman in the Woods
The Threat
The Specter
The Mafia Trilogy
A Murder in Time
Frequency of the Dead

Co-Authored Novels

Collision Course (Written with Gary Ponzo)
There Will Be Blood (Written with Rania Stone)
The Soulless (Written with Rania Stone)

Short Story Collections

Twisted Fate (Tales of Horror)
Twists of Fate (Tales of Hope)

5

Chapter 1

The human cargo being shipped in the back of his truck were people who exchanged one set of difficult circumstances for another. Their way of life, their customs, something intrinsic and ingrained since birth, conditioned into them, now ripped away, stolen, due to economic conditions, political strain, or bad choices. Nomadic, in search of hope—a plight humans suffer from the most as it's such a flimsy god to worship—and for what? In the end, it's all just more struggle.

An empty stomach for years turns into a full stomach but an empty wallet. An empty wallet becomes an empty heart. Just like energy, hope never seems to die. Wherever, whenever we all end up suffering in some way, some fashion, regardless of how *hope*less—or *hope*-filled—our situation may become.

Yet, there's something about *choosing* our individual form of suffering. Left alone to make that choice, it seems we can handle it better. We can *live* with it—or at least try to—providing it doesn't kill us.

His family would be safe. He had made sure of it. He could live with that. Even if he'd suffered anxiety, lost sleep, and a pound of nervous sweat, he had arranged for their safe transport, their *safety*.

No one had to die because he was behind the wheel. A real, documented American, a man with pride and honor.

At least, he *hoped* not.

José Luis eased into the truck stop on Interstate 35 North as scheduled. He had done everything they said. He'd done it without complaint. And now, it was time for the final act, the final transaction. Then, everyone would be safe as documented citizens in America.

He eased his semi into a spot with easy access to the interstate and waited, engine running. Even though his heart beat double-time and his perpetually wet brow made him blink away the sweat, he held the wheel with confidence. He'd made it over the border with barely a second glance at his bill of lading. A truck full of coffins didn't garner much attention from the Mexican authorities or the Americans. Sure, they inspected the underside of the truck with mirrors attached to poles, they examined his papers and even his sleeper but waved him through without opening the rear doors. And even if they had, any inspector would've been greeted by a wall of large boxes containing actual coffins.

His *real* cargo was trapped in the front, hidden in a safe room hastily built by the people who promised to get his family to safety. A soundproofed small area with oxygen pumped in through tiny holes drilled into the underside. Water was supplied. A bucket secured to the side wall for a piss; heaven forbid someone needed it for something else. Papers were coming, as promised.

Across the parking lot, a man exited a black SUV and started toward him, a coffee cup in hand. The summer sun had set an hour before, but this guy wore sunglasses. José thought the guy would've resembled an FBI agent if he wasn't in a T-shirt and jean jacket. The slick back hair, the shades, the strut. Even the black SUV fit the role.

These guys had money. That was evident from the beginning with the renovations to the truck. It made sense they'd be driving an expensive Suburban.

The passenger door cracked open, and his contact climbed into the seat.

"Drive," he said. The word came out as the order it was intended to be.

Without a word, José put the truck in gear and eased back onto I-35 North, heading away from Laredo, Texas, from the border patrol's white SUVs with green stripes, from danger, from imprisonment. With each mile on the darkened highway, his anxiety lifted like a plug was removed in a clogged sink. It was a slow process, but it was going down.

"In two miles, take a right," the man said.

José glanced at him. "A right?"

The man met his gaze, then looked away.

José slowed the truck, watching for a road he couldn't see in the dark. He'd driven this highway a thousand times. That was why he was chosen. Well, that, and he wanted his family brought over from Mexico, too. As far as he was concerned, there was no right-hand turn on this stretch of I-35.

"Slower," the man said, his tone hardening.

The man eased forward in the passenger seat as if looking for something. The man's open jacket offered José a glimpse of the butt of a large weapon holstered at his waist.

Why bring a gun?

"Now," the man said abruptly. "Turn." The man pointed.

José slowed the truck, saw a small opening on the right between the brush, and made a wide turn onto a dirt road, his clogged sink of anxiety filling back up. This wasn't the arrangement. They were supposed to drive north to Dallas. The specific instructions were to pick up a man named Alejandro Hernándes at the truck stop shortly after leaving Laredo and then drive to Dallas, where he would be instructed to leave his *cargo*.

"Are you Alejandro?" José asked.

The man glared at him, nodded once, and then returned to the road.

The truck made the turn well as the ground was hard, baked by the relentless sun. There were tire tracks as well. Someone had driven this road as recently as hours before.

"Where are we going?" José asked.

The man—Alejandro—looked at him again, then looked away. He retrieved a cell phone from his pocket, texted something, then dropped it back in his pocket.

They rode in silence for several more minutes while José wondered if he could turn the large truck around to get back out to the interstate, provided they *were* going back to the interstate.

Was this the end of the road? Did he fail his family? He'd heard of these kinds of people, these human traffickers. Moving people through tunnels, over borders, from whorehouses to strip clubs. But the people in the back of his truck weren't like that. They'd all paid thousands of dollars to catch a ride to freedom, to America, to hope. Alejandro's people assured them they'd get there. Alejandro's people assured José they'd get there if he did what he was told.

So he drove.

Up ahead, headlights flashed once. Then again.

"Slow down. Stop by that vehicle."

José did as instructed, slowing to a stop beside a large box truck, possibly twenty-four feet in length. Some brand of fish was advertised on the side of the box.

A cloud of dust filtered into his headlights as his truck came to a complete stop.

Alejandro was looking at him. "Everyone gets in that truck. You drive. In several hours, this'll all be over."

Alejandro opened his door and dropped from sight, leaving his coffee cup in the holder. The passenger door slammed with finality.

As José got out, he wondered why they didn't tell him they were changing vehicles. Why would it matter? New details—changes in the plan—worried him.

Alejandro came around the front of the truck and gestured toward the other truck. "Go. Get in the driver's seat and wait for the cargo. Then wait for me. Do not watch. Understand?"

"Don't watch? Why? What's going to happen?"

Alejandro eased his weapon from the holster. Open carry in Texas. Something José was used to.

Alejandro kept the gun beside his thigh, a subtle threat.

"The truck. Driver's seat. No other option. Don't watch."

José hesitated as men strode past them, headed for the rear of his truck. In seconds, they had the back doors open and were inside, headed past the coffins toward the front where over thirty people waited for rescue, for America.

When José turned back to Alejandro, the gun was up and aimed at his eyes. José stepped back involuntarily, surprised at the sight of the barrel so close to his face.

"I don't need you," Alejandro said, his tone void of emotion. "Drive or don't drive." He waited a moment, then added, "Three … two …"

"Drive," José blurted and started for the smaller truck's cab. He kept his head down as he crossed the dirt, waiting for a bullet to enter his back. Shot out here, buried behind a pile of brush, covered in sand, his body would likely never be found.

He made it to the truck's door without a bullet. After climbing in, he rested his arms on the wheel and snuck a glance outside. Alejandro was at the back of the long semi, watching what was happening inside. Moments later, he helped the first of the undocumented individuals out of the truck and directed them to the fish truck.

Intent on following directions and not watching, José kept his head down as much as he could. Perhaps it wasn't such a big deal that Alejandro didn't want him to see the cargo transfer as much as he didn't want José's family to see him.

A fast operation, the human cargo was loaded, and Alejandro climbed up into the cab beside him, the gun back in the holster.

"Drive back toward interstate."

"What about my truck, my load of coffins? They were a legit contract."

Alejandro faced him, his jaw tight, eyes slit. "It will be safe. My man will drive it to Dallas. No one will suspect a thing." He adjusted himself in the seat, placing a hand on the dash, angling his body toward José. "Now drive."

José eased the truck forward, back toward I-35. As he passed his truck, two men were closing the rear doors. One of them glanced up at José, and their eyes locked. The man stopped moving and glared at José, a menacing steel glare. José saw death in the man's gaze.

"Eyes forward," Alejandro shouted.

José jerked in the seat as if he'd been shot.

"We are turning soon. No interstate."

"No interstate?"

"You have too many questions. Just drive."

With both hands on the dash now, Alejandro leaned forward as if scouting for the road.

"There. Turn here."

Another break in the bush revealed tire tracks turning right, which, as far as José could tell, ran parallel with I-35.

The smaller truck handled the turn easily; moments later, they bounced along a dirt track cut through the land.

His anxiety was back, that sink filled to overflowing. He couldn't quell the shaking in his hands. The plan had changed without reason and without answers. He dared not ask another question. How this night would end was anyone's guess. All he could do was what they told him to do.

Alejandro grunted. "Like *Breaking Bad*, yes?"

José turned to him. "*Breaking Bad*?"

"You with the questions again. Yes, *Breaking Bad*. Have you seen that show? Mr. White and Jesse?"

José shook his head. He was about to ask, *what show?* but kept his mouth shut.

"They took their meth trailer—well, it was an RV—onto dirt roads far from people to cook." Alejandro seemed more relaxed.

"Meth trailer? I don't understand."

Alejandro frowned, looked at him again, his upper lip curled in a snarl, then said, "Just fucking drive."

Soon, the road smoothed out. The headlights didn't offer much to illuminate where they were headed, so José kept his speed down. Alejandro checked his watch several times.

Not unexpectedly, he looked at José again and said, "Drive faster. You waste time."

José eased the pedal downward, increasing their speed. Soon, they were going dangerously fast, in José's opinion, but Alejandro seemed to know what he was doing. Although, whether he knew what he was doing or not, he was the one with the gun.

Something moved at the corner of his vision. José glanced to the left, but it was gone.

The truck jolted like it had hit something, bouncing hard on its shocks. A loud bang, like a punctured balloon, resounded throughout the cab. José let out a small shout as he gripped the wheel tightly, trying to keep the truck on the makeshift road.

Then another, even louder bang followed the first. The front of the truck canted forward and slightly to the right. A second later, it dropped to the left as well.

Alejandro shouted something, but the second noise drowned it out.

José turned to his passenger as the damaged truck came to a complete stop, the engine running. The gun was already out, and it was pointed at José.

"What did you do?"

José moved away, his left shoulder pushing into the window, hands raised.

"I did nothing. This isn't me."

"Get out. Inspect the truck. Tell me what we hit."

José fumbled with the latch, opened the door, and dropped to the ground, where he stumbled and almost fell. He caught himself, stood to his full height, and took in the truck. The front tires were completely flat. The back tires were, too.

They had to have driven over something sharp enough to cut through all the tires.

The door opened on the other side of the cab as Alejandro exited the vehicle. He came around the front of the truck, his weapon aimed at José. "What have you done?" The man's tone was less confident. José thought he detected doubt, or perhaps worry in it. Or was that fear?

"I did nothing, Alejandro," José pleaded. "I drove like you told me. That was it."

"I didn't tell you my name." The gun clicked.

"They did, they did," José blurted, hoping his last words

wouldn't be punctuated by fear and desperation. "They told me I was meeting a man at the truck stop. They said your name was Alejandro Hernándes." José held up his hands, eyes squeezed shut, waiting for the bullet.

After a moment, he opened his eyes and lowered his hands.

Alejandro strode past him, headed for the back of the truck. José reluctantly followed, the tension of the moment leaving his legs feeling like jelly over bone.

Alejandro checked the back door. It was locked. José noticed the heavy-duty lock they'd placed on the door. No one was getting in without a key, which undoubtedly Alejandro carried on his person.

All of the truck's tires were flat. They were stuck out here. And even if they went back for the rig, there was no way his semi would make it up this smaller, winding dirt road.

"Can we let everyone out to breathe?" José asked. "We can wait together, no? It must be stuffy inside there."

Alejandro moved away, staring off into the darkness behind the truck.

"I've never killed a man for asking questions," Alejandro said. "Tonight, I might make an exception."

He pulled something out of his jacket and clicked a button. The light from his cell phone illuminated the tracks behind the truck. He walked slowly, methodically, watching the ground, kicking at the dirt.

José leaned against the rear of the truck, the anxiety and tension exhausting him. He was suddenly so weary, wondering if he'd make the night without some form of a nap. Maybe sugar would help. He would eat one of the candy bars he always carried with him in the—ahh, but they were in his rig, his truck. Not in this fish truck.

"What the fuck is this?" Alejandro said.

José pushed off the truck, moved a couple of steps toward Alejandro, and then stopped. He didn't want to get too close to the man if he decided it was time to shoot him. At least fifteen feet separated them, and José could use the truck to hide behind.

"A spike belt …" Alejandro turned back to José. "Tell me, José Luis, what is a spike belt doing out here, laid in our path." He waited a heartbeat, then started toward José, his weapon raised again and aimed, ready to fire. "What the fuck have you done—"

Something shot up from the dirt to the left of Alejandro. It was so fast José only saw a blur of movement, a black shadow, moving upward as if bounced off a spring-loaded board. The object—a person dressed in black—launched into Alejandro as he was about to walk by. The person's gloved hands wrapped around Alejandro's wrist, yanking it toward the dirt, the gun's tip facing the ground. Their shoulder shoved into his elbow at the same time. The result was Alejandro's arm torqued backward in a way an arm should never go. His grip relaxed in the scuffle, his hand opening wide. The gun dropped harmlessly into the dirt. Alejandro's scream of pain came at the same moment José registered the distinctive sound of a bone cracking—more like popping—as his elbow caved in backward. In the dim light, José could see Alejandro's elbow tented upward in the unnatural opposite direction from the pressure of it being yanked that way by the other person's shoulder thrust.

Then, as fast as the figure launched upward, they dropped, spun in the dirt in a circle, legs long and strong, and knocked Alejandro off his feet. He dropped at an angle, and as the brain is hardwired to do, he raised his arms to break the fall.

There was an undeniable scream of absolute agony as Alejandro landed on his newly broken arm, collapsing it under his body.

The figure in black dove atop the man and did something to his face.

Then Alejandro fell silent.

The figure got to its feet, turned, faced José, and started toward him.

He recalled the movement that caught his eye before the tires burst. It was this person throwing the spike belt in their way.

"Wait, wait …" he raised his hands. "I'm not with him. I mean," he stammered. "I'm not a bad guy. I'm just the driver."

He couldn't believe what he was saying. What did that mean anyway?

The figure stopped in front of him. From the way she moved, the smooth, graceful edges, and the bumps in the front of her black suit, he could now see the figure was a female.

A woman?

She held out her hand, palm up.

He frowned. "You want the keys to the truck?"

Her head jerked once toward the back of the truck. The

hand jerked with impatience.

"I don't have the key for that lock."

She spun on her heels, jumped twice, and landed back on top of the unconscious Alejandro.

Something roared in the distance. José glanced over his shoulder, the sudden urge to release his bladder overwhelming him.

When was the last time I went to the bathroom?

Engines revved somewhere up ahead. Could it be the people she worked for? Or the people she worked *with*?

He snuck a glance back at the woman. She was just getting to her feet, a series of keys dangling from her hand. She ran to the back door and started working on the lock.

Curiosity made José walk a few steps forward to see what she was doing. She tried key after key. There had to be a dozen small keys on the ring.

Lights flickered in his peripheral vision. He looked left and saw large vehicles—probably SUVs—approaching them. A quick count got him to seven of them.

The lock snapped open.

The woman shoved the clamp out of the way, tore open the door on the right, and then shoved the door open on the left.

She snuck a glance around the truck.

"Get them out," she shouted, her voice an order not to be questioned. "Do it now."

The fear he felt for this woman seemed to be more than he had felt for Alejandro and his gun. She was like a magic woman, having risen from the dirt to destroy men in a single blow.

He acted upon her command without a second of hesitation—or any questions.

When he looked inside the truck, everyone was sleeping. That was odd. They'd only been inside the fish truck for ten minutes.

"Hey," he shouted. "Wake up."

No one moved. He frowned, then grabbed the handle on the right and hopped up into the back.

"Everyone, wake up."

He nudged a man closest to him. Dead weight. No response.

"No, no, no …" he muttered under his breath.

He dropped to his knees and grabbed what felt like a woman.

"Wake up!" he shouted at her.

After not getting a response, he checked her pulse. It was faint, but he felt one.

Drugged? Poisoned?

Vehicles had pulled up outside. He heard them stop hard with the sound of gravel and dirt crunching under their tires. The doors of multiple vehicles slammed shut. Men were giving orders to one another. Secure this, secure that.

In the darkened interior of the back of the truck, all José could think about was his family. He searched, but it was too dark to see who was who.

Then lights flooded the back. He glanced over his shoulder as multiple flashlights bobbed near the open door.

"Down on your knees," one of the men ordered. "U.S. Border Patrol. Hands behind your head where we can see them."

"But I have to find my cousins, my family."

"Down. Now! I won't tell you again."

The distinctive metallic sound of a weapon being readied convinced him to lower to his knees. It wasn't sweat in his eyes making him blink anymore; it was tears.

Someone grabbed his arms and yanked them back painfully. Handcuffs were snapped on his wrists, and he was drawn back up to his feet.

"My family …" he muttered as they ushered him to the open door.

Other men were rushing by him wearing paramedic shirts. The men who lowered him from the truck were in full tactical gear.

Three other men stood over Alejandro, talking.

It was over. They had been stopped, caught. He would go to jail. An American jail. And his family would be sent back to Mexico. It was all for nothing. He had failed his family. And the people Alejandro worked for would hear about it. They were powerful, rich men. José hung his head as he realized his life was forfeit.

"José Luis?" a man asked as he stepped into view.

José nodded.

"Bring him over here."

Two large men half dragged, half walked him toward a white U.S. Border Patrol SUV. Once there, the man who had asked his name moved in front of him again.

"I'm Chief Patrol Agent Michael Wilson with the U.S. Border Patrol. We know a small amount of what happened here. You will have to fill in the rest of the details. Will you do this?"

He nodded. There was nothing left to do but tell them everything. Remaining silent or talking made no difference to the people Alejandro worked for. José Luis was as good as dead.

"There was a girl here?"

It sounded more like a question, so José nodded again.

"You can speak, Mr. Luis. Was there a girl here a moment ago?"

"Yes."

"Where is she?"

José looked around, then met the border patrolman's eyes and shrugged.

"She was here. She stopped Alejandro from shooting me and then opened the back doors with his keys."

Two men ran up beside Wilson, who turned to address them.

He nodded toward Alejandro. "Status?"

"Alejandro is knocked out cold. Arm snapped in two. It's bad. Medics are working on securing it now before they move him."

"Weapons?"

"None that we could find."

Wilson glanced back at José. "You said he had a gun on you."

José nodded. "In the hand of the broken arm. He was about to shoot when that woman jumped up and broke his arm. He dropped the weapon in front of him. I saw it land in the dirt."

Wilson faced the men. They shook their heads.

"Gun's gone, sir."

"Find Sarah. Now!"

Sarah? José considered the name of the woman who had saved his life, then doomed him all in one moment.

Another man ran up to Wilson, shouldering his way past the other two as they left to look for the missing gun and that Sarah woman.

"The filter has been turned off. She was right, sir."

"Casualties?"

The man shook his head. "None, sir. Some of them are waking now."

"Good. Get them out of here. I want all of them checked out and deemed safe."

"Yes, sir." The man bolted off.

"Filter?" José asked. "What sort of filter? What was that woman Sarah right about?"

Wilson had pulled out a phone. He typed on it briefly, then looked up and met José's gaze. "The truck you were driving had a built-in filter to remove the oxygen from the air in the back. There was just enough to keep these people alive." He glanced at his watch. "By the time you made it to Dallas, many would be dead, if not all of them."

José could no longer trust his knees to keep him standing. He stumbled once, bumped the side of the SUV, and was righted by one of the men on either side of him.

"What …?" he managed to say. "No, that can't be. They were offered a new life."

Wilson was shaking his head. "These people weren't going anywhere. And neither were you."

"But that doesn't make sense," José protested. "These people paid a lot of money to be on this truck. They paid for transportation to a new life." He heard the plea, the desperation in his voice. "You must have it wrong. Maybe they got them to sleep to be quiet."

Wilson tapped on his phone again, then slipped it into the breast pocket of his Kevlar. "José, we understand you're upset. And I'm sorry you had to go through this, but those people weren't going on to new lives. Their money is gone." He paused, staring into José's glazed eyes. "Do you know how much money it is to garner fake documents? These people are undocumented from Mexico. Concealing them on American soil takes resources. Guys like Alejandro and his people take your money and get you over the border. Most times, they leave them to fend for themselves. Sometimes, we find an abandoned truck filled with bodies." He paused again, probably wondering how much more to say. "Look, when we find Sarah, you can thank her. But not until I smack her first."

"Uh, what?" José didn't know how he'd ever gotten so confused in his life. "Why would you smack her?"

"We were set up five hundred yards down the road. It was a perfect ambush. She didn't have to play a lone ranger. That was fuckin' dangerous." He placed a hand on José's shoulder. "She does *not* work for me. If she did, she'd infuriate me so much I'd probably end up killing her."

José considered what Wilson had said. Ambush, down the road. Had Alejandro seen the ambush, wouldn't he just shoot José? Or would he use him as a hostage to get away? Making Alejandro get out of the vehicle, singling him out, had worked much better.

But how could this Sarah girl have known where

Alejandro would be in order to hide in that exact spot in the dirt?

"I was as good as dead, too, wasn't I?" José asked.

Wilson nodded, his lips tightening and rising in a gesture of sympathy. Then he turned away and shouted, "Mack! Ron! Did you find Alejandro's weapon?"

"It's not here, sir," the men shouted back. "Sir, we've covered a full fifteen-foot radius. The gun's gone, sir."

"What about my spike belt? Have we retrieved that yet?"

"No sir," someone yelled back. "Spike belt is gone."

Wilson stepped away from José, moving closer to the edge of light strewn from the truck's headlights. He glanced up at the night sky.

Then he shouted like a wolf baying at the moon.

"*Saaaarrrrraaaahhhhh!*"

José dropped to his knees, then fell over and rolled into the fetal position on the Texas dirt. He wept for the family he almost lost and the role he had played in their near-death experience.

Chapter 2

Aaron Stevens set down the phone and stared at it, confused. What the hell was that all about? It didn't make any sense whatsoever.

He rubbed his clammy hands together as a pang of acid filled his stomach. Who should he call first? Who *could* he call?

He glanced out his home office window overlooking the city. They had settled on the tenth floor of an apartment building off of Bloor Street in an area of Toronto called Mississauga. Over the past six months, after almost a year of the nomadic lifestyle, they had gone through a deeply personal tragedy. Then Sarah had said she was leaving for a bit. She had to go. Don't follow. She would return when she was ready.

That was two weeks ago.

He'd promised to honor her request. After what they'd been through during their year off—their year away from Vivian's bidding—he was surprised Sarah was still functioning. Who was he to argue if she needed a little space to clear her head?

He spun his chair to look at their wall of pictures and memories. His eyes stopped on Sarah's smile, the one caught on camera at her surprise birthday party. She hated surprises and almost punched him when he flicked the light switch in the hall he'd rented, and everyone shouted at the same time. Prepared, he'd hit the switch and dropped back several feet, missing her lunge by mere inches. Sarah's reflexes were like that now. Raw, ready, a noise too loud, a sound too close, hands up in a defensive posture, fists moving to ward off whatever was coming at her. Assess later. Apologize later, if necessary. Remain safe. Her personal training had evolved her into something entirely different than the original goal foresaw. Lately, she'd embraced it, enjoyed it, and worked in the dojo with blindfolds, listening for danger, sensing it. Alex enjoyed those sessions too much for Aaron's liking because Alex had morphed into something else entirely.

Aaron glanced at another photo, then closed his eyes for a moment. Last February was the hardest month of his life— but it was worse for Sarah. He held her, tried to soothe her, wrapped her in his arms, and whispered how so many people loved her.

She endured, she drank, and she let it all go for several weeks. All the pain, all the history, the dwelling on the past, her mind a vacuum of emotion.

But it had only helped for a while.

They needed better, more advanced help. The idea of contacting a therapist came up, but she refused. When he asked her to talk to him, she refused.

After *It* happened (he was so used to calling it *It* that he was even doing it to himself), once they got settled in their new apartment, Aaron felt he'd lost her.

And now, perhaps he *actually* had lost her.

Two weeks ago, after she left, and out of a healthy curiosity on where she might have gone, he checked her browser history, went through her closet and drawers for any sign of notes, and searched for anything that would let him in on where she had gone and why. He'd found a couple of useless notes that made no sense to him. In the meantime, if she called, needing him, he would be ready. Until then, he was forced to give her the space she needed because he had no clue where she was, having hidden her tracks too well.

In his heart, he was fine with that. If she needed time away, maybe that would help her deal with last February. He never suspected her of doing anything crazy like infidelity. Sarah was just too honest, too honorable.

Yet, the phone call he had just hung up on scared him. Fear spiked through him as a mild shock settled over his system.

He thought about calling his three brothers—teachers at the dojo and dear friends who had become brothers over the years—to join him at the apartment and figure this shit out.

While Sarah and Aaron had done the nomadic tripping around the States when they first took off, his three teachers had set up a new dojo. They waited for Aaron, and when he and Sarah returned to Toronto and rented this apartment, they got him in training and teaching again. It was just like old times.

Although, not so much for Sarah. She'd gone rogue in the dojo, training with styles and weapons and all sorts of shit only Alex could relate to.

The boys would be in class. Before calling them, he wanted more information. He would call Parkman first. If anyone knew anything about Sarah, it would be Parkman. And if he didn't know what was going on, maybe Darwin Kostas would. The last he'd heard, Darwin was back in Italy with his wife, Rosina, leading a comfortable, relaxed life.

All this shit was supposed to be over.

He snatched up the phone and hit Parkman's picture on the screen, then placed it on speaker, not wanting to hold it in his wet palms. With the phone lying on the desk beside him, he stared at Sarah's smiling visage on the wall while the phone rang at Parkman's end.

It was answered on the second ring.

"Aaron?" Parkman's familiar voice.

"Parkman. You doing well?"

"Calling about Sarah?" Parkman asked.

Without formalities or asking how he knew that, Aaron simply said, "Yes."

"Sorry, man. Don't know much."

"What do you know? There has to be something."

"I know she's in Texas."

"Texas?" he shouted, leaning toward the phone on the desk. He ran a hand through his hair and eased back in the chair a moment later to stare at the sky through his window. Now, his stomach was doing belly flops in a toxic mix of nerves. "What the hell is she doing in Texas?"

"She called me. Asked me to come down. In truth, it was to throw my weight around."

"Parkman, try to make sense. Throw your weight around what?"

Parkman cleared his throat. "Aaron, it's not really a good time. All I know is when we talked, she asked me—no *ordered* me—to keep you out of it."

His stomach dropped further if that were possible. Was he losing his precious Sarah? His chest tightened at the thought. It couldn't be. They were a forever-and-always couple. Till death did they part, even though they hadn't exchanged vows officially, there were unspoken vows. There was an unspoken commitment, a bond, a love beyond this realm. He couldn't lose Sarah. In fact, he couldn't even consider it for fear of losing a piece of his soul. Sarah was life. Sarah was *his* life. Sarah was everything.

"Look, you've heard her say this before," Parkman was talking again. "Trust the process. Aaron, just stay where you are and trust the process. I'm sure she'll make it all clear to you when she returns."

"Parkman, has she told you what happened last February …" he faltered, unable to finish the sentence.

"Yes," Parkman said, his tone even.

"What she's going through …" he swallowed involuntarily, cutting himself off, "…shouldn't be a burden anyone can carry alone."

"I understand, Aaron. I'm truly sorry—"

"Well, I just got a phone call."

Now, there was a pause on the other end of the line. Then

Parkman asked, "Who called you?"

"The United States Border Patrol. Specifically, a man named Chief Agent Michael Wilson."

There was a pause on the other end of the line. Then Parkman said, "And?"

"He wanted to know if Sarah had returned home."

"What did you tell him?" Parkman's tone was clipped now, short.

"The truth. She left a few weeks ago, and I hadn't heard a thing. No email, no text, no phone call. And now I have the Texas authorities looking for her."

"Stay home, Aaron. You have to trust me on this—no, wait—trust Sarah. It's her edict."

"Explain it to me. Tell me why. Then I'll consider it."

"Only Sarah knows why."

There were several moments of silence while Aaron studied the wall of pictures, going from Sarah's smile to one of her opening Christmas presents last year. Never much for material things, he searched hard for a gift for her and came up with a new MacBook Pro and a gift card big enough for twenty to thirty books at the local Indigo bookstore. All that and a return flight to Santa Rosa to see her parents. She'd needed that trip. They'd gone several months ago in the spring. It had grounded her and made her feel better somehow.

"Parkman."

"Yeah?"

"That border patrol guy said she stole a spike belt from them and went against some kind of protocol."

"Yeah." He cleared his throat. "Well, you know Sarah.

Always working on her own. On her own, Aaron. We need to keep it that way."

"Parkman, they're considering pressing charges."

"That's hyperbole. They won't press charges after what she did for them. That's only to heighten this shit so they can expend more resources in finding her."

"What did she do for them? And how does that lead to them hunting her?"

Another pause. Then Parkman said, "Aaron. We've known each other for a long time. I have worked with you countless times, and it pains me to say, but I have been asked to respect confidentiality."

"By whom?"

"Sarah."

"What is she hiding from me?" He tried to control his voice, keep it from raising, but he did a piss-poor job. This kind of concealment went against everything they were. It made him feel like she was forcing him out of her life. And if so, then tell him, and he will respect that. Saying nothing other than to stay away wasn't like Sarah. "I'm her partner, her man," he continued. "I'm with her all the way." He realized how pathetic that sounded, but it came out before he could rein it back in. What happened over six months ago happened to him, too. Sarah wasn't the only one hurting.

"I know," Parkman whispered. "She knows that. We all do. But she called. Asked me to do something. I did it. She also asked for confidentiality. I made a promise."

"Does it have anything to do with something called True Legacy?"

The pause on the other end of the line came with a slight

intake of breath this time.

"Where did you hear that name?"

"I found a piece of paper in the kitchen garbage the day after she left two weeks ago. It was torn to bits. After a little reconstruction, the paper had those two words on it."

"Leave it alone, Aaron." Over the line, Aaron heard a car starting. "Let it go. She'll be in touch."

"What is Sarah's true legacy, Parkman?" He licked his lips and glanced around the room for his water glass. It felt like sand coated his tongue. "I'm really scared over here. What is she doing?"

"Even I don't know what she's doing. She's mostly on her own."

"Then where are you right now? I'll come hang with you until she needs us."

"Aaron ..." Parkman's engine revved through the phone's speaker. "Please. I can't. It doesn't work like that."

"Then answer me this. Why did Sarah fill out an organ donor application online the day before she walked out? Organ donor, Parkman, and true legacy? What the hell am I supposed to take away from that?"

"How do you know about—"

"It doesn't matter *how* I know. What matters is what I *want* to know."

Parkman's engine slowed. Aaron thought he heard a turn signal, and the engine revved again.

"You're right. You are owed an answer. And you'll get one. Just know that Sarah loves you and will be in touch when she's ready."

Angry, Aaron hovered his finger over the red button to

end the call, then eased it away.

"Listen," Parkman said. "I have to go. I'm sorry—"

The line died.

"Fuck!" Aaron shouted and bolted up from his chair. The desk chair caught the backs of his knees and shot away, banging against the far wall.

He bent at the waist, hands on his knees, and breathed in and out, in and out.

After several minutes, his heart rate back to something more reasonable, he got on his computer and opened WhatsApp. After checking the time, he saw it would be early evening in Umbria, Italy, where Darwin and Rosina lived.

He dialed Darwin.

Luckily, he was home and answered right away.

"Aaron," Darwin's familiar voice resonated throughout Aaron's office. "Great to hear from you."

"Hey, Darwin. Is there anything you can tell me about Sarah? Where she may be? What she's up to?"

"Right to business. I like that."

"I'm sorry. That was rude of me. Let me explain."

"Sure, I'm listening."

Aaron told him about the call from the Texas border patrol guy, his call with Parkman, and the note on true legacy and organ donor application.

"That got me thinking," Aaron continued. "Since you've been known to track us, I thought maybe you could tell me more."

"Let me put you on speaker. I have Rosina here with me."

"Hello," Aaron said.

"Hi, Aaron." Rosina's soft voice traveled through his speakers. "You holding up okay?"

"As best as I can," he lied. "Getting through one day at a time."

"Isn't that all you can do?"

"Indeed it is."

"Okay, Aaron, here's what I've got. Sarah called about three weeks ago and asked for a favor."

"A favor? What kind of favor?"

"She asked to borrow Bruno."

Aaron frowned. "Bruno? That guy who helped her when she was in Denmark? The same huge guy I met here in Toronto?"

"That's him."

"Did she say why she needed Bruno?"

"Aaron, when Sarah asks for something I *can* do, I do it. I only ask questions when it's something I *can't* do."

"Fair enough. Anything else?"

"Yeah, she's using burner phones, so we haven't been able to trace her. But I can see Parkman is in Dallas, well, an area of Dallas called Desoto, at the moment. According to my system, he was parked outside a house on Hillside Lane for over an hour. Looks like he just left that area several minutes ago."

"You're actively tracking Parkman?" This came as a surprise.

"When Sarah asked for Bruno, and we're footing that bill, I'm tracking anyone and everyone in the Texas area in case Bruno or Sarah need us. Think of it as passively tracking them. They're in our system and being watched. We aren't staring at screens all day. Italy is too nice this time of year." Aaron heard something that sounded like a kiss.

"Are you seeing anything else?"

"Now that you ask, we are getting a few hits with the Texas authorities. They are looking for her, probably for the same reasons they called you. That's it. That's all I have."

"Has Sarah asked you for confidentiality?"

"No, but she might've asked Bruno to stay quiet about whatever they're working on. He likes her. He'll do what he's told. He's one of the best I've ever employed."

"I wonder what she's doing that would require him?" Aaron asked out loud.

"I thought the same but didn't ask." Aaron heard them whisper something to each other. "Listen, Aaron, you want me to come to you? Rosina can handle all this tech shit here."

"The more help, the better, but don't come here. Go to Texas. Dallas, to be exact."

There was a short pause, and then Darwin said, "I don't think that would be wise, not after what Parkman said. Sarah's working some plan of hers. She'll be okay. Besides, she's got Bruno and Parkman."

"You're right. I should leave it alone."

"Look, I'll book a flight to Toronto. Be there by the weekend. We'll have a few drinks, talk about old times, and wait for more news together."

"It's okay. Really. I'll call the boys at the dojo. We'll spar, hang out. Just promise to call when you have something new. I'm really worried about her."

"Okay, Aaron. I promise to try."

After several niceties, they hung up. Aaron closed his

computer, tugged at his lower lip as he considered his options, then snatched his phone off the desk and called the dojo.

Daniel answered right away.

"Aaron."

"Daniel."

"What's up?"

"How fast can you guys be ready to go on a trip?"

"A moment's notice. No issue. There are only a few classes this week. Why?"

"Sarah might be in trouble." Aaron filled him in on the call from Texas, his call with Parkman, and Bruno being summoned to Texas. He conveniently left out the part about Sarah not wanting his help, or anyone else's for that matter.

"Shit. Okay. I'll tell Alex and Benjamin. When are we leaving?"

"We fly out tomorrow morning for Dallas, Texas. We're going to find Sarah and figure this shit out."

"We'll be ready."

"Meet you all at the dojo."

The line died.

Chapter 3

Sarah Roberts sat low in the back seat of her rental car. From the rear of the SUV she'd rented using Bruno's ID, she could watch the house and street without anyone seeing her as the back windows were tinted black. Any curious passersby would just see an empty front seat.

The house she watched sat back from the road, pied out at the corner between Southwood Drive and Hillside Lane. The late afternoon sun was taking forever to drop after the oppressively hot Dallas day. After an hour of watching the house, giving Parkman a break, her phone rang. He was ready to return.

She climbed over the seat, turned on the SUV, and eased away from the curb. As she did, headlights came down Hillside Lane behind her. The vehicle eased to the curb where she had been, and then the light died.

Their phone was still connected.

"You in place?" she asked.

"I am."

"No one in, no one out while I was there."

"Okay. Sarah, Aaron called me."

She stopped at an intersection and stared off into space. "What did you tell him?"

"To let it go. You'd be in touch."

"Okay." She waited a moment, feeling Aaron's warmth on her neck, his hands encircling her, holding her. Something about that made her want to cry. "Did he sound okay?"

"No, but he'll live."

"He had a million questions?"

"Yeah."

Someone honked their horn. She looked up. The light was green. The horn honked again. She eased forward, two hands on the wheel, making sure to drive safely. Thoughts of Aaron and what they'd been through over the past six months scared her, and not much scared her these days.

"Gotta go, Parkman."

"You okay?"

"Yes. I'll be at the motel with Bruno. He will spell you later tonight."

"I'll be here."

She disconnected the call. She would have to make it up to Aaron if they survived this trip to Texas. She would have to go a long way in helping him understand what she did and why. Quite possibly, her consequence for keeping him back in Toronto and out of the loop on this job could potentially hurt their relationship. As long as they were both alive, a hurt relationship she could deal with. If one of them were dead, or both of them, then there was no relationship anymore, hurt or not.

She could live with that. For whatever it was worth, Aaron had to stay in Toronto, as well as his dojo teachers, all of them dear friends. They'd helped out on so many occasions she had lost count. Aaron was missing a finger because of the Enzo Cartel in Mexico. Benjamin had been shot countless times over the years—it was a wonder he was still upright. They'd all been kidnapped, abused, shot at, tortured, and lived to tell the tale.

Then Sarah and Aaron took a much-needed break, only to go through the toughest time of their lives. She never wanted to go through that again—ever.

She wiped a tear and continued south, the motel no more than ten minutes away.

This thing, this job Vivian had told her about, wouldn't take long. A couple of more days, max. In and out of the States. Sure, she'd been gone about two weeks, but that was prep time. She needed to convince the U.S. Border Patrol to work with her and Parkman to help.

They did, and lives were saved. Almost three dozen people. Sure, they'd be sent back to Mexico, but they were alive. And maybe they'd try again one day. That wasn't her concern. All she needed to do was stop Alejandro, and she'd done that.

Phase two will start tomorrow afternoon. She was ready. Parkman was ready. And Bruno understood the risks.

Nothing would stop them.

She eased into the motel's parking lot, drove to the back,

parked, and waited. The engine ticked while she sat in silence, watching the building. No one moved toward her vehicle. There was no trap set.

She listened for her sister and called her name inside her head.

Vivian responded, a word reverberating throughout her head: *Clear.*

Sarah opened the door and got out. She wore a hat to conceal her hair and baggy clothes to shield her body type. Unless they had facial recognition cameras—which they didn't—no one would recognize her.

At the room, she knocked on the door twice. It shot open, and Bruno stepped aside. He closed the door.

"Not good," he said.

Sarah turned to him as the pit in her stomach became a jumping bean of worry. Bruno was so tall he had to lean forward so as not to bump his head in their standard motel room.

"What's not good?" she asked, already fearing the answer.

"Darwin called."

"And?"

"Aaron's coming."

Sarah spun around and slammed a fist into the palm of her other hand. She grit her teeth together and held her breath a moment to avoid tears. After a large intake of breath, she turned back to Bruno.

"Call Darwin," she said. "See if there's anything he can do to stop Aaron. Flag his passport. Send someone to stop him. I don't care, just stop him. Aaron cannot come to

Texas."

Bruno nodded, already pulling his cell phone from his pocket. "Four people coming, Darwin said."

"Daniel, Benjamin, and Alex, too?" she asked, her voice taking on a shrill as she realized how fatal this news was.

Bruno nodded. He watched her, his phone in his hand, waiting to place the call.

She stared into space momentarily, contemplating what this meant, listening for Vivian.

Nothing came. Her sister was gone for the moment.

Her eyes refocused on Bruno. "Stop them at any cost. Find a way. Tell Darwin if he can't find a way, make one. Aaron and the other guys cannot come to Texas. If they do, they'll die here." Now, she couldn't hold back the tears. "Please, Bruno, tell Darwin." She placed a hand on Bruno's forearm. "Please." The last word came out, sounding like she was begging.

It was so unnerving and unbecoming that she turned and strode to the bathroom as Bruno dialed out. After slamming the bathroom door, she crumpled to the floor and curled into a ball. Outside the door, she heard Bruno talking to Darwin in clipped tones, relaying Sarah's message.

She heard Aaron's name a couple of times.

Then she fell apart, curled up on the cold tile floor, weeping for all the loss, the missed opportunities, the pain, and what had happened to them over the past year.

Why did life have to be so unfair? Why did people have to suffer so much? And how much was too much?

If Aaron came to Texas, he would die. Vivian said so. She had seen his death. She had shown his burial site to

Sarah.

"Please, please, please, Aaron," she mumbled through her tears, mucus dripping from her running nose over her top lip. "Please, baby, stay home. Just stay home."

She was still curled up on the floor an hour later when the phone rang out in the room.

"It's Darwin," Bruno said through the closed door. "There's nothing he can do in such a short time. Aaron bought four tickets to Dallas from Toronto. They are flying in twelve hours."

Sarah shouted, "Isn't there someone Darwin knows in Toronto who could kidnap Aaron and hold him until this is over?"

After a few moments, Bruno said, "He hung up. He's working on it."

Sarah wrapped her arms over her head and gripped her hair from behind.

Vivian, tell me what to do.

There was no response.

"Vivian," she whispered. "You know me. I may appear weak right now, but I'm stronger than ever. I'm ready to go back into this full-time. You want me. You got me. But Aaron is off-limits. He gets hurt, or worse—" She choked up, took a deep breath, and stared at the bathroom ceiling. "I'm done if something happens to Aaron." Her hands curled into fists, her teeth came together, jaw clenched. "You hear me, sister? I'm fucking done. Fix this, or fuck you."

There was no response.

Chapter 4

A ARON GOT UP EARLY, poured coffee, and got on his computer to read the news. Nothing coming out of Dallas with Sarah's name on it. He googled her name to be sure he didn't miss anything, then settled his nerves with a lukewarm shower.

Once he was packed and ready to go, he locked up, headed down to his car, and drove to the dojo on Queen Street after stopping at a Starbucks drive-thru.

All three teachers were packed and ready. He emailed their plane tickets to each man, and they quietly added the electronic ticket to their wallet on their individual cell phones.

"We're all on a direct flight, Toronto to Dallas. It leaves at 12:40 p.m. and lands just over three and a half hours later at 3:14 p.m. Dallas time."

His men, team, and brothers nodded, collected their bags,

and stepped out into the bright morning sunshine.

A long black stretch limo waited with its four-way lights flashing.

"I'll call a cab," Aaron said.

"We're taking this." Daniel pointed at the limo.

Aaron hesitated, phone in hand. "Who ordered a limo?"

"Darwin called. Said he knew we were heading to the airport and wanted to pitch in."

Even though Darwin was part of the family, someone he could trust with his life, something felt wrong about this. He hadn't told Darwin he was going anywhere. Darwin had offered to fly to Toronto, have a few drinks, and talk about old times. Before hanging up the phone yesterday, Aaron said something about leaving it alone for now.

Yet, a shiny black limousine was parked outside the dojo, waiting to ferry them all to the airport.

He turned to Daniel. None of them had made a move for the long vehicle.

"Did he call once?"

Daniel nodded. Benjamin did, too.

"Just this morning," Benjamin said. "Why? What's wrong? I can verify it was Darwin. Daniel put him on speaker."

Alex had lowered his bag to the sidewalk and was moving away from it. With Aaron's hesitation came caution, and Alex always seemed to be the first to investigate.

His movements caught Daniel's and Benjamin's eyes, too.

Alex stopped in front of the limo and bent over to glance in through the windshield. Then he smiled and waved at the driver. From where Aaron was standing, it looked like the driver waved back, but the windows were too dark to be sure.

Alex placed his hand on the hood ornament. Then he bent it back.

The driver's side door opened, and the driver got out.

"Hey, what are you doing? Get the fuck off my car."

Alex smiled innocently, shrugging, as the driver stepped up to him and made to push him away.

The driver's hand never got the chance to touch Alex. He swung his arms around the driver's elbow, pulled him closer, then reversed his arms like the parody of a windmill, spinning the man in front of him and locked his arms around his neck.

With his mouth close to the man's ear, Alex asked, "Who's in the vehicle with you?"

"Hey, let go of me," the driver said.

Alex squeezed. The man made a choking sound. Aaron moved to say something as two pedestrians had stopped to watch, one recording with their cell phone out.

"Who is in the vehicle?" Alex repeated the question, then eased up on his chokehold.

"No one," the driver spat.

"What's waiting for us in there?"

"Nothing," the man shouted. "A ride. That's it. I was hired to drive you to the airport. Paid upfront from some guy in Europe."

Alex turned just enough to look at Aaron, who nodded. Then Alex's arms flailed open in dramatic fashion, and the driver stepped away from him, grasping at his throat. A few side steps later, the driver was back behind the wheel, his door shut and locked.

Alex moved back to his bag and shouldered it.

The pedestrians shuffled their feet and then carried on.

"Your move," Daniel said. "Looks like a nice gesture to me. We can thank Darwin from the airport."

Aaron shook his head. "Thanks, Alex, but I still feel like there's something wrong with this. If he only called once, he's tracking us—or tracking me—and I don't know why. And not just that, he felt I shouldn't go to Dallas as well."

"Then why are we going?" Benjamin asked. "There won't be any guns, right?" He glanced at Alex, then back to Aaron. "No one's getting shot, right? We all know how that'll end."

"No one's getting shot," Aaron assured him. "Okay, fuck it. Let's go."

They opened the back door and climbed inside the limo one by one.

The partition between the driver and his passengers had been raised. They could push a button to speak with him through a speaker, but what looked like a reinforced piece of Plexiglas separated them.

Moments later, the driver eased into traffic on Queen Street and headed for the Gardiner Expressway West to take them toward the 427 North and, ultimately, the airport.

Definitely something wrong with this, Aaron thought.

Chapter 5

IT WAS NOON WHEN Bruno relieved Parkman on Hillside Lane. Parkman was back in the motel room within a half hour with lunch. He'd stopped at a Greek place and bought them a couple of pork gyros.

Without much to say, they dove right in, eating with gusto as breakfast had been a meager sampling of biscuits and dried bread.

Sarah sat on the edge of the bed while Parkman sat at the small desk by the TV. The gyro reminded Sarah of her time in Athens, then in Nafplio, where she'd eaten her first one—what felt like a decade ago.

Nafplio was also where the ancient prison, *Palamidi*, sat upon a hill. The same prison where Aaron was shot and almost killed all those years ago. Years later, as that city was once again thrust into their lives, a man approached her at a restaurant in Nafplio and gave her a package. Inside was Aaron's detached finger. A Mexican cartel had kidnapped Aaron and cut off his finger as a message to Sarah. Even though she had been warned harm would come to Aaron if anything happened to the finger messenger, she had killed that man. And yet, Aaron and Sarah had survived that ordeal.

They wouldn't survive this one. At least, according to Vivian.

Memories of Aaron, past events, and pain flitted through her mind.

She set the half-eaten gyro on her lap and waited a moment before resuming eating.

"You okay?" Parkman asked.

She nodded, her mouth full.

He set his gyro down and addressed her. "What are we doing here?"

She chewed, waited a moment, swallowed, wiped her mouth, and looked up. "I don't know," she whispered.

After a moment, she took another small bite while he watched her. She waited for more questions, ones she would answer as best she could because Parkman, of all people, deserved the truth. But the truth was, she had no idea.

Get Darwin to send Bruno. Call Parkman and have him influence the border patrol to listen to her. Then stop that truck off I-35 in Texas. After that, watch the house on Hillside Lane. A man, his wife, and their young daughter lived there. But why watch the house? Was a robbery going to happen? Was the husband a bad guy?

The need to get out of Toronto, to get away and be working again, had been driving her mad. So Vivian gave her an out. Amid other details, here she was, doing as she was required, waiting for other missives from her dead sister.

"Instead of asking pointed questions, is there anything you can tell me?" Parkman said. "Anything about that house we're watching? I'm assuming this has everything to do with human trafficking after you stopped that truck."

Sarah lifted one shoulder in a half-shrug. "I thought the same, but that doesn't feel right."

"How so?"

"Just a feeling I get from Vivian."

Parkman resumed eating. She scrunched up her wrapper and tossed it in the garbage beside Parkman's chair. After a moment, she leaned back and lay on the bed, staring at the ceiling.

"You worried about those border patrol guys? They're looking for you."

"No, not worried. That air filter would've caused permanent damage to some of those people in that truck. I couldn't wait until their ambush to get that back door open. I had to stop the truck early. I knew Wilson would be angry with me, but I had to do what I had to do. Lives were saved, and they know that."

"But that's not it, is it? Just because of the breathing apparatus in the truck?"

She waited a heartbeat, then said, "No. Vivian showed me a shootout. We would've lost men on both sides. Doing it my way saved every single soul." She leaned up on one elbow. "Besides, I'm still the same old Sarah. You know that. I'll do what it takes, consequences be damned. I can live with that. I sleep quite well. What happened in February is over.

I'm past it." She dropped back onto the bed, closing her eyes. "A strong woman will always be judged as bitchy or bossy. Being female, confident, and not relying on others' opinions isn't rude. It's called commitment. I'm happy with who I am, which bothers some men—not you—but some men. Don't ever feel that it changed who I am fundamentally."

"I wouldn't make that mistake, fundamentally speaking." The sudden noise of his gyro wrapper being balled up made her jolt slightly. A soft thunk and it was in the trash can. "But it changed you, Sarah."

She frowned, wondering what others saw that quite possibly she hadn't seen.

"How so?" she asked, her tone more inquisitive than accusatory. She was interested in what changes Parkman saw in her.

"You're more emotional."

She jerked upright, a smile playing across her lips. "Emotional? Aren't girls always more emotional than guys?" Now, her tone was playful.

"You know what I mean. And I wasn't being gender specific."

She sat up fully and stared out at the window. "You're right. I have been more emotional. Not *monthly* emotional, but I *feel* more than I used to." She wrung her hands together. "As if I care more, which scares me."

She got up and went to the window, watching the parking lot. Only a few vehicles left as it was checkout time. Her rented SUV was parked at the back. Parkman's was parked out front, and Bruno was still watching the house on Hillside Lane.

"Why would that scare you?" Parkman asked, his tone soft, slightly above a whisper.

"When I did this thing with Vivian for nearly a decade, all over the world, I didn't care about anything but getting the job done." She pivoted to look at him. "But now I care about everything. Sure, getting the job done, but I care about you, too."

Parkman smiled. "Well, I've always cared about you."

"Oh, Parkman," she blurted, acting dramatically exasperated. "You know what I mean. For example, that's why Bruno is here and not Darwin."

"You don't care about Bruno?"

She moved to sit back on the bed. "Of course, I care about Bruno. But he can handle himself. He's a serious professional."

"And Darwin isn't?"

"You know, this verbal sparring with you can be a good thing. It opens up one's understanding. But I hate it. So stop."

"Not a chance."

They exchanged a smile, a knowing glance.

"Look, I just need to work alone, or as close to alone as possible, so no one I love gets hurt. I mean, I care for Bruno, of course, but Darwin and Rosina are family to me."

"Is that why you want Aaron and the boys to stay in Toronto?"

She felt her face harden, cheeks tighten, jaw lock, her teeth pressed against themselves. Aaron and the boys. In Toronto, where they would stay safe.

"No, there's another reason."

"Then tell me so I don't conclude shit on my own. After

the year you two have had, I really think I need to know."

She suppressed her first *emotional* reaction to Parkman's question by remaining stone-faced. There was no issue with telling Parkman what she knew, or rather what Vivian had told her. If there was anyone she could trust, it was Parkman. It wasn't so much in the *telling* as it was *how* to tell him.

Her hands were wringing themselves into a frenzy. She glanced down, then released them.

"Vivian showed me their gravesites." She locked eyes with him. "All four of them die if they come to Texas. I can't lose them. That would be the end of me. And if it was my fault? I could never have that on my conscience, the burden too heavy to bear. Nor can I focus on what I'm here for if I'm trying to save them constantly."

Parkman didn't reel back in surprise. He didn't gasp or panic. He simply leaned forward and said, "So, just change the future like you do for everyone else. Like stopping that truck early, before the ambush by Wilson and his men. You saved those people from being oxygen-deprived. Just save Aaron and the boys by altering what's coming."

She nodded. "I am, by not including them down here." Now, she shook her head. "Although, it's not that simple."

"Why not?"

"It just isn't."

They allowed a lull in the conversation. Sarah went to the bathroom and brushed her teeth. When she came out, Parkman was standing by the window.

"Why are we watching that man's house?" he asked.

Sarah dropped onto the chair beside the desk Parkman had just vacated. "I don't know yet. Vivian hasn't told me anything more than I've already—"

Vivian cut her off. Her sister had been listening the whole time, waiting, watching them talk, and now she explained to Sarah what would happen next. Then Vivian widened the picture for Sarah, explaining some of the end game, even giving her a new address she needed to know.

Sarah gasped, clutching at her stomach.

"No," she grunted, staring off into space. "It can't be true."

Parkman lurched over from the window and dropped to one knee beside her.

"What can't be true, Sarah? What's going on?"

"Vivian …" She inhaled. "Just told me … more." Sarah used Parkman's shoulder to hoist herself to her feet. "Hurry. I have to leave."

"Leave?" he gasped. "Where are you going?"

"To the airport. I need to buy a plane ticket. But I have to hurry."

"Sarah, you're freaking me out. What about Bruno? Do we just leave him here?"

"In the car. I'll call him and give him further instructions."

"You're going to the airport," Parkman said. "Where do I go?"

She opened the motel room door and turned back to him, blinking away the tears caused by the vision her sister had shown her. "I need you to drive. I can't be trusted behind the wheel in this state."

"You going to tell me what Vivian said?" he asked.

Sarah nodded. "On the way. And I have an address I have

to write down. You drive, I talk."

"Deal. Let's go." On the way out the door, Parkman said just loud enough for her to hear, "See? More emotional for sure."

Chapter 6

Traffic was busier than usual as the limousine left Toronto's downtown core on the elevated highway. By the time they'd passed Islington, traffic opened up, and soon, the limo was moving at highway speeds.

No one spoke. The interior of the expensive vehicle was quiet except for the sound of the traffic outside the windows.

Aaron couldn't deny the feeling in his gut that something was off somehow. Darwin hadn't told him about the limo. To have a car waiting like that implied too much: too much spying, too much protection. But from what, or whom? And why?

Aaron was quite confident the four of them could take care of themselves without help from Darwin or anyone else. Sure, if help was needed and being offered freely, he'd accept. That's what friends were for. But a ride to the airport?

That wasn't as much help as it was an unnecessary intrusion and an obvious announcement that Darwin knew what he was doing, even after Aaron had been told countless times not to go after Sarah.

That said, this wasn't a ride to the airport after all. It was something else entirely, like a message, and Aaron was determined to figure it out.

He watched the highway and checked the signs they passed, making sure they were going the right way. However, sign-checking proved difficult because using the front window wasn't an option with the dark partition raised. Using only the side window, he had to read signs fast as they zipped by his window.

"You're bothered," Daniel said.

Aaron shook his head. "Still just feeling like something's off, but it's probably nothing."

Movement caught his eye as Alex crawled over the seats and maneuvered himself close to the partition, where he began an inspection of the wall.

"It's nothing, really," he said, loud enough for Alex to hear.

He'd do no harm checking things out. Knowing Darwin set this up, and Darwin was a friend, put him at ease regarding their safety. But the question of why still nagged at him. Why tell him he needed to stay home and then deliver them to the airport?

He shot up in his seat when it hit him. How could he have been so stupid? It was the obvious move.

"Guys, we're not going to the airport."

Daniel and Benjamin looked out the windows. Alex

continued to inspect the partition as if Aaron hadn't said a word.

Outside, the limo traveled north on the 427, still heading toward the airport.

"Kinda looks like we are," Daniel said. "What makes you say that?"

"Parkman told me to stay home. Said it was Sarah's *edict* that we all stay home. When I spoke with Darwin, he wasn't as adamant but suggested we stay home, too."

He glanced out the window. They were over the 401, making the wide curve to continue north on the 427.

"And?" Benjamin asked. "We're a minute from the airport. What else did they all say?"

"I don't know," Aaron blurted, frustration tightening his stomach and his grip. "Dammit, something's off. I feel it." He stared up at Alex as he moved away from the partition. "Locked in?" he asked.

Alex nodded, not one for words. He gestured toward the ceiling. Aaron looked up at the sunroof as Alex flipped a button, and it slowly began to ease back.

Halfway open, it stopped, the tiny engine sound dying off. Then, inexplicably, the window began to close. Before anyone reacted, gasped, or drew any conclusions on why it would slide back closed on its own, Alex snatched his gym bag off the seat beside him and shot it skyward as he dove upward without regard for where he would land. The gym bag wedged in the sunroof window, grinding the mechanism to a halt, wind ruffling the handle as Alex landed half on Benjamin and half on the floor.

He righted himself and reached over for the button on the

door to lower the side window. It didn't work.

Without a word, Aaron tried his button.

Nothing.

He looked outside. The Toronto airport slid past their windows on the left as the limo continued north on the highway.

"Fuck!" Aaron shouted. "I knew it." The partition was up, and all the windows had been shut down from interior use, but the driver had forgotten about the sunroof—until he didn't.

Alex's gym bag was buckled under the pressure, leaving no more than a foot of room. Certainly not enough for anyone to climb out.

Even at this speed, Alex crawled over Aaron's lap and yanked on the door. Nothing happened.

Their eyes met. If Aaron were a betting man, he would've put his life savings on Alex getting them out. The look in his eyes wasn't defeat. Nowhere close. All he saw was a challenge, one fitting for Alex's brand of fun. He sparred, he taught—body language, as Alex didn't talk much in class either—and he hung out with them, drinking occasionally. But day to day, he was never tested. And Aaron didn't know anyone who enjoyed a test of his knowledge and abilities like Alex did. The thing with Alex was that if someone else wasn't testing him, he tested himself, which scared the hell out of Aaron. Sarah loved it, but Aaron feared it. He didn't like some of the shit Alex did, like dangerous parkour from one building to another.

"The 427 ends at the 407," Daniel said. "The driver will have to slow down. All we have to do is kick out a window and jump when he gets to a red light."

"Technically," Benjamin interrupted, "it ends at Highway 7, but we've only ever driven as far as the 407."

"Okay, well, the driver'll have to stop." Daniel leaned closer to the window. "I'm all for jumping, but not at this speed."

Alex met Aaron's gaze. Then his eyes flicked to the sunroof, and Aaron got it.

"Guys, everyone, get behind the sunroof." He rose from his seat and dropped into the one facing the back directly under the sunroof. "All hands on this window. When I say so, we all pull it back to allow Alex a large enough spot to exit through."

Alex was already sliding on the limo floor, stopping directly under the partially opened roof, staring up at it, a hungry look on his face from the outside.

The limo slowed as it neared the junction at the 407 or Highway 7—Aaron had stopped watching.

"All hands," he said. Daniel, Benjamin, and Aaron grabbed the small window. "Pull back," he grunted as three pairs of hands leaned into the window.

The limo slowed more, no doubt coming to a light.

The window resisted, then eased back in stops and starts.

Alex's gym bag dropped beside him, and then he was up, squeezing his head through, his ear rubbing rough against Aaron's knuckle.

They couldn't let go now, or Alex would be caught in the window. Redoubling his effort, Aaron brought his feet up and used the back of the chair to his right for leverage.

Even though they weren't successful in opening the

sunroof all the way, they could open it enough for Alex to climb through. As if pulled upward by someone on the outside, Alex launched up and out of the limo just as it slowed to a stop.

They all released their grips from the glass in unison, deep red indents in their fingers left behind to prove their effort.

Gravel crunched under the tires as the driver pulled over onto the shoulder of what looked like Highway 7. A speaker sounded inside the confined space.

"I'm sorry, guys," the driver said through the speaker. "I was ordered to detain you for a couple of hours, then drop you off at Canada's Wonderland. There, you'll have free passes for the day, all courtesy of some guy in Europe. No one is getting on a plane today. No one is going to the airport. I hope you understand. This wasn't me, guys. I don't make the decisions—"

The sound of glass breaking somewhere up front cut him off. The limo jolted, bouncing on its hinges. The three of them exchanged glances, staring outside but not seeing Alex. The speaker had cut off. A scuffle was happening in front of the black partition, but none of them were privy to it due to their confined space.

As fast as it started, the bouncing limo settled. A car door opened, and then, after a moment, it closed. They waited, collectively holding their breath.

Not five seconds after the limo door closed, it started moving again. A wide U-turn, and then Aaron saw they were heading south on the 427, back toward the airport.

He checked his cell phone. Plenty of time to clear

security and still make the plane.

The speaker engaged with an audible click. There was silence at first, then the soft lull of Alex's voice.

"Destination: the airport. Five minutes."

The speaker died.

Aaron dropped back in his seat. Alex had done it again. He hated the risks that guy took, but man, what would he do without him—or Daniel and Benjamin? These guys were his life, his blood.

Just like Sarah. She was everything to him. Absolutely everything. Whether she needed him in Texas or not, he was going. He'd wait in the hotel then. He'd buy dinner. He'd drop her off, pick her up. Whatever it was he did, he was going to help. He needed this. She needed to *feel* his level of commitment to her.

For life, baby, he thought. *We're in this till the end. I'm coming to Texas, even if it kills me.*

Chapter 7

ONCE THEY WERE IN Parkman's car, Sarah retrieved her cell phone from her pocket and hesitated before calling Bruno.

Parkman glanced over. "What?"

She faced him with a deadpan stare.

"What?" he asked again, louder. "Why aren't you calling him? What's wrong?"

"I just, I can't." Sarah felt like she was mumbling. "I'm just feeling a little shocked at everything Vivian said."

"Shock? That's not the Sarah I know." Parkman watched the road ahead. "Unless it is the Sarah I know, and what Vivian showed you was an imminent nuclear holocaust."

"Not nuclear." She shook her head. "But close to the other thing."

"She showed you a holocaust?" Parkman asked, his tone poised on the edge of disbelief.

"Not exactly." Sarah started to dial. "Look, don't react to what I tell Bruno." Her finger hovered over the call button. She waited, then, after a moment, glanced up at Parkman. "Understand? No comment until the call has disconnected."

Parkman nodded. "Yeah, sure, make the call."

She hit dial, and it connected. "Parkman, I need you to listen. I'll explain more when I'm off the phone."

She caught his nod beside her as she stared at the phone. Bruno answered with a grunt.

"You still outside the house?" she asked.

"Yeah."

"The husband left sometime in the last twenty to thirty minutes, right?"

"Yeah," he said again. This time, he sounded more awake. Like he was surprised she knew.

"Okay, here's what I need you to do. Bruno, listen closely, and please do it without asking why. I will explain later."

"I'm listening. I will do as I'm told, or Darwin would kill me."

Parkman seemed nervous or jittery as he struggled to listen and meander through traffic. She was about to explain Bruno's tasks when Parkman revved the engine and ran a yellow light.

"Parkman," she said, caution in her voice.

The car immediately slowed.

"Okay, okay, I know. I got this."

"Ma'am?" Bruno said in her ear. "What is it I'm to do?"

"I need you to go inside the house we were watching. Secure the two occupants"—Parkman snapped his head toward her—"and wait for my call. But Bruno, do not hurt them. After my phone call, you will release them and leave the area. Head toward the airport. You still have the spike belt in your car?"

"Yes, ma'am," he said without hesitation.

"Good, here's where to meet me." She explained the rest in as much detail as Vivian gave her.

She wondered how many people he'd *secured* in his day and that this was just another can-you-grab-me-a-Coke-from-the-fridge request. Through the earpiece, she heard Bruno's car start.

"Moving the car to a hidden location now," he said. "I'll be inside the house in five minutes. Assets secure and waiting for your call within ten."

The line died.

As much as she needed someone with Bruno's mercenary abilities and militant precision, working with him at times was still unnerving. Not a single question as to why he was supposed to secure a housewife and her young daughter. No personal issues with it, either.

A shiver ran through her. She set the phone down and glanced at Parkman.

He shrugged. "I figured they had something to do with our future. What's next?"

Parkman is always the same: no challenging questions, either. Just roll with it, play it out. Why would she expect anything less of him?

"I need a disguise." She padded her pocket. Passport and small wallet in place. She had everything she needed. It had been so long since she'd done anything like this—just shy of two years—twenty-one months to be exact—that she felt woefully unprepared.

"What kind of disguise? If you're talking hair dye and makeup shit, I think that ship has sailed. We haven't the time."

"I wish we had the time. A hat would do. Something to tuck my hair up, offer some sort of cover."

"Where are we flying?"

"We aren't going anywhere."

He looked at her as the airport came into view. "Okay, now I'm confused. The call with Bruno I get. Vivian's asked some wild things of you in the past. But we're going to the airport because you said you needed to buy a plane ticket." He faced the road, slowing at a light. "That's the airport." He stopped the car behind a loud pickup truck that had a modified muffler. "But we're not going anywhere."

"No, I just need inside the terminal."

"Inside," he repeated as if rolling her words around inside his head, mulling them over. "The terminal."

She nodded as Parkman started forward on the green light. "I need to kidnap an airline pilot."

"Oh, right. No big deal."

"No choice, Parkman. Too many people die if I don't."

"Then let's do this. Fuck it."

Chapter 8

The limousine stopped outside Terminal 3 at Toronto International Airport. The locks on the doors popped open. The three of them exited the back, with Aaron taking Alex's bag with him. By the time he got to the front of the limo to hand it to Alex, his friend was already outside, leaning against the vehicle.

Aaron took a look inside the front of the limousine. The passenger side window was gone, glass strewn on the seat and floor. The driver cowered in the passenger seat, the seatbelt wrapped around his body at least twice. He stared at Alex like he was some kind of demon.

"It doesn't look like he moved after you got inside," Aaron said, even though that was obvious.

Alex shook his head, then muttered, "Didn't move."

"Smart to break the passenger side window." Aaron

looked at the driver's seat. It was clean of debris.

Alex stepped away and joined Daniel and Benjamin, who both smacked him on the back. It was likely the only time anyone touched Alex without his consent. It had to be one of the boys from the dojo, and it had to be in moments like this.

As a unit, they started for the doors. Once inside, they found the security access, showed their electronic boarding passes, and quickly got through security.

By their gate, Aaron said he'd spring for food. They all got large coffees, bagels, salads, and a few sweet items, then found chairs by power outlets.

Aaron plugged in his cell phone and dug into a herb and garlic bagel.

"What are we expecting in Dallas?" Benjamin asked.

Aaron shrugged. With his mouth half full, he said, "Sarah's there. Parkman too. Oh, and Bruno. That's all I know."

"Why are we going?" Daniel asked. "Sarah call for help?"

"No, she didn't call. The U.S. Border Patrol called."

Benjamin spun toward him. "The border patrol? What the hell for? She trying to escape into Mexico?"

Alex sat beside him, staring down at his salad as he ate, taking it all in, listening, evaluating.

Aaron took a long drink of coffee and said, "She stole one of their spike belts."

"Spike belts?" Daniel said. "Did he say why?"

Aaron shook his head, his mouth full again.

"And we're going to Dallas to try and find Sarah and return a spike belt?"

Aaron wiped his mouth. "No, we're going because Sarah —"

His cell dinged as a text came through. He grabbed it.

Darwin said: *Sorry. Was acting on Sarah's request.*

Aaron typed: *Understood. No issue. But I'm still going.*

"Who's that?" Daniel asked. "Something we should know?"

"In a sec," Aaron said, eating with one hand, holding the phone with the other as three tiny dots danced on the screen, indicating a new message being typed.

Darwin said: *She wants you guys safe. Claims something in Texas isn't safe for you.*

Aaron typed: *That's the reason I'm going. If it isn't safe in Texas, then she'll need help.*

Darwin: *She has all the help she needs. But since you're going, I'll meet you there.*

Aaron: *I wouldn't try to stop you ...*

Darwin: *I deserve that. My apologies. Acting on intel. See you there.*

He set the phone down and took the last bite of his bagel. When he looked up, all three of them were staring at him.

"That was Darwin. He apologized. Just doing what he was told. Acting on intel." Aaron filled them in on the rest of the conversation.

"So now he's coming to Dallas, too?" Benjamin asked, a smile broadening his features. "Looks like we're having a reunion in Texas, boys."

No one matched his smile, which faded as fast as it appeared.

Daniel smacked Aaron's arm. "You were going to tell us

why we're going to Texas in the first place before Darwin texted."

"We're going to Texas because Sarah needs us. She's in trouble with the authorities again. She has Parkman and Bruno down there with her, and she's listening to Vivian. We're going because of what happened last February. And we're going because that's what we do, regardless of what Sarah might think. We're family. We stick together. There's nothing that would stop me from going to help her, and I appreciate you three agreeing to join me."

"Of course," Daniel said. "We'll always be there for you and Sarah. Any idea what we're walking into down there? Has she indicated what Vivian's been having her do?"

Aaron shook his head. "Zero."

Benjamin raised his hands, then dropped them to his lap. "Oh great. So it could be guns and bullets and shit."

Two people to his left glanced at him.

"Sorry, talking about video games." He twirled his hand in a motion for them to look away.

In a voice slightly above a whisper, Aaron leaned closer to them. "With Sarah, anything is possible. So yes, there could be weapons."

Alex's eyes seemed to sparkle.

For the first time since he'd known Alex, he considered the man might be mad. Either he had an unusual penchant for danger, reveled in near-death experiences, or was a psychopath and didn't *feel* anything—it had to be something. Or did he just like to constantly test his skills? Aaron decided to lean toward skill tests because Alex loved them, and he loved Sarah.

On that note, Aaron didn't know much about Alex's past. Where was he born? Were his parents still alive? When this was over, he decided to pay more attention to Alex and find out if something happened to him to give him such a hunger for self-defense and violence. Although, with Alex's penchant for love, psychopathy was ruled out.

Sarah's missive to Darwin to stop them from coming concerned him. Had Vivian told her to stop them? Was there a legitimate concern for them, their welfare, their lives?

Aaron motioned for them to lean in and listen to prepare them for whatever was coming. "I should say, though," Aaron started, waiting for all three of his dojo teachers to give him their full attention. "There's definitely a chance we could all die down there." His lips tightened, then he added, "We may not be coming home."

Daniel nodded and looked away. Faithful, without remorse, without rancor. He was going as Sarah was in trouble, and Aaron needed him.

Benjamin's body had a subtle jerk when he heard the words. Then he settled, checked Daniel's response, and emulated it. But Aaron could tell those words unsettled him. Benjamin was an excellent fighter, worthy of being a teacher at the dojo. But he was just as good as a lookout, someone who stayed behind to watch their asses.

Alex didn't budge. The sparkle in his eyes increased until they glistened and danced. Even the edge of a smile played across his lips.

Perhaps Aaron misjudged him. Maybe all this time, the guy was insane.

But maybe, just maybe, they needed insane on this trip.

An announcement came over the speakers, telling them their flight was starting the process of pre-boarding.

The four men got to their feet, lugged their bags to their shoulders, and filed one in front of the other, headed to the back of the line to board their non-stop flight to Dallas, Fort Worth International Airport.

"One more reason we're going," Aaron said.

The four of them huddled by a pillar as two mothers with strollers and a man in a wheelchair were boarding first.

"Before Sarah left, she wrote the words *True Legacy* on a piece of paper. She also signed an organ donor card for the State of Texas."

"Organ donor?" Daniel asked. "On the surface, admirable, but why write about her true legacy and decide to fill in organ donor shit just before taking off suspiciously? She planning on going to Texas to die?"

"Why Texas?" Benjamin asked. "I mean, why not die right here in Toronto?"

Aaron gave him a cold stare.

"What?" Benjamin protested, arms out in defense. "I'm just saying."

Aaron pushed through them, headed for the line forming by the gate. "That's what we're going to find out."

I'm coming, Sarah. I love you, and sure hope you're still alive and not pissed at me.

Chapter 9

Sarah asked Parkman to drop her at departures and leave. She would call when she needed to be picked up, but Vivian had mumbled something about picking someone else up, although she wasn't quite sure yet.

Without question, Parkman did as instructed and dropped her at departures. After rushing inside, she checked the time on her cell phone. She had less than thirty minutes.

Not enough.

She half ran, half walked toward a small store. In under two minutes, she'd bought a baseball cap with Dallas Cowboys written on the front and a Dallas newspaper. Inside a restroom, she shoved her hair up inside the cap, checked the little makeup she wore, and then headed for a nearby counter. A ticket, any ticket, would do. All she needed was a boarding pass.

At the counter, *Vegas* popped into her consciousness.

"I need a ticket for Las Vegas," she told the woman at the counter.

The woman wore glasses that went out of fashion in the fifties. The outer edges on each side of the spectacles were raised. Horn-rimmed, she thought they were called.

"Checking any bags?" Horn Rim asked her.

Sarah shook her head. The woman frowned.

To offer some sort of explanation that would make sense for this woman, Sarah said, "My girlfriends all went before me and took my bag. I had to stay behind at the last minute. Missed my flight yesterday." She shrugged innocently. "My fault entirely. Always late for everything." She tried to laugh it off, but it came out as a nervous giggle.

"Would you like me to pull up your flight history and see if we can do something about yesterday's ticket?"

"No," Sarah said so fast, the woman jumped. "Sorry, just charge me for a new fare. I need to get on the next flight out."

Horn Rim typed on her computer for what seemed like a half hour, asked about rates, typed more, confirmed a rate, typed, and then printed a boarding pass.

Sarah almost snatched it from her grip and ran, but she still needed to pay.

"I've got you on American Airlines. You have an aisle seat, as that was all that was left."

The sense of urgency made her perspire. She felt it slide down her back and ring her forehead where the new baseball cap clung to her skin.

"Your flight leaves in—"

"How much again?" Sarah said, cutting her off.

The woman made it obvious she didn't like being cut off but didn't respond right away. She typed on her system agonizingly slow, then gave Sarah the price with taxes.

She was fine with paying slightly over three hundred to fly nowhere. After processing her card, she slipped the boarding pass into the pages of her passport with her picture for easy access later.

"Which way to security?" she asked. "I'm always getting lost in airports."

Horn Rim told her, pointing to her left.

Sarah thanked her and got to the security area quickly but was held up by multiple lanes of people all crushing each other to get to their gates. The TSA employees worked fast, shouting out about liquids, computers out of bags, and everything they needed to say, but still, as travelers approached the conveyor belt, they left their shoes on and belts clipped securely to their waists. Buzzers sounded on every other person, making them walk through the detectors repeatedly. Randomly, people's hands were being swabbed for residue of some kind.

Sarah would jump the line if it were anywhere else and not an airport. She had to enter the airport within five minutes, or she would miss her opportunity. Unnecessary delays were driving her mad. She hopped from one foot to the other, waiting, anxiety building in her stomach. There were still a dozen people in front of her.

She took a moment to text Bruno.

I will call within five minutes or so. Be ready.

According to her phone, she was almost out of time.

She slipped past the last three people in line and walked directly to the bomb-detecting machine because she wasn't wearing a belt, had no carry-on, and wore running shoes. After showing her passport and boarding pass, she tossed her cell phone on the belt in front of five other trays.

Inside the large machine, she stood on the feet diagrams, raised her hands, and waited. After a moment, she got the TSA agent's okay and exited.

She'd done it. She had a plane ticket and was through security. She just needed her cell phone and could do exactly what Vivian had asked her to do.

The man watching the conveyor on his computer monitor took his sweet time, pointing at someone's luggage on the screen. Another TSA agent stepped over. After a whisper between them, the conveyor started moving again.

Sarah felt like screaming. She took in her surroundings and focused on her breathing. She watched the area, looking for the man she needed to meet. If she missed him, untold numbers of people would die. She couldn't have that on her conscience.

The belt moved.

She reached around the partition, grabbed her cell phone, and headed toward Gate 35 in a run, even though her ticket said Gate 32.

She kept an eye out for anyone wearing a pilot's uniform while jumping around slow-moving travelers and wheeled carts jammed with bags, meandering past people standing in groups in the middle of the walkway.

The man she was looking for was Captain Mark Hewlett. He lived on Hillside Lane in Desoto with his wife, Joanne, thirty-five, and their six-year-old daughter, Anna, now currently secured by Bruno and waiting for her call.

"Sarah?" someone shouted.

Out of reflex, she ducked a foot and spun around, looking for the woman who called her name.

"Sarah Roberts? I can't believe it. What are the odds?"

A woman pushed off the wall by the washrooms, moving toward her. Sarah had no time whatsoever to stop and chat with anyone. She was still seven gates from Gate 35 and Mark Hewlett.

"Do I know you—" she stopped, recognizing the woman's eyes. They'd met before, done something important together. This woman did something nice for Sarah. *Detective Marina Diner*, Vivian whispered. *From Toronto.*

"Detective Diner," Sarah said. "Of course. Wow, long time."

"What are you doing in Texas?" she asked, suspicion filtering into her tone. She leaned closer. "I thought you'd stopped all this."

No time! Vivian shouted, making Sarah jerk.

"Right, yeah. No, I've been busy." She stepped back once, then again. "Just staying out of trouble, mostly."

"You seem in a hurry," Marina said. "I can see that. But tell me," she leaned even closer, moving in step with Sarah. "What are you doing here? Maybe I can help."

Sarah shook her head as she turned to go. "You can't help. Not this time." Then she spun around and continued toward Gate 35.

Ten feet from Marina, Sarah glanced over her shoulder. She wasn't being followed. Detective Diner had resumed her spot on the wall beside the women's restroom, watching her go. Marina had a cell phone in her hand. She was dialing out. When their eyes met, Marina didn't smile.

Sarah spun back around and ran for Gate 35. If Detective Diner were here for some reason related to Sarah, she would deal with that later. Kidnap pilot first.

Vivian shouted *Go!* in her head so loud it made her clasp her hands over her ears like that would do any good.

She ran, passing Gate 31, then Gate 32 with its sign LAS VEGAS on the board with the flight's time below it. Horn Rim was already at the booth waiting to board people. Before Sarah got to Gate 33, Horn Rim glanced up, saw her running by, and frowned.

Shit! Drawing too much attention.

Sarah got to Gate 34 and saw the next one coming up. Two attendants stood by the doors where people would board.

She almost tripped, caught herself, and then her heart sank as she saw the doors closing, a man wearing a pilot's uniform having just slipped through.

Captain Mark Hewlett was already heading to the cockpit. She'd missed him, and she didn't have a ticket for that plane.

Why Vivian? Why didn't you have me buy a ticket for his plane?

She almost tripped, caught herself, and slowed down to get her breathing back under control. Hewlett was in the cockpit. Nothing would change that now, and she had no way to get to him. She could collect herself for a minute or two and then talk to the attendants at the booth. If they wouldn't let her in to speak with him, she would buy a ticket. If the plane were sold out, she would buy someone else's ticket.

If she didn't speak with Mark within the next twenty minutes before he settled in the cockpit and got ready to leave—too many lives were at stake to contemplate that further.

A bomb scare would be her last resort.

But she didn't want to go that route. It would end in her arrest, and no one would believe her story because those lives would be saved, but hers would be forfeit in a U.S. prison.

Shit, Vivian, when I agreed to this, you said it would be easy.

No response.

She started for the attendants. At the counter, she waited for one of them to look up.

"Excuse me," she said. "Is there a way I could speak with the captain?"

The attendants exchanged a glance. One was young, mid-twenties, and pretty. The other was in her mid-forties, with no ring on her finger.

"Boarding pass, please," the mid-forties attendant said.

"What for?" Sarah asked. "I'm not on this flight. I just want to speak with Captain Mark Hewlett."

Awkwardly, they exchanged another glance. This time, the younger one stopped typing on her computer. Sarah had their full attention.

"I just saw him get on the plane." Then she added, "We go back." She offered a large, fake smile. "Way back. Like years. His wife, Joanne, and I are friends." That should be an easy sell. There was only a six-year age difference.

"I'm sorry," the older woman said, shaking her head. "He's on duty, prepping for a flight. This isn't a time for a social call. But if you leave your name and number, I can pass a message along—"

Sarah leaned against the counter with her stomach, her knees bumping hard against the lower area. She whispered, "Call him out here for one minute. It won't be long." She held up her cell phone. "I've got a message from his wife and daughter." Then she considered another angle. "It's an emergency."

The woman smiled, but it wasn't pleasant. It was one of those snarky smiles where the center of the mouth dipped, and only one edge rose. The urge to smack it off the woman's face made Sarah's hand twitch. People would die because this woman wouldn't tell the captain Sarah needed him for one minute, and she was acting put out, bothered. The urge to grab the woman and scream overwhelmed Sarah.

Instead, she gripped the edge of the counter and waited.

"Ma'am, if you're not on this flight, please head to your own gate. We're busy and preparing to board at any time. If you need assistance, I'd be happy to call airport security, and they can take you where you need to go."

That was it. The line had been drawn. She wasn't going to get access to Captain Mark Hewlett. She'd missed him by less than a minute.

Her phone vibrated. She checked it. A return text from Bruno.

We are secure. Waiting.

She slipped her phone back into her pocket and realized there was nothing left for her to do but push the envelope.

Just like the old days.

Sarah Roberts was back, and she was ready. Lives hung in the balance. This was literally a do-or-die situation.

She knew this was coming because Vivian had told her to have Bruno bring the spike belt after letting the family go. The entire picture wasn't clear to Sarah, but did it ever have to be?

She had to fight for what was right, regardless of the consequences.

By the time she barged through the doors that led to the ramp, made it to the captain, and spoke with him, airport security would just be arriving to apprehend her. He would call them off once he heard her elevator pitch, her call to action.

So she went for it.

Sarah jumped to her right, and in one large step, she was at the doors, tugging on them.

"Hey!" the attendant yelled at her. Then she turned to her colleague and said, "Call security."

The doors remained locked. She glanced up at the rectangular magnet at the top of the glass. She was not getting to Captain Mark Hewlett unless they let her in.

And now security was being called.

"What's the problem here?" a woman asked.

Sarah turned around at the familiar voice.

Detective Marina Diner stood there, her ID up and out, showing it to the two attendants.

"I'm Detective Marina Diner. This woman," she pointed at Sarah, "she's with me."

Chapter 10

Parkman decided to browse a bookstore. He figured Sarah would be at least an hour, possibly longer. There was a Barnes & Noble, a short drive from the airport on Belt Line Rd. It was only twenty minutes away, and until Sarah needed him, he would browse books, buy a few, and drink coffee.

As he pulled into the parking lot, his phone rang.

"Shit."

He snatched it up without checking caller ID.

"Parkman here."

"It's Darwin. We have a problem."

Parkman eased the car to the right, found a safe spot, then stopped. "What sort of problem?"

"Aaron's coming."

"What? That's not good. Sarah didn't want that."

"I know. He's pretty messed up about being excluded. I

feel he's taking that shit personally. I mean, most people would."

"Are you worried about Sarah?"

Darwin hesitated. "No, Sarah's not stupid. If her sister wanted her to do something that required extra danger, even more than normal, she would call for help. In fact, she did call me. That's why Bruno's there. And you're there."

"Exactly." Parkman stared at the bookstore sign, knowing how upset this would make Sarah.

"Does this have something to do with them? I mean, are Sarah and Aaron on the outs?"

"You mean, are they breaking up?" Parkman asked.

"Yeah, you know, because of last February."

"No, they're fine. But that definitely sent a shock wave through their core. They're still growing together, having to relearn things since then." Parkman stared at the bookstore sign again, needing a coffee now. He was so close to the hardcovers he could taste the coffee and smell the pages. "Look, we have to stop him from coming."

"I tried. Sent a limo to drive them to the airport—"

"How's that trying to stop them?" Parkman blurted.

"Listen," Darwin said without a note of impatience. "I sent a *hired* limo to drive them to the airport. This vehicle was decked out to contain the occupants. His task was to wait until their plane left, then drive them to a secure facility where I had people waiting to explain the situation to them. The driver was supposed to take them to Canada's Wonderland so as not to make them feel threatened. We all know how those four will act when feeling threatened. My guess is I would have Sarah on the line by then telling Aaron to stay home."

"What happened to the limo?"

"Somehow, they got out. Broke one of the windows and drove themselves to the airport."

"Your driver?"

"Fine. Banged up, but fine."

"Aaron know it was you?"

"Yeah. I apologized."

"That's good. Once things calm down, Sarah will talk to him. It'll all work out."

"So she's okay with Aaron coming to Texas now?"

"Absolutely not. Aaron dies if he comes here. She said she's seen it."

"Well, he boarded his flight a few hours ago. They're landing at Dallas Fort Worth within the hour."

"Shit," Parkman shouted, smacking the steering wheel with his free hand. "There goes the coffee and hardcovers."

"The what?"

"Nothing. Sarah's gonna be pissed."

"Tell her I tried."

"Not at you. At Aaron."

"If it means anything, just remember that he loves her, and she's not talking to him. Consider that what happened last February killed something in their hearts. He's searching for it as much as she is."

"Yeah, but I'm afraid it won't just be Aaron's heart that's killed when he gets here. At least that's what Sarah's saying."

"That's why I'm on the next flight out of Rome. I'll be in Dallas tomorrow around lunchtime. I'll text you the itinerary."

"Everyone's coming to Dallas," Parkman said out loud, although he meant to say it to himself.

"Wait, did Sarah say anything about me coming? Like she saw something about my ... future?"

"No, just Aaron and his three teachers. They have to stay away until this is over."

"Too late for that."

"Okay, I have to go. I have to warn Sarah."

"See you tomorrow, Parkman."

"Wait, when do you land? Where do we meet?"

"I just told you. I'll text the itinerary."

The line died.

Parkman tossed the phone into the passenger seat, spun the car around, and headed back toward the airport.

Everything was getting out of hand.

Sarah may have returned to the vigilante business helping strangers stay alive, but she had to solve her friend's and family's issues, or they would be the people who ended up dead.

Chapter 11

"I'M DETECTIVE MARINA DINER. This lady, Suzann Scott, is traveling with me to Oregon. We're on this plane. You don't need security. This woman"—she pointed at Sarah as she lowered her ID—"is with me."

Marina had gestured at the woman standing behind her when she said her name. Suzann Scott's eyes flitted from Sarah to Marina, then back to Sarah. Something about Suzann looked badass, like if push came to shove, she *could* be a badass. Was Suzann Marina's prisoner? That didn't make sense. Marina was a detective with the Toronto Police Force. She had a partner named Niles Mason. They came after Sarah years ago when a cop's daughter had died.

Vanessa Simmons, Vivian whispered.

That was it; Vanessa Simmons had died after falling from the CN Tower in downtown Toronto.

That, and I shot her before she died. A lifetime ago.

"I'm sorry, Detective," the woman was saying. "But she was trying to break into the—"

Sarah moved a few steps toward them. "Not *break into* the ramp. I need to speak with the man about to fly that plane." She turned to Marina. "I have a serious matter to discuss with him, one of massive importance." She held up her phone. "Captain Mark Hewlett's wife and daughter are waiting for his call." This last bit was only half true. They were waiting, but they didn't know what to do. With Bruno there and both of them secured in some fashion, they probably thought they would be dead soon.

"You haven't started boarding yet," Marina said to the older attendant. "What does it hurt to allow this young lady to simply give a message to the captain?"

The attendant bristled like she couldn't handle being talked down to, even though Marina just asked her a simple question.

"I offered to pass the message myself, but she refused—"

Marina smiled. "Look, I know a little about Sarah. If she needs to speak with the captain herself, you passing a message along won't work." Marina pointed at the doors. "Let her in." She flipped open her ID to show it to the attendants again. A small crowd was gathering behind them. "I'll go with her. We'll be out in a minute, isn't that right, Sarah?" She raised her voice for this last part, her eyes not leaving the attendant's face.

"That's right. One minute."

More people gathered behind Marina, some whispering to each other. Several of them held up cell phones, no doubt recording. This was something Sarah would have to get used to. Everyone was an amateur Spielberg with their devices.

"Fine," the attendant said. "You've got one minute. But I do this against protocol."

"Oh yeah," Marina said, a warning tone in her voice. "What's protocol when the captain has a family emergency and is not actively flying the plane? When we come out, I'll want your name. I'm in a letter-writing mood. Perhaps there are people above you who would want to know what you impeded here and why."

The doors unlocked.

Sarah tore them open and stepped through, waiting for Marina. Suzann Scott came up behind Marina. Looks like all three of them were going. Made sense that Suzann would go with Marina. For all she knew, Suzann could be a friend and not Marina's prisoner. In fact, that was more likely as Marina had no legal jurisdiction in the States.

"What's this all about?" Marina asked as they scurried along the ramp.

"Long story. You'll hear it all in a few moments." And what exactly would Marina do when she did hear it all? That was another problem Sarah would deal with when the time came. The first step was to talk to Hewlett.

Once inside the plane, Sarah turned left toward the cockpit, where the door was still open as they hadn't started the boarding process yet.

"Can I help you?" a flight attendant asked. She had been bent over the chairs, placing seatbelts into a V position on seats two rows back.

"We're here to speak with the captain," Sarah said.

The woman stepped between them and angled herself in front of the cockpit door. Sarah read her nametag.

"Look, Nancy Bibb, we just need a minute of his time, and then we're gone."

Behind her, Marina opened her ID again. "Family emergency," she added.

Nancy read the ID, looked at Suzann, and then back to Sarah. "Captain Hewlett is about to fly—"

"We know, to Oregon," Sarah said, cutting her off. Then, in a voice loud enough for the men in the cockpit to hear, Sarah said, "Captain Mark Hewlett. I have a message from Joanne and Anna. Can you please come out here to take their call?"

Nancy appeared flustered. She wasn't sure how to handle the intrusion but stepped aside and let the captain handle it as he got up from his chair, set a clipboard down, motioned to the copilot that he'd be right back, and stepped out of the cockpit. She recognized him instantly. She'd seen him come and go, even cut the lawn two days ago, as she'd watched his house as well for a few days alongside Bruno and Parkman.

"Sir, I will call your house now," Sarah said.

"What's this all about?" he asked.

Marina shrugged and gestured at Sarah. "She knows."

Sarah stepped back to have some room. It was crowded, with them all standing around such a tight space.

"Who are you people?" he asked, a note of worry in his voice. "Has something happened to my wife and daughter?"

How does shit get this fucked up? Sarah thought. To do what she was about to do in front of so many witnesses, one a detective out of Toronto.

There was no other choice, no other plan. This was it.

"You may want to take a seat, sir," Sarah suggested. She hit the send button on the screen, and then Bruno's cell started ringing. He answered right away.

"Yeah?" he said.

"Put Joanne on the phone first. Her husband is here. Once the phone call has ended, you know what to do."

"Yes. I will be watching for you."

"Good, see you soon. Now, put Joanne on."

Sarah lowered the phone and turned to Nancy Bibb. "Please step back." Then she motioned for Marina and Suzann to give her some room. "Everyone, step back."

The tinny sound of a frantic voice eked out of Sarah's phone. The captain frowned, looking at it in her hand.

"Marina, Detective Diner," Sarah said as she edged toward Hewlett, "you know who I am and what I can do. I need you to trust me on this."

Marina also frowned, turning her head slightly to the side as if thinking harder would give her the answer to what Sarah was up to.

"Do not react until the phone is turned off," Sarah added for everyone's benefit. "Or a lot of people could die."

It sounded like a collective gasp, but it was only Nancy, the attendant, and Suzann. Marina and the captain remained quiet.

Sarah brought the phone to her ear. "Joanne, calm down. This will all be over soon."

That caught the captain's attention in a negative way. "What have you done?" he asked, his tone accusatory.

Sarah raised her hand, palm facing him. "Calm down,"

she said sternly. "This is a proof-of-life call. Once you speak with Joanne, you will speak with Anna. Both of them are safe. Both of them are at home on Hillside Lane. Once you hear their voices, return the phone to me, and I will explain what you need to do."

Mark moved to launch at Sarah, but Suzann stepped between them.

"Hey, take it easy," Suzann said. "If Marina trusts this woman, then she's good in my books. At least hear her out."

Badass Suzanne Scott. Sarah had pegged her right.

"Sarah …" Marina said beside her. "What have you done?" Those four words were just above a whisper, a tone of disbelief seeping into her voice.

She handed Mark Hewlett her cell phone.

He put it to his ear, staring at the carpeted floor. "Baby?" he said. "Are you hurt?" Then, after a moment. "A big guy? What big guy?" Then his voice rose when he said, "A monster?" Hewlett glanced at Sarah, a scowl changing his youthful middle-aged face to something demonic. "Are you hurt?" he asked again, continuing to stare at Sarah. In fact, they were all staring at Sarah now. "Did he hurt Anna?" A pause. "Okay. Just hold on. I'll be home soon."

The phone lowered from his ear, but he didn't attempt to hand it back. Sarah didn't care. It was one of ten burners she'd bought for this Texas trip, and she had Bruno's and Parkman's phone numbers memorized.

With all eyes on her, Sarah cleared her throat. "Several dozen people will die today if you don't do exactly as you're told, Captain Mark Hewlett."

Chapter 12

MID-AFTERNOON, AND THEIR plane was starting its descent to the Dallas airport. Aaron stretched, yawning. Alex had drifted off to sleep as soon as the plane left Toronto. Daniel had spent the flight reading something on his phone, and Benjamin had opted for the inflight movie.

"You think Darwin's going to try and stop us again?" Benjamin asked, folding up his headphones.

"How?" Aaron said. "We're already here. Besides, we're friends. He's not an enemy. He was just trying to fuck with us because Sarah wants to do whatever it is she's doing here on her own."

"Yeah, but we haven't met up with Sarah yet. He could have people waiting for us to deplane. He's got the resources and money."

"Well, we've got resources, too. We've got each other."

"That wasn't the question." Benjamin laid his head back, staring at the ceiling. "There are always so many unknowns."

"Yeah, but you know what's good about that? As soon as we land, find Sarah and Parkman, ask the right questions, and deal with everything, whatever the hell we're dealing with, all those *unknowns* become *knowns*."

"Yeah, that's what I'm afraid of. The *knowns*."

Daniel set his phone down and chuckled. "The *knowns*. Sounds like a disease."

"It can be," Benjamin said. "And it affects all of us. It's so contagious. Sarah's got a nasty case of it and can infect us from anywhere in the world."

"And we'd find a cure every time," Aaron added.

Benjamin nodded. "I know, I know, because we're family. It's not coming to help that's bothering me. Or the fact that there might be," he lowered his head as if whispering wouldn't be enough when he said, "guns. It's the fact that Sarah didn't want us here. That scares me."

Aaron glanced out the window, watching Dallas below them as they flew over the airport.

"Looks like the airport below us."

The man in the seat in front of him half-turned. "It is the airport. I live here, in Fort Worth. Looks like the pilot's circling to come back."

"Circling to land in the wind, probably," Benjamin added.

"Could be," the guy said. "This happens often when the airport gets busy. Just waiting our turn to land."

Benjamin's knees were bouncing. Aaron shot a glance at Alex. He was awake without having looked like he'd slept at all.

A moment later, Daniel dropped a hand on Benjamin's leg. "Calm," was all he said.

Benjamin stopped bouncing. This nervousness was out of character for Benjamin. He holds a second-dan black belt in Shotokan karate. Nothing much bothered him except being shot and earthquakes. Maybe flying freaked him out, and Aaron had never noticed before. Daniel and Alex had probably noticed how unsettled Benjamin was as well, but they were letting it go for now. No one wanted to out him, embarrass him.

But Aaron felt a growing concern. Maybe he should have come alone. Why did he ask them to close the dojo? Was it a moment of uncertainty on his part, a moment of weakness?

What's done was done. They were family and all here, in Dallas, Texas. Whether Sarah wanted him here or not, he was here, and he would prove his love by showing her how he felt. They were all here, a unified front supporting the woman that brought them together.

And maybe, just maybe, that unified front would go a long way in healing the scars of the past. Maybe they'd be able to work past last February. All the tears, the dreams ripped from them. At times, the pain had been unbearable. For a few months, Sarah had turned to whiskey to silence the voice in her head. Aaron had joined her. By June, they felt like alcoholics, dehydrated and fighting with daily hangovers.

Then Vivian was back, and Sarah would disappear for a few hours. When Aaron asked her about it, she said it was a small, easy task for Vivian, nothing dangerous.

It sounded like Vivian had Sarah back in training, preparing her for bigger things, like whatever the hell they were doing in Texas.

Or the alternative, which Aaron refused to think about, was Sarah had signed that organ donor thing to come to Texas and find her *true legacy*, her reason for living, and quite possibly, her reason for dying.

Sarah's death was not something he could live with.

The plane banked to the right, and after several minutes, Aaron noticed they were flying by the airport again.

The speakers beeped above their heads. "Good afternoon, ladies and gentlemen. This is your captain speaking. We're hearing from the tower that the Dallas Fort Worth Airport is a little backed up at the moment. It appears our landing schedule has been pushed back. We've been ordered to circle the area and burn off more fuel. I'll let you know when I get the all-clear to land. Shouldn't be long now, folks." The speaker beeped as the captain disengaged.

"They're not backed up," Benjamin said, leaning over Aaron to stare down at the empty runway. He sat back in his chair and looked up at the overhead bins. "This is Darwin, through and through. I told you guys, but no one would listen. No one would fuckin' listen. This has Darwin Kostas written all over it." His legs started hopping again.

No one tried to correct him or dispute his claims. Daniel didn't try to stop Benjamin's bouncing legs.

Alex snuck a glance at Aaron. Their eyes locked for a moment, a brotherly moment of we'll-figure-this-out-soon-enough.

Aaron nodded slightly, with Alex nodding back.

Maybe Benjamin was right after all. Maybe Darwin was stopping their commercial airline from landing.

But how could he do that? How the hell was that even possible?

Chapter 13

"Tell me," Captain Mark Hewlett said. "What is it you want me to do?" He leaned against the seats beside him, probably to remain upright. Once he'd realized what had happened and spoken with his wife, he understood he was now in the middle of some kind of kidnapping-for-ransom deal. At least that got his attention, and that's what Sarah needed.

She glanced down at his legs, wondering if he'd fall. They were shaking so badly. That almost made her stop everything, get arrested, and linger in prison for a few years. How would Vivian feel then?

She blinked herself back in the room, back in the moment. How many people would die if she did that? How many innocent children have gone because of her selfishness? No, she would see this through till the end, consequences be damned.

"There's another plane scheduled to take off out of Gate A12 with your airline. You're the new pilot of that plane. Do that, and my man walks away from your house."

"What?" he managed to say. "Wait, why? What's wrong with the pilot that plane already has?"

"You have rank. You're something called a *training* captain. You walk in that cockpit and outrank the captain who is scheduled to fly today."

"No, why kidnap my family to make me fly another plane? What's in it for you?"

Nancy, the attendant, had eased several feet away from Sarah, but Sarah kept her eyes on her in case she hit some kind of alarm.

"Okay, everyone, listen and listen closely." Sarah glanced at Marina's blanched face and gestured toward her. "I'm happy you're here, Detective. An unexpected surprise but welcomed all the same. You can vouch for what I'm about to say." Marina nodded, but it was clear she wanted no part in this. Regardless of the goal, this was criminal and went against everything Detective Diner stood for. What Sarah did for Marina all those years ago in Toronto probably gave Sarah some wiggle room with Marina's conscience, though.

Sarah turned back to Hewlett. "Your family is safe at home. My friend was only there to facilitate that call. Understood?"

"But if I refuse to do as you ask—"

"You won't refuse. Neither one of us wants to face those consequences." Which meant two different things to both of them. "That plane cannot take off today."

Now Mark's brow knitted together, giving him a not-so-pretty unibrow. "You want me to take over the captain's seat to fly a plane to ensure it doesn't go anywhere?"

"Precisely."

"Why?" Hewlett asked. "Doesn't make sense."

Something rustled behind her. She snuck a peek and saw the copilot watching them. His face twisted in a concerned scowl.

"Someone tampered with the landing gear," Sarah said.

"Oh great," Hewlett almost shouted. "So you hurt my family unless I fly a broken plane and die. Is that it?"

Sarah suppressed the urge to grab his collar, yank him nose to nose, and shout at him. She clenched her hands into tight fists, calming herself. It seemed only Marina glanced down as Sarah's hands unclenched.

"Listen closely. I said, take over the plane, then, during your pre-flight safety check, explain you want the landing gear checked. I don't fucking know or care how you do it but do not let that plane fly anywhere today. Or tomorrow, or any day, until it's been properly inspected. The current pre-flight safety inspection missed the landing gear issue. That's it. That's all I want."

"Why not just tell someone—"

"Because I can't let the people behind the tampering know I'm here, whoever they are. Besides, who would listen to me? I'd be locked away for weeks of questioning how I knew that information. The paranoia would be intense. I'd be asked what other planes are being tampered with. When should we this, when should we that—"

Marina raised a hand, stopping her rant. "Sarah, we get

it." She angled her body to stand directly in front of Sarah. "Call your man back and tell him to walk away. Let the captain's family go." She nodded at Hewlett. "I'm sure he'll do as you say now that he sees how serious you are."

Sarah checked on the flight attendant. Nancy Bibb hadn't moved. Suzann Scott stood rapt, watching everything, listening, taking it all in. Detective Marina Diner had adjusted into full professional mode, attempting to take over the situation and calm it all down.

Hewlett nodded at her when she glanced his way.

"I'll do it," he said. "Just as you say. Just let them go first."

"Please," Marina said. "We'll see this through and call it a day." She pointed at the ramp that led back into the airport. "Let's go stop that plane from taking off." Then she gestured at the phone that was still in Hewlett's hand. He handed it to her, and she handed it to Sarah. "Make the call. End this."

Ideas ran through Sarah's mind. Vivian was gone, leaving her directionless without advice.

So Sarah went with her only option.

She dialed Bruno's number. He answered right away.

"Yeah," he grunted.

"I will call back in two minutes. If I don't, kill them both."

She disconnected the call, dropped the phone, and stomped on it, making it useless, all in one quick motion.

A collective gasp resonated from the small group assembled around her.

Detective Diner's eyes hardened. "You shouldn't've done that."

"The plane," Sarah said. "Now, Captain Hewlett. I need to see and hear your intentions. We have a minute and a half to save your wife and child."

He sprang to his feet, holding the seats on either side of him. How someone's eyes could go bloodshot on cue was beyond Sarah, but Hewlett's eyes sparkled red where the sclera had lost its previous whiteness.

"I'll do it, I'll do it," he gasped. "Just make the call." Hewlett pushed past Marina, then edged Suzann aside, making his way for the ramp. "What gate again?" he asked.

"Gate A12. You've got less than twenty minutes. When I see you running, I'll make the call to leave your family alone."

He spun around, walking backward up the tunnel, about to turn and be lost from sight. "On what phone?"

Marina yanked hers from her inner breast pocket and held it up.

Hewlett nodded, then pivoted back around and ran up the ramp.

Sarah started after him, but Marina grabbed her arm and leaned in to her ear. "You're in a lot of trouble, Missy."

Sarah glanced down at Marina's hand wrapped around her elbow. "Take your hand off me, or I'll break it off."

Marina waited a heartbeat, and Sarah let that go for old time's sake. Then, the hand opened and moved away.

With everyone on her heels, Sarah started back up the ramp. Marina fell in close behind, with Suzann at her heels. Even Nancy Bibb joined them. Near the doors that led back to the waiting area of Gate 35, Sarah glanced back once and saw the copilot trailing them all.

She smacked the doors open, hoping she wouldn't see Captain Mark Hewlett anywhere close. She was ready to grab Marina's cell phone to make the call, but that wasn't what happened.

Hewlett stood to the side, surrounded by half a dozen security officers and four uniformed police officers. Before the door to the ramp even closed behind her, three men jumped on her, their combined weight slamming her to the carpet. It was natural for Sarah to resist, but with one pull, one tug, she realized it was useless. They would use a Taser, they would subdue, they would cuff her.

It was over, and there was nothing she could do.

"Cuff her hands in front," Hewlett shouted, leaning in close as the men scrambled to secure Sarah's arms.

A knee dropped on the back of her neck, shoving her cheek into the carpet. Another knee pressed down on the small of her back, and someone grabbed her ankles and bent her knees, pinning her legs in a V formation, applying weight to the point that pain shot up from her knees and thighs.

A moan escaped her lips against her will. She would rather be subdued with more dignity, but sometimes, the body had other plans.

Dignity, isn't that all anyone really wanted in life, a little dignity?

On the Dallas Fort Worth Airport floor, dignity was nothing but a dream as no one listened to Hewlett. They had her cuffed and jerked up to her feet, pins and needles rushing to her shoulders and lower extremities.

"Wait!" Hewlett screamed in a near panic. "Guys, she has to make a call."

Marina was already providing her ID for everyone to see and holding out her cell phone. "She has to make a call," she stammered as well.

"She can make her call when we get her secured away."

Marina stepped in front of the men holding her. "No, she makes her call now. Or this man's," she pointed at Hewlett, "wife and daughter will be killed."

The men holding Sarah looked at each other, frowning.

"What?" the older one said.

"It's true," the copilot said, stepping forward. "I heard the whole thing. I'm the one who called you guys. This woman has Captain Hewlett's family hostage."

So you're the one who fucked me, Sarah thought. *Missed that.*

"Okay, make the call," the older cop said. "But make it quick."

A huge crowd had gathered. Not dozens of people, hundreds. Over half of them were holding cell phones up, chattering among themselves. If Sarah weren't right beside the older cop, she would have trouble hearing him with all the commotion.

"What's the number?" Marina asked.

Hewlett had broken into a full-body sweat.

Sarah told her the number. Marina dialed and held the phone close to Sarah's ear.

"Yeah," Bruno said, the sound of his car in the background. He was already on the way.

Good Bruno.

"Leave them alone. Don't hurt them."

"Got it. See you soon."

"Destroy your phone. Hang up now."

There was a faint click as Marina pulled the phone away and to her ear. Bruno was gone. She slipped the phone back into her breast pocket.

Hewlett dropped into an empty chair beside him. The whole row was empty. Probably cleared by the authorities before grabbing Sarah.

"Let's go, miss," the older cop said as they started to drag her away.

"Hewlett?" she shouted over her shoulder. "You still going to A12?"

"Fuck you!" he shouted.

The crowd cheered, roaring their approval of the captain in his full regalia, epaulets adorning his shoulders as he swore at the bedraggled female criminal as she was dragged away.

It dawned on Sarah that she'd lost her *Dallas Cowboys* hat somewhere. Her hair was probably a complete mess.

Then someone shouted something, and a smile broke out on her lips.

Suzann Scott, that badass after all, had shouted, "There's a *bomb* on the plane parked at Gate A12. Get everyone off immediately. A *bomb*, a *BOMB!*"

Chapter 14

THEY WERE STILL CIRCLING the airport. The tension, frustration, and general annoyance for their prolonged flight were bothering other passengers and had seeped under Aaron's skin as he watched Dallas from the window. Why couldn't they just land? If Darwin was involved in some twisted way, what could he have done to make their plane circle endlessly?

Aaron hoped Darwin hadn't overstepped and got himself caught up in something so big that there would be serious repercussions. Messing with American airports was tricky and dangerous.

"I'm convinced this is Darwin," Benjamin said. "Sure as shit."

Aaron turned to face them.

Daniel shook his head. "Somehow, I don't think so. Not

this."

"He tried to stop us in Toronto. He's finishing the job now."

The couple in the seats in front of them half turned again. Aaron waved his hand toward the floor at knee level, indicating they should keep it down.

"This has nothing to do with Darwin," he whispered. "Would he go this far? Could he?"

The speakers clicked. "This is your captain speaking. We've been cleared to land in Dallas, Fort Worth. Flight attendants prepare for landing. Cabin crew, please take your seats for landing."

"See, all good," Aaron added. "If this were Darwin, we wouldn't be cleared to land."

He watched from the window as the ground drew closer. Minutes later, the wheels touched down on Texas soil.

The plane erupted in a chorus of clapping and cheering. It seemed as if everyone was happy that it was over. Once they deplaned, they could call Parkman. He would direct them from there or at least let Sarah know they'd arrived.

How mad could she be? If they weren't needed for help, they could wait in the hotel until Sarah was done with whatever she was doing. At least she'd know they were there and feel their support from afar.

Once the plane had taxied in and stopped and everyone jumped up to grab their carry-on from the overhead bins, Aaron was ready to leave, feeling rather claustrophobic after over four hours stuffed in a small seat by the window.

Inside the airport, circulation returning to their legs, they followed the signs to the exit as they'd cleared customs in

Toronto before leaving, and none of them had checked any bags.

Aaron kept a watchful eye on everyone they were passing in case Darwin popped up out of nowhere. He wouldn't doubt it. Or it could be Parkman. If Sarah truly didn't want them in Texas, she would make a point of letting them know.

He wondered if Sarah herself would show up and tell them to get on the next plane back to Toronto.

And Aaron would honor that request and leave. But not before knowing a good reason. They'd worked together in the past, taken risks in the past. How was this any different?

Twenty minutes later, they were headed for the taxi stand. Out front, a dozen police vehicles lined the arrivals doors.

"Looks like something big went down," he muttered as he slowed to watch.

Daniel gave Benjamin a friendly shot in the arm. "Quite possibly the reason for the delay in landing."

"Yeah, yeah," Benjamin said, finally realizing their delay probably had nothing to do with Darwin.

Alex remained quiet and watched. Because that's what Alex did. He watched. He listened.

At least ten cops were coming up a walkway with someone jammed between them. Aaron couldn't look at their prisoner well, so he started forward, slow at first, out of curiosity, then faster because the officers were reaching their vehicles.

"Hey, Aaron," Benjamin said behind him. "Taxi stand is that way."

By now, he was fifteen feet from them. "I know, just one sec."

If Darwin actually had anything to do with their delay in the air, he wanted to eyeball the person the authorities were escorting off the property for later reference.

"Aaron?" Daniel said, closer to him.

Of course, his boys would follow.

Then Alex moved up beside him, probably as curious as Aaron was.

The officers rounded the corner to exit the open doors of the airport terminal and stepped up to a cruiser. Two men opened doors and stepped aside.

The prisoner was jostled forward.

Panic rose in Aaron's stomach.

"Sarah!" he shouted.

She stopped and looked at him, her eyes wild, searching. They locked eyes as Aaron started to run, but Alex stopped him by wrapping his arms around his waist and lifting him off the pavement.

"Sarah," he bellowed this time, like shouting the word hurt.

"Get out of here," she shouted back, then was manhandled into the back of the police cruiser. The door closed, and the vehicle started away from the curb.

Several officers started toward them.

Daniel stepped forward to talk to the cops, and Benjamin went with him. Alex stayed with Aaron as they watched the police cruiser drive by them, Sarah glaring at them from the back seat.

She was crying when she mouthed the words, *please, go*

home.

Chapter 15

Sarah waited. In cuffs, in the back of the cruiser, there was nothing she could possibly do until Bruno arrived.

She could brood. She could think about how everything always seemed to come together and then fall apart again. The plane at Gate A12 did not fly today. She had done it, but barely. And really, it took a village, as the saying goes.

What would she have done without that woman, Suzann Scott? And Detective Diner. Where the hell did she come from? Why was she even in Texas?

To think how crazy everything was and how it all still came together. Real life was truly stranger than fiction. There were no two ways about it.

The cruiser braked at a traffic light. The officer took the opportunity to look at Sarah in the rearview.

"You've got yourself in a bit of a pickle now, haven't

you?"

Sarah turned away and stared out the window. She'd be out of this *pickle* in minutes if everything went as planned.

Aaron.

What the hell was he doing with his team of black belts? She had sent instructions—no, orders because it was that serious—that they were to be stopped from coming to Texas.

As soon as she was back with Parkman, she would have to find Aaron, talk to him, and convince him to leave. She only hoped it wasn't too late.

The cruiser stopped at another red light. Sarah snuck a glance out the back window. A large black SUV edged close to the cruiser. She spun back around, looking for Bruno.

Then she saw him, the spike belt neatly wrapped up in his large arms.

The traffic signals for the other direction switched to yellow. This was it. Breakout time. Whether she'd done this sort of thing a million times or not, it still got her heart racing in anticipation because anything could go wrong.

The lights switched red for the other direction.

The cop's light switched to green. He hit the gas, and Bruno unfolded the spike belt directly in front of the cruiser, then jumped back.

All four tires popped as the police vehicle vibrated with the concussion of expended air. The cop hit the brakes, causing Sarah to almost smash her forehead on the screen, separating the back from the front.

They were parked in the middle of the intersection, with several cars driving around them. Others had stopped, some honking their horns.

"What the fuck …?" the driver shouted as he fumbled for his radio, somewhat dazed at what had just happened. He spat a number of some kind into the radio as Bruno walked around to the driver's side.

"In need of backup at the corner of—"

A siren wailed somewhere close behind them. With as many cruisers as they had at the airport, there were bound to be several more cops coming this way.

The driver's side door was ripped open from the outside. Bruno had a grip on the cop as he screamed in protest, his right hand going for something on his belt.

Sarah waited and watched. She was too constrained to do anything else.

A moment later, the cop was out of her line of vision, and Bruno leaned inside the front of the cruiser. Then he stood up and came around to her door, yanking it open. He gently lifted her out of the car, placed the handcuff keys in her palm —not pausing to unlock them himself as time was limited— and walked her to the large SUV behind the cruiser.

Over a dozen people stood and watched. People in vehicles at the light, blocked vehicles, pedestrians, virtually everyone saw them enter the SUV.

The second the door closed with Sarah and Bruno safe in the back, protected from further gawking by tinted windows, two more cruisers shot by on their left.

The driver eased up on the sidewalk, angled past the ruined cruiser, and turned right. By the time they were twenty feet from the vehicle that had held Sarah, she had removed the cuffs. Palm out, she asked for a cell phone.

Bruno handed her one.

"No trouble at Hillside Lane?" she asked. "The woman and girl were compliant?"

Bruno nodded. "I did as you asked. No harm was done to them. We made the call, and then I left. They are safe."

It was her turn to nod. "Good."

Rationally, she knew it didn't matter how she got the job done as long as it got done. Stopping that plane from taking off today saved dozens of lives. The man who sabotaged the plane was another story. Why couldn't she be directed to stop him first? It would've been a lot easier than kidnapping families and getting arrested at airports.

But Vivian had a plan, and Sarah made a pact a long time ago. It had to be done Vivian's way. She was the one who saw what was coming. Sarah didn't. Actually, Sarah often didn't want to know what was coming, but sometimes Vivian offered her dark visions of the future. Like Aaron's death if he came to Texas.

She shuddered, then dialed Parkman.

"Where are you?" he asked as soon as he answered.

"I'm with Bruno. We're heading back to the motel."

"You know the airport was almost placed into lockdown? Some reports of a bomb on a plane. A woman was arrested."

"Yeah, I'm aware."

"Wait, was it you? Arrested?"

"Yeah, but we're good now. There are other problems, bigger problems we need to deal with."

"Like what?"

Sarah heard Parkman's car door slam. Then his engine turned over. Parkman was at the airport, looking for her.

"Aaron and his teachers are at the taxi stand in arrivals at

Terminal D. They're still in line. It was pretty long, and nothing was moving in that area when I was there. Please pick them up and bring them to the motel."

"I'm at Terminal D right now."

"I figured. That's where you dropped me off."

"Okay, I'll loop back around and look for the taxi stand line." He paused, then added, "You pissed?"

"No."

"Oh, thought you'd be angry he came after you told him not to."

"I'm not angry, Parkman. I'm scared."

"What? You? Scared? That's new." His tone was lighthearted like he was trying to make her laugh. She didn't respond for a moment, and then he said in a more serious tone, "Yeah, sure, I'll find them."

Sarah hung up and passed the phone to Bruno. "Who's that?" She jerked her head toward the driver.

"One of Darwin's friends."

"Darwin has a lot of friends." Then she asked, "You didn't hurt that cop, did you?"

Bruno shook his head. "No. He'll be awake by now."

Bruno stared at the windshield. His job was done. She'd told him to leave Hillside Lane as soon as the first call was made and bring the spike belt to that corner in the event she got arrested. Wait for a vehicle—cruiser or otherwise—with her in it, then extract her without killing anyone. Why could Bruno do his job without fail, and Sarah's jobs always got screwed up? And she had a dead sister to guide her, too. Something had to be done to fix that.

We're changing the future, Sarah, Vivian whispered,

startling her. *Much more involved. Fate always pushes back.*

Then, change the future for Aaron or expect pushback from me.

Vivian disappeared again. Silence filled the void her sister always occupied. There was certainly a difference when Vivian lingered in her consciousness. Sometimes, they carried on conversations as if Vivian was in the room with her, loud and clear. Five minutes, ten, didn't matter. Like getting a good signal on a ham radio at four in the morning.

Other times, nothing. Dead silence. Not even any white noise. As if she wasn't there at all or never was. To the degree that Sarah couldn't even *feel* her sister, which was something she almost always felt as her sister hovered close, listening and watching everything Sarah did.

Her own personal spirit guide.

But wasn't Vivian breaking the rules by changing the future? And her comment about fate pushing back. Didn't that imply that what they were doing *shouldn't* be done?

If so, that plane would've crashed. Every life on board would've perished. At least, that's what Vivian told her. As much as Sarah didn't want that to happen, wasn't it *supposed* to happen?

She never once considered her sister lied to her about the end results. To do that would risk everything, even her sanity, after all she'd done, all she'd been through.

Before she was distracted further, before everything she planned to do in Texas went to shit, she would have to talk to Aaron and make him see that he had to leave. Would she tell him what Vivian showed her? Would she *need* to? Wouldn't it be enough to ask politely or request it from the woman he loved?

Aaron's sense of protection had always gotten him in trouble with her, but secretly, she liked it, even admired it. As much as his ways went against hers in that department, she didn't always want to be the tough one. It was nice to be taken care of sometimes, to know someone else would deal with a confrontation. It was nice to be loved enough that someone else would risk something for you. After all, wasn't that what she did all the time? Take risks so others don't have to? It wasn't just nice. It was warm, special, and a sure sign of love. Sacrifice, compromise, and even danger.

Aaron needed to leave Texas, or she would never see him again.

Unless visiting his grave was considered seeing him.

Chapter 16

AT THE TAXI STAND, they were two away from getting into a yellow minivan.

Daniel had spoken with the officers who had approached them after Aaron had called out Sarah's name. They acted like they'd all seen a celebrity.

"Was that really Sarah Roberts, Officer?"

"How do you guys know her?" one of the cops had asked.

"Oh, we just wanted her autograph. Never thought we'd see a celebrity in Dallas. I mean, she's in all the papers in Canada."

"Okay, guys, just carry on. She's gone now."

Lucky for Daniel's quick thinking, the cops didn't pursue any sort of line of questioning from four guys who had just gotten off a plane and were headed for the taxi stand.

When they'd first joined the long line for a cab, several cruisers had pulled away from the curb and exited the area. After one of their radios blurted something unintelligible from where they were standing, every cop in the area ran to their cars, squealed their tires, and raced from the area with their sirens on full.

That was when Aaron had asked Daniel to step back inside the airport and ask around to see what he could gather about what Sarah had done.

Daniel eased back in line and leaned in close to the group. "Sarah kidnapped some pilot's family and held them ransom until he flew her out of the area, is what one woman told me."

"Kidnapped a family?" Aaron repeated in disbelief. "That doesn't sound like Sarah. There has to be more to it."

"There is." The foursome shuffled sideways as the group ahead of them entered a taxi. One more group remained in front of them. "She was working with some detective—"

"Probably Parkman," Benjamin cut in.

Daniel shook his head. "A *female* detective from Canada who's still being questioned by the airport authorities."

"Female detective?" Aaron said. The more he heard, the more ridiculous it all sounded.

They stepped to the front of the line.

"Is there more?" Aaron asked.

Daniel nodded. "I'll tell you about the bomb threat she called out on the way to the hotel. Man, the information booth sure knew a lot about what had happened back at the gates beyond security. News travels fast in this airport."

"Anyone know where we're going?" Benjamin asked.

"You want me to google a nice hotel in the area?" He lifted his phone and shook it left and right.

"Aaron," a man shouted. "Hey guys."

They spun around as a unit, Alex lowering his center of gravity. Parkman waved at them from the other side of the minivan taxi parked in their way. The cab driver was just opening the back door.

"I'll give you a ride to our motel," Parkman added. "Come on, guys."

They all looked at each other.

"How the hell did he know we were here?" Aaron asked.

"Darwin," Benjamin said in a pitch higher than he probably intended.

They shuffled toward Parkman as he opened the car's doors.

"Had to be Sarah," Daniel muttered under his breath. "She saw us and asked him to come get us."

"That fast?" Benjamin exclaimed. "She just left in a cruiser, handcuffed too." He shook his head as they approached the front of Parkman's car. "No, this has Darwin written all over it." He stopped at the hood, appraising the car. "This is a trap, Aaron. This car is a death knell, one hundred percent. Darwin is still determined to stop us from being in Texas. Beyond determined."

"Great, now everyone in," Parkman said.

"Just get in, Benji," Aaron said. "We're all friends here. And besides, we're already in Texas, dumbass."

"I won't be if someone starts shooting." He stepped around the car to get in the back. "No more bullets for this guy. I'm as serious as an earthquake."

"A what?" Daniel asked.

"He said earthquake," Parkman said, then shrugged. "He's that serious."

Aaron took the front beside Parkman while the teachers piled in the rear. When Parkman pulled away from the curb, Aaron fastened his seatbelt.

"Guys, get secured. We don't know what's coming."

Benjamin grunted. "Stop fucking with me."

Parkman gave Aaron a sidelong glance but then focused on the road.

"Where are we going?" he asked Parkman.

"To the motel."

"The motel? What's at the motel?"

"Sarah. She wants to talk."

"Sarah's at the motel?" he asked, disbelief coating every word. "How's that possible? We just saw her get arrested not fifteen minutes ago."

"Well, she'll be at the motel before we arrive."

"Still in custody?"

"No, that's all done. She was released."

"Released? How?"

Parkman looked at him again, then faced the road, placing two hands on the wheel. "Bruno helped."

"Oh my fuck."

"See," Benjamin said, his voice rising. "Darwin all the way. We're fucked."

Chapter 17

ONCE SAFELY INSIDE THE motel, with the SUV parked at the back, Bruno made a phone call, and the driver Darwin hired drove away, taking the easily identifiable vehicle with him. They wouldn't be seeing that man or the SUV again.

They were back inside the room, and all Sarah had left was the new address Vivian had given her in one of her last communications. The address led to what? Another house to watch? Someone else to kidnap? More from Vivian would have to be forthcoming before she did anything else.

In the meantime, she would speak with Aaron, stay low, and keep off the radar as every law enforcement officer this side of each border, north and south, would be looking for her after what happened at the airport. Escaping custody was something the authorities didn't take lightly.

Someone would have to go buy hair dye, makeup, and an

assortment of other items to change her appearance. Leaving the States was going to be tricky. They probably knew by now that she lived in Toronto and would be watching the border.

The trouble she was in would be worth it if she only knew the stakes. What was Vivian not telling her? Why not justify her presence in Texas with valid answers about what she wanted her to do, to fix?

It frustrated her to no end, having zero idea of her purpose. But it is what it is, and she was here and wasn't leaving until it was over, whatever it was.

A knock sounded on the door.

Parkman was here. With Aaron.

Her stomach dropped as she nodded at Bruno. "Let Aaron in. But then can you take the rest of them for food or something? Give Aaron and me half an hour or so?"

Bruno nodded back at her and opened the door. "Aaron only," he said.

"What about our bags?" She heard Daniel's voice even as Aaron edged by Bruno.

Their eyes locked, and desire filled her. Desire to be held by him, to be swept away and leave everything behind, forgotten.

But they'd done that once before, and it almost killed her.

They all filed in, dropping bags in the corner, hugging Sarah, and asking if she was fine. Moments later, Bruno gathered everyone and, without much resistance, had them outside, and the door closed.

"Sarah," Aaron said.

"Aaron."

"What's going on?"

"I don't know."

He plopped down on the edge of one of the queen beds, hands on his thighs, staring at her.

"I know you didn't want me here."

She nodded. "It's not safe for you."

"What about you? I just saw you arrested at the airport. Is it safe for you?"

She glanced up, meeting his eyes, forcing back any sign of tears. "It's not safe for anyone, especially not for you." In order not to cry, she would have to get angry. "Why did you come?" She shook her head. "You shouldn't've come. On this job, you're not needed."

"Gee, thanks. Always nice to hear from the woman you love that you're not needed."

Heat rose to her cheeks. "Really, you want to play it that way? You fucking know what I meant. I even said, *on this job*."

"Still, whether I'm *needed* or not, I'm here. Even if there's no task or job for me, I can at least be with you, get you a coffee, help you stargaze, think."

"Be my rock?" she asked, steel entering her voice. Maybe anger was what he needed.

He watched her a moment, not responding.

"You are my rock," she went on, calming a notch. "Whether you're here or back home. So go home and be my rock there."

"No."

"Damn you, Aaron. You can't stay."

He shot up from bed, moved to the window, glanced past

the closed drapes, and then started pacing.

"Why? Tell me why?"

"Because I asked. Isn't that enough?"

"Well then, answer a few questions, and I'll leave."

She looked down at the floor, staring at the cheap motel room carpet.

"Why did you sign an organ donor card for the state of Texas before coming here?"

He had gone through her computer history. He had snooped and investigated her. Could she blame him after she just left over two weeks ago, with only a few parting words? A part of her heart loved him for that. He wanted to take care of her and protect her. One of the qualities she loved about Aaron—mostly because he actually could do that—but it also pissed her off.

"I don't know."

"You don't know?" he asked. "How's that possible? You're the one who did it. You must have had a reason."

She blinked and looked away from the carpet. In his eyes, she saw pain swirling there. "I had a reason. Vivian."

"So Vivian asked you to do that and then come to Dallas, Texas?"

She nodded, afraid she would blow up at him if she opened her mouth. He knew how this worked. When listening to Vivian, she was on the job, doing what her dead sister asked of her, no matter how confusing or stupid it seemed.

"Do you know why you're here?"

She shook her head again.

He stopped pacing and placed his hands in his pocket to

offer her a non-threatening pose. It concerned her for the next question.

"What does *true legacy* mean?"

He'd gone through the garbage, too. Pieced together that tiny paper she'd written on.

"What the fuck, Aaron?" she shouted, launching off the bed.

His hands shot out of his pockets as if to defend himself. She stared at them, the left, then the right.

"You want to fight?" she asked. "You may be trained," she leaned closer, "but I'd kick your ass. Passion, pain, and the fact that in your heart, you wouldn't want to hurt me puts me on top." She blinked several times. "But no, I won't use those advantages. Not me. We never come to blows. We fight until the end. One of us leaves in a coma, or worse."

Aaron stepped back, out of reach. "What the fuck are you talking about, Sarah?"

"I'm talking about death."

He retreated farther until his back hit the wall. "Death," he repeated. "Whose?"

"Yours."

That was it, she'd said it. All the anger seeped out of her body, and she crumpled to the floor, her arms reaching for the edge of the bed. Aaron shoved off the wall to come to her, but she lifted a hand to ward him off. Then she buried her face in the crook of her arm and sobbed.

Minutes later, when she got herself under better control, she wiped her eyes and nose but kept her face on the bed covers.

"Vivian sent me an image," she said, her voice still

choked with tears.

"An image?" he asked, his voice soft and loving.

Why does love have to hurt so much? She loved and hated the man in her motel room at that moment. He was her world, but she couldn't act without him, think without him, love without him.

"An image of your grave." She wiped her eyes and faced him, knowing she looked a mess. "Vivian inferred that you and your three teachers, Daniel, Alex, and Benjamin, all die if you come to Texas. I'm afraid if you don't leave now, I won't be able to bear it."

Aaron smiled. He actually smiled. And she felt that familiar anger stirring again.

"What's so fucking funny?" she blurted.

"That's what you're all about."

"What?" she shouted, her tone close to a scream. It sometimes infuriated her that this man made her feel so weak and sensitive.

"You've changed the future for strangers for over a decade." He opened his arms wide. "Just change the future. Vivian's offered you a challenge."

She shook her head. "No, it's not like that. Not this time."

"Why not? Just do it. You've certainly done it before."

An idea struck her. It would fail, though. Mostly because it was her idea and not Vivian's, who was suspiciously absent again. She never stuck around during the few arguments they'd had.

"Aaron, listen to me. Something terrible will happen to you if you stay. Something I can't see, I can't stop, and I can't reconcile with."

"Then come with me if it's that dangerous. We'll leave together."

"I can't. I have more to do here."

"Like what? Save more lives?"

She understood what he meant, what he was inferring. The lives of people she didn't know were more important than him.

"It's not like that, and you know it."

"Then why are you here? Help me understand it."

"I already told you. I don't know."

"So you signed an organ donor card for this state, flew down here, and with Bruno's and Parkman's help, you're doing shit, and you don't know what's going on?"

She thought about the only lead she still had—that address—crumpled up on a piece of paper in her pocket. "About sums it up."

"And you don't know what true legacy means?"

She shook her head. "I found I'd written that down while sleeping the day before I left."

"Just like old times," he said. "Automatic writing again."

She nodded.

"You know, this is scaring me. I keep hearing full circle in my head. Back to square one. Automatic writing, donor card, your legacy—"

"We don't know that it was referring to *my* legacy," she blurted.

He clucked his tongue and went back to the window.

"Expecting someone?" she asked.

"Yes," he said, turning back to her. "Our friends. I was

kind of hoping to have more answers before they returned, though. So far, we're just going in circles."

Sarah moved toward the small desk and sat at the tiny chair in front of it. "How can I convince you to leave? Head straight back to the airport and fly home, where I know you'll be safe?"

"You can't. I love you too much."

"You love me enough to die?"

Their eyes locked. "Absolutely."

"Wrong answer." She reconsidered. "Well, wrong answer for this scenario." She ran a hand through her hair. "Look, after what happened in February, I can't lose you, too."

"Is that what this is about? February?"

"You know it isn't."

He came to stand beside her, placing a comforting hand on her shoulder. As much as she welcomed it—yearned for his touch—she almost batted it away.

"But we haven't really spent a lot of time talking about it, discussing our future. How does a couple move on after losing a baby?"

"Certainly not by just making another," she said, jumping up from the chair, thereby knocking his hand off her shoulder. "We were supposed to be done with all of this. Having a baby, raising a family by now." The tears started again, unabated. She always cried when the word *baby* rolled off her tongue. "But that's all gone, and it's my fault."

He rushed to her side, wrapping his arms around her before she could fall or push him away. She fell into him, her face in the comfort of his neck, where she often slept. She wept in his arms for the loss of their baby. It was her fault.

Her past coming back to haunt her. The doctor said it might have had something to do with the multiple injuries she'd endured over the years. All the stabbings, the gunshots, the broken bones, and a multitude of other injuries to her abdominal area. Her skin was covered in more scars than Post Malone had tattoos. Or maybe she did something wrong during the early stages of her pregnancy that caused it. She overheard someone at the hospital say that some people just weren't meant to have kids. That woman's voice, echoing down the hall in the hospital at four in the morning, had broken not just her heart but her spirit.

When Vivian reached out a few weeks ago, telling her to come to Texas, she'd asked Vivian if it involved children. Her sister said it did. Sarah could save the lives of kids.

So here she was, in Texas, not just ready to risk her life to save children, she was ready to die for them.

They would've made bad parents anyway. The life they led, the violence, the danger. Who knew when something she had done in the past triggered an old enemy to come after her or her family?

Her birthday had come in April. She was another year older, her clock ticking. Would they try again? She didn't know. Was there still time? Absolutely. Did she want to try again? Of course, she wanted to have a baby. But could she try again, knowing another miscarriage was apt to happen? No fucking way.

They had processed the issue differently, too. She wanted to be left alone to heal, contemplate, read, and escape. Time would heal everything. He wanted to talk about it, get it all out in the open, and plan the next pregnancy with healthy food, regular exercise, and a positive attitude. As much as she understood and saw his motivation and heart, they just drifted apart.

And now here they were, holding one another in a dirty motel room in Dallas, Texas, with every law enforcement agency hunting her and Aaron's life in danger.

"What the hell are we doing?" she asked.

He pulled away from her, lowered his head, and wiped the wetness from her cheeks. "What do you mean?"

"What kind of a mess have we gotten ourselves into?"

"Nothing we can't get out of." His voice was soft, soothing. "That's all we do. We're fixers. Sometimes it's other people's messes, sometimes our own."

"Why couldn't you have stayed in Toronto?"

"Because I love you too much."

"Men. Sometimes you're so stupid." She eased out of his grip and wiped her face. "Don't you know a woman can love her man to death until her heart stops beating, even if she never saw him again, never talked to him again? We suffer love. It's beautiful, and it fucking hurts."

"Never see me again?"

"Yeah, because you're dead if you stay. I know it, and Vivian knows it. That should be enough for you to run to the airport and wait at home for me."

"I'll stay out of the way. You won't even know I'm here."

"And if fate has made the predetermined choice?"

"If my time has come, then there's nothing I could do to stop it."

"Yes, there is. You could go home."

"But isn't it too late? I'm here, aren't I?"

She grabbed a Kleenex for her nose, then blew it. "And what about Daniel, Benjamin, and Alex? You're okay with what happens to them?"

"C'mon, Sarah. They're big boys. They can take care of themselves."

"There's no convincing you, is there?"

Aaron shook his head. "Mostly because I believe in Vivian and her power to change things. When the time comes, you'll be able to do something. We'll fix this."

"If Vivian could change things, we'd both still be in Toronto, and we'd have our baby—" she stopped as her throat closed at the thought.

To his credit, Aaron waited a few moments before responding.

"With all the future telling she does, she undoubtedly saw I would come to Texas. We've worked together since I met you that fateful night you ran into my dojo when those guys with white-painted faces were chasing you."

"The Rapturites."

"Yeah, them. I was in that hot yoga studio when their crazy boss died, a needle still sticking out of your neck. We've been to Italy, Mexico, even Vegas dealing with shit. Why wouldn't Vivian know I'd come to Texas? Well, I submit to you she did know."

"So you think your death prophecy is a ruse to keep you away?"

"Not necessarily, but there's definitely more to it because she knew I'd come."

"This isn't a game, Aaron. She showed me your death."

He frowned. "My actual death. A bit morbid, don't you

think?"

"Your gravesite. Not how you died."

"Still morbid. And it further proves my point."

"Which is?"

"She could have easily showed you my gravesite. I'd believe that. But she didn't tell you at what time."

"What do you mean, what time?"

"It could be my gravesite in sixty years. Did she actually tell you I would die in Texas on this particular trip?"

"Not in those words, but you know how she communicates. She's clear without being exact. I know what she said, and it was a warning."

Someone knocked on the door. "You guys okay in there?" Bruno.

"Yeah," Aaron shouted. "A few more minutes."

Movement on the other side of the door indicated they were edging away. Bruno wasn't a big talker.

Aaron moved to hug her again, but Sarah stepped back. He stopped moving.

"What now?" he asked. "What's your next move?"

She inhaled deeply to collect herself. "I don't know. I have an address Vivian gave me, but that's it."

"And you don't have a clear idea why you're here, who the enemy is, or what's going on?"

Sarah nodded. It sounded ridiculous, but that was all she had.

"And you don't know what true legacy meant or why Vivian wanted you to fill in that organ donor card shit?"

Again, she just nodded.

"Then let's go home together."

"I can't."

"Why?"

"I don't know, I just can't. I'm supposed to be here, and I know how that sounds, but I'm not leaving. Not yet."

Another knock on the door. "We're coming in."

The door opened, and all five of them bustled in. Bruno led, then Parkman, Daniel, Alex, and finally, Benjamin.

"Sorry," Parkman said, heading to the drapes to peek by them. "Catching unwanted attention standing outside our own room."

Sarah headed for the bathroom to collect herself. People like Bruno and Parkman rarely saw her like this. They were all here because of her. She needed to be strong for them.

When she stepped back into the room, the soft susurration of voices stopped.

"We should find another place," she started. "A motel with two rooms. Parkman should rent them. I don't think Bruno and I should be showing our faces around for a couple of days."

"Aren't we heading back to Toronto?" Benjamin asked.

Aaron gave him a sharp look.

"What?" he said, shrugging. "Darwin sent people to stop us from coming. I just think if Sarah feels we shouldn't be here—"

"We're staying," Aaron said. "Unless anyone wants to leave. They are welcome to do so."

No one moved.

"I'm sorry for what Darwin did," Sarah said. "That's on me. He didn't like doing it because we're all friends, but I told him it was necessary."

"Why?" Daniel asked. "We've helped in the past. Why's this time different?"

He deserved answers. They all did. But Vivian wasn't forthcoming, and Sarah didn't have any.

"All I know is whatever's happening here, or will be happening, is dangerous. I've been told you four"—she pointed at the four black belts in the room—"don't fare well."

"You mean we're killed?" Benjamin said.

Sarah just looked at him.

"Well, that settles it." Benjamin clapped his hands. "I vote we head back to the airport." No one moved or seconded that motion. "For fuck's sake. It'll probably be me, and it'll be because I'm shot. Fate has been after me for years."

Sarah moved toward the door. "Aaron brought you here. Aaron will protect you all. Now, let's move. Bruno, check us out. Parkman, I'll ride with you. Find us a new motel a dozen miles out of the city, and then after a short nap, we need to go look at this address Vivian gave me."

She wrapped her hand over the door's knob, then stopped.

"Vivian keeps whispering about time. Like we're running out of it." She turned back to face the men in the room. "When we're in the car, I need to make a call."

"Who are you going to call?" Parkman asked.

"Chief Patrol Agent Michael Wilson with the U.S. Border Patrol in Laredo."

"Why call him?"

"It's time to make a deal."

Chapter 18

ONCE BRUNO CHECKED THEM out and collected Aaron and the dojo boys, Parkman and Sarah got in his car and led the way. The oppressive Texas August heat caused her to break out in a whole-body sweat within the first mile.

Parkman had turned on the air conditioner, but Sarah flicked it to high, max air.

"What happened at the airport?" he asked, raising his voice over the sound of the air conditioner.

Sarah told him what she needed to do and how Bruno helped. She also told him about the bizarre meeting of Detective Marina Diner, who he remembered, and that woman Suzann Scott.

"Sounds like you pulled it off."

"It could have gone smoother, though. Didn't need to end so badly."

Another mile passed, and the car's interior was better, more tolerable. She adjusted the air conditioner down a notch to be able to hear the phone, then pulled out one of the burner phones and dialed Wilson's number.

"Wilson here," he said. "Who's this?"

Sarah kept her eyes on the road, focused. "I want to make a deal."

"Sarah Roberts?"

"It's deal time."

It sounded like he laughed, a soft chortle, but then it was gone as fast as it started.

"Too late for that," he said.

"It's never too late."

"Why would anyone make a deal with you?" he asked. "Last I've heard, you've got the U.S. Border Patrol—my guys—wanting to talk with you about a spike belt theft, among other things. You've got the FBI looking for you and the local authorities at the Dallas airport. I just got off the phone with some special agent out of Dallas named Melanie Sullivan."

"The FBI?" Sarah asked. "Seems a bit much, don't you think?"

"Kidnapping is a bit much?"

"Well," she glanced at Parkman, then back to the road, "I wouldn't say kidnapping. All we did was make sure they stayed home for a phone call. Once that call was placed, they were free to go."

"Stay home?" he retorted, his tone one of surprise. "I wonder what the judge will say with that defense. Tied up, secured to a kitchen chair, held against their will by a monster of a man while you're at the airport coercing a pilot, the man whose family is all tied up, to fly you out of the country. Unlawful confinement, kidnapping, left hand, right hand. It's all the same."

"I wasn't trying to fly anywhere—"

"Every law enforcement agency is gunning for you, Sarah. A, why call me? And B, why not turn yourself in and see if this Sullivan agent will give you a deal?"

"You sound angry. I saved a truck full of people who would have surely died—"

"I am angry. Sure, you did good. And I trusted you because my old friend Parkman called and vouched for you. But now, we're all at a new place in time."

"Wilson, stop interrupting me, shut the fuck up, and listen."

He didn't respond. Maybe his tantrum was over. It was her turn.

"Why did they call you?"

"They didn't. Well, not at first. I called to see if anyone had seen you. I have friends in Dallas. I was informed the FBI had taken over after the airport thing. The phone was handed to Sullivan."

"Earlier, you said, *among other things*. What were you referring to?"

"The spike belt pissed me off, but it was Alejandro's gun that made me have to find you. The man had one in his hand when you broke his elbow backward."

She snuck another glance at Parkman. When she sunk lower in the car seat, she felt Alejandro's gun in the back of her pants. She'd had one there so often over the past decade she almost forgot it was there.

"So you know what happened at the airport?"

"Mostly."

"Did they tell you the plane at Gate A12 was tampered with and unfit to fly, even though it was cleared in security checks?"

He cleared his throat. "No, they didn't tell me that. And now you're lying to me. There was a bomb threat on the plane. It was grounded until a thorough inspection could be completed."

"The landing gear was tampered with," she said, her tone even, like she was stating a known fact and annoyed she had to remind him of it. "There's no bomb."

"Then why the bomb threat?"

"Because people don't listen to me the first time, and that was the next option to keep it on the ground."

"They arrested the woman who warned of the bomb threat—"

"And they'll release her shortly as she was only helping me once the situation became untenable."

"Okay, so why call me? We're back to that. Just go to the authorities in Dallas. Better to turn yourself in than be found because they will find you. Have no doubt."

He said it with such certainty. She didn't like that.

"I called you because you know Parkman and trust him. I called you because I came through for you with that truck. And I called you because you can tell them I can prove the plane was tampered with. I will find the guy who did it. Get him to confess."

"As much as all that's great, you've still broken laws.

You'll have to face that."

"Hence the deal."

There was a moment of silence. Sarah felt a chill and lowered the air another notch. She glanced at Parkman. He nodded, rubbing his arm to indicate it was getting cold for him, too.

"I'll call Sullivan back and tell her what you've told me. You should know, though, that this Special Agent Sullivan isn't in the deal-making mood. There's too much heat. It's one thing to save a bunch of lives in a truck, and by all rights, you get credit for that, but it's something else entirely to kidnap a pilot's wife and young daughter. Sarah, you won't be able to walk away from this."

"Tell Sullivan I want a deal, or I disappear."

"No, I won't tell her that because it's a threat with no room for negotiation. She'll never deal with you on those terms. But I'll talk to her. And not because I owe Parkman. I'll talk to her because no matter how much of a badass you are, or who the fuck it is, you know that would do all this kidnapping shit with you. I will talk to her because you saved a lot of people from certain death the other night and stopped a murderer from killing an innocent driver. For that, I'll give you one phone call."

"I'll be in touch."

She ended the call, dropped the phone on the floor of the car, stomped on it until it broke nearly in half, then grabbed it and tossed it out the window.

"How'd that go?" Parkman asked.

"Not good. He seems to think a deal isn't going to happen."

"Is he going to make the call?"

She nodded. "He said he would."

"Then he will. I know Wilson. He will." Parkman was nodding.

"Even if he does, we have to do whatever Vivian wants and get the hell out of here. He was right about one thing."

"What?"

"There's too much heat."

After a few minutes, Parkman turned up the air again. Sarah didn't object.

"What are we doing about Aaron and his team?"

"I've got an idea. Still working on it, though."

"Tell me about it. Maybe I can help."

Sarah told him what she thought might work to remove Aaron and the three teachers from the equation, thereby keeping them safe.

Parkman thought it was a lovely idea. "He's going to be pissed, though."

"Pissed, but alive. That's good enough in my book."

Chapter 19

After checking into a new motel, Sarah took a power nap, and then she left with Bruno. With nothing new from Vivian, they had driven to the address she'd given Sarah. So far, all they'd seen was a man in his mid-thirties walking by the living room window several times while on the phone. Bruno also saw a dog dish by the front door, indicating they may have to deal with the occupant's pet if they approached the house.

The man they were watching could be anyone. Vivian hadn't offered any explanation with the address, which was maddening to Sarah as she still had no idea what their next step was.

Darwin was scheduled to arrive tomorrow, Sarah was in a serious amount of trouble with the authorities, and Aaron's questions about what she was up to were starting to make her doubt her intentions in Texas as well.

After they'd all got settled in the new motel, Parkman had headed over to the local Walmart for supplies while she napped. Tonight's stakeout had no time limit, as she had no idea why they were watching the house.

Her hair was still damp from when she dyed it a dark black. It almost turned a purplish black, but she was fine with it as long as it was dark. She applied a ton of makeup and even added clip-on earrings to appear to have multiple piercings when, in fact, she only had one hole in each ear.

Bruno didn't do a single thing to disguise himself. There's little he could do when someone's that tall and big.

Parkman had also bought a large thermos, and when he arrived back at the motel with take-out food from a restaurant called Azteca, the thermos was filled with Starbucks. Grateful, they all ate, and then Sarah and Bruno left, but not after a few words with Aaron.

He apologized for coming. Said he'd stay out of the way. He just wanted to be near her. She apologized for her role in the argument but told him he had better start learning that she didn't just say shit for the sake of saying it. If she needed him to stay home, there was a reason.

He'd nodded as if to say he understood, but she knew he didn't.

Then he said something that pulled her heartstrings and reminded her she wasn't alone, but it hurt. He said he was devastated at the loss of their baby. He understood it was her body, her personal experience, her desire to be a mother, but to not forget that men hurt, too. Men didn't carry the baby to term, but some men wanted to be fathers as much as women wanted to be mothers. They hugged, they held each other, and she loved him all over again.

At that moment, she knew the plan she'd told Parkman in the car on the way to the motel had to go forward. She was not willing to lose Aaron or the three men he brought with him, his dojo teachers, who had been through so much with them all over the years. She would have to get them into isolation until this was finished, and Parkman was willing to help. At least he still trusted her, still trusted what Vivian prophesied.

The sun lowered far enough that the streetlights flicked on. Bruno had parked between two lights to avoid direct illumination on their vehicle. He also angled the car in a way that their trunk was aimed at the house they were watching. Both of them studied the house using the rearview and the side mirrors.

Other than the occupant walking by the windows several times, they had nothing to go on.

Is that a message in itself, sis?

Sarah couldn't deny the pit in her stomach at the thought that Aaron was in Dallas. She had *seen* his grave, and it devastated her. Aaron would be furious when he discovered what she planned to do, but at least he would be alive. And knowing him like she did, he'd come around. They survived black February. They would survive this.

And maybe once back on Canadian soil—if that was even possible with all the heat she had brought down on her head in Texas—they could consider trying again for a baby.

That would mean ending what she had been doing for a decade, though. Reckless behavior and risk-taking weren't an option for a mother. At least not a responsible mother.

"We wait?" Bruno asked, startling her out of her reverie.

"We wait."

"For what?"

"Don't know."

She glanced his way but didn't see a single muscle in his face move. The man never seemed to frown or scowl like an expressionless robot.

"Girlfriend back home?" she asked.

He didn't answer right away. He just sat there blinking, watching the mirror. Just when she thought he hadn't heard her, he responded.

"Before."

"Before?"

"Years ago."

"Were you in love?" This was the most she'd talked to him since they'd known each other regarding anything personal. She wondered why that was and determined to change that in the future.

"Yes. Much love."

Curious to know how it ended, she asked, "What happened?"

"She died."

"I'm sorry." Now, she regretted asking. "Anyone since?"

This time, he turned toward her, his eyes small orbs in his massive face. Without a scowl, a brow pulled down, or a clenching of the jaw, Sarah actually saw an expression in those eyes. Pain, hurt, loss, even remorse.

"There was one woman for me. She is gone. I am an island now, deserted. I find love with Darwin and Rosina, family. That is all I need." He turned back to the mirror.

How could her heart break for this man and swell simultaneously? The dedication to that lost woman was admirable, but to stop searching, to live the rest of his life without anyone else, wasn't noble. It was emotional suicide.

But she couldn't fix everybody, nor was she apt to try. Before extolling advice, she had to fix her own home and heart. And with that thought, she realized she was about to strike out against Aaron and make him rage at her, swear at her, and probably curse her name. But he'd be alive, which is what he didn't understand. The love she felt for him meant she would do anything—absolutely anything—to keep him alive. Even make him hate her because her love would never change. Ever.

"Movement," Bruno said.

The front door opened. With the windows cracked an inch on either side, she could hear the house's single occupant as he cooed a name and let his small dog outside for a toilet break. The name was unclear but had a Y sound, like Smokey or Tokey. The door shut while his dog sniffed the ground, lumbering slowly toward the edge of the yard. The man was inside the house, the dog on the front lawn.

"Enough waiting," Sarah said. "Get the dog, keep him quiet, and hide between the houses in the dark."

The door opened on her last word as Bruno was already moving into action.

"Don't hurt the dog," she added, then the door shut.

The vehicle's interior remained dark as they'd disabled the light function when the doors opened.

Bruno strode across the street rather obtrusively as how

could a man as large as Bruno be *un*obtrusive?

Scanning the houses to her right and left confirmed no one was watching them. No idle curiosity, no neighborhood watch nosey busybody about to call the cops.

Maybe they could be in the house and out within fifteen minutes. Then, we could go back to the motel for a solid sleep and meet Darwin in the morning.

Within a couple of days, this would all be over. A girl could hope.

Her phone vibrated. The only person who knew the phone number of this burn phone was Parkman.

She leaned down to watch Bruno in the mirror as she answered.

"Yeah?"

"Sarah, Rosina called."

"And? We know Darwin's coming."

"It's not that. He's still on the way."

"What is it, then?" She wasn't sure she wanted to hear what he had to say.

"Rosina tracked chatter in the area. She was able to gather enough intel to confirm a warrant for your arrest has been issued."

"I figured that was coming."

"We did, too. Kidnapping that pilot's family, attempted kidnapping of the pilot, and a slew of other charges have been added, like flight from lawful custody and on and on, but that's not it."

"What else, Parkman? But make it quick. I have to go."

"Man, I have to marvel at your peaceful tone. I mean, I know you and how you are, but telling anyone else what I just said would freak them out.”

“Parkman, I’m out of time.”

“Right, okay. Well, it said to consider you armed and dangerous, and you know what that means, right?”

“Yeah, shoot on sight.”

“Unfortunately. And there’s a reward for anyone offering information that leads to an arrest.”

“How much am I worth?”

“Fifty grand.”

“That’s it?” She let out a pfft sound. “Bastards. Thought I’d garner more.”

“They’ll likely raise it in the coming days. The media were apprised. It’s scheduled to hit the morning papers, internet news sites, and anywhere anyone will post it, like Facebook, Instagram, and everywhere. Sarah, your face will be shared a million times within hours of daybreak.”

“Likely. Look, gotta run.”

“Stay safe.”

The line died.

Sarah checked the mirrors, but Bruno and the dog had disappeared.

Chapter 20

SARAH CRACKED THE DOOR, then slipped out into the night. With the gun in her waistband and a burn phone on silent in her pocket, she strode across the street, aimed for the darkness between the two houses where she'd directed Bruno to go.

Moments later, the darkness enveloped her.

"Here," Bruno said in his husky version of a whisper.

She moved toward the sound of his voice, her eyes adjusting to the inky blackness, then stopped an inch before bumping into his thick forearm. She could barely see the small dog wrapped in Bruno's meat hook arms. He had a hand clamped over the dog's snout, which allowed the tiny animal to breathe, but he couldn't bark. She could still catch the dog's feeble attempt to squirm in the dark, matched with a small internal whine. Bruno hadn't hurt the dog. He had only secured him.

They waited in silence. It wouldn't be long now. It was less than a minute before the front door opened, and the dog's owner stepped out onto the porch.

"Snaky, come on, boy. Time to come in." The screen door slammed shut.

The dog thrashed in Bruno's arms at the sound of his master's voice, but nothing changed regarding his captivity except a slightly louder whimper.

Was the dog's owner inside, or did he step outside?

Sarah eased the weapon from her waistband and held it by her leg.

"Snaky?" he called again.

Outside. Good.

"Snaky?" This time, it was more of a question.

The man's silhouette broke the streetlight glow between the two houses as he stepped around the corner. There was no way he could see them standing there yet, as it was simply too dark between the houses.

Slowly, Sarah raised the weapon.

The man turned away to walk toward the road. The dog whimpered. The man stopped.

"Snaky?" he said, turning back to look between the houses. "You okay, buddy?" He started directly toward Sarah, leaning forward to squint into the darkness.

With the weapon pointed at him, she eased forward, too.

When he saw her, he jerked back, hands raised. Credit to him. He didn't shout or try to run.

"What the fuck?" trickled from his mouth in a mumble, as if he said it over a cookie crumbling on his tongue.

She moved farther until the gun was just inside the light.

"Stay quiet, and this'll all go away."

"Yeah, sure. No issue." His eyebrows were knitted together in a serious frown. "You want to steal my dog?"

"Lower your hands and head back inside the house. We will bring Snaky with us."

He did as he was told without resistance. Sarah slipped the gun away and stayed close to him in case he pulled out a cell phone and dialed the cops before she had a chance to knock it from his hands.

Bruno clumped along behind her.

In seconds, they were all inside the house with the front door shut and locked. Bruno released the dog and stepped back to the door to lean against it.

"On the couch," Sarah said.

The man moved to the couch while Sarah examined the place. A modest, small home, the dishes from dinner still on the counter. The TV cast Liev Schreiber in a suit carrying a baseball bat as he entered a building on the screen.

"Anyone else here?" she asked.

"No. I live alone."

She moved closer and sat on the edge of the chair beside the sofa, keeping her weapon in easy reach. The man's dog had jumped up beside him and sat staring at her.

"What's your name?" She had to start somewhere. Vivian hadn't given her anything other than the address.

"Luke Roland."

"Where do you work?"

"The airport … Dallas/Fort Worth Airport." His gaze went from Bruno and then back to Sarah. "Is that what this is about?"

It had to be the connection. But how and why?

"What specifically do you do at the airport?"

"I'm an AMT. I work on the planes."

His voice took on a different tone when he spoke those last few words. *Work on the planes.* As in, fix them and, perhaps, sabotage them?

"What's AMT stand for?"

"Aircraft Maintenance Technician."

"In other words, you're a mechanic."

He shrugged. "Yeah, you could say that."

"Did you work today?"

"What's this all about?"

"This is about you answering my questions. When we learn what we need to know, we'll leave."

He glanced at Bruno again.

"Yes, I worked today."

Something about his voice had changed again, but it was subtle. He worked today, but on what? Could Vivian have sent her to the man who actually sabotaged the plane at Gate A12?

She decided to take that gamble because who else would Vivian have sent her to meet?

Sarah pulled out the weapon and placed it on her lap. Luke watched it the entire time.

"Explain what you did to the landing gear of that plane."

Luke looked down at his hands as he fumbled with a nail. His dog turned to him, sensing a change. When Luke raised his head, a tear was in his right eye.

"They made me do it."

"Who?"

He shook his head. "I had to do it," he said, a level of desperation in his voice now. "There was no other choice."

"There's always a choice."

Now he was fully crying, but Sarah felt she was finally getting somewhere. She needed to learn who *they* were.

"No, you don't understand." He looked down at his lap. "I did not have a choice."

She waited.

Without raising his head, he whispered, "I owed them."

"How much?"

"It wasn't a number." He looked up and met her gaze. "It was a favor."

She almost glanced at Bruno to see if he was getting all this but trusted that he was. A favor? Who would require such a favor? Sabotaging an aircraft that would have resulted in a devastating crash isn't a favor. It's mass murder. Nothing was making sense. Sarah was starting to feel this whole thing might be too big for her. She was in way over her head.

Vivian, where the fuck are you?

She let him have a moment to collect himself. When his sobs abated enough for him to talk again, she asked, "How were you indebted to them? Why would you owe someone a favor like that?"

"Who are you people?" he asked. "Are you cops?"

Sarah shook her head.

"You can't barge in here and just fucking ask questions —"

"Actually, I can." She held up the weapon.

"Then fucking kill me because if they find out I talked to

anyone, they'll kill me for sure. They're too powerful."

"Who are they? Tell me that, and we'll leave. No one needs to know we were here or that you were the one who told us anything."

"They probably already know you're here."

A box of tissues was on the table beside her. She tossed them at him. "Wipe up your tears and man up because I'm going to hurt you so bad that you'll scream answers to my questions. This," she held up the gun, "is a reality." She pointed over her shoulder at the huge man standing by the door. "He is a reality. Whether they come later is still up for debate." She leaned closer to make her point while he dabbed at his eyes with tissue. "The people on that plane would've died." She raised her voice. "Do you fucking hear me? You almost killed all those people because of a favor. So, you're going to tell me who wanted those people dead. As soon as I know a name, I will leave through the back door if you like. You know, in case anyone's watching the house."

Luke was already nodding. "Okay, okay, I'll tell you because I should've been dead already." He glared at her. "Do you know how hard it was to cut the line on that landing gear, to know I was dooming all those people? I also considered the NTSB investigation that would follow the crash and wondered if there would be enough evidence in the wreckage to see the cut in the line I'd made. The pressure was intense. But did I waver? No, I didn't. And for that, maybe I don't deserve to live."

"Pity party over?" she asked. "Look, I have no beef with you personally, although I don't agree with what you did, and yes, there are consequences you should face for what you did, but feeling sorry for yourself won't stop the people who made you do this. Tell me who they are. We can stop them and help you. Now talk. I'm done waiting."

"Can I stand up?" he asked, looking down at her gun, then back at her face.

"Why?"

"I have to show you something."

Heavy footsteps edged closer as Bruno took up a position beside Sarah. It told Luke to be careful, and it told Sarah he would protect her. Bruno could never face Darwin—his family—if something happened to Sarah on his watch.

She gestured with the tip of the gun in an upward-jerking motion. "Go ahead."

Luke got up from the couch slowly, then lifted his shirt. A long scar arced like a thin waxing crescent moon, pink and raised, dotted on each side from staples taken out long ago, started slightly below his belly button and arced up with the tip of the scar fading near the edge of his lower ribcage.

The shirt dropped over the scar as Luke retook his seat on the couch.

"Who did that to you?" Sarah asked.

"They did, but it's cool. I wanted it done."

Bruno eased back slowly and reclaimed his position at the door.

"That scar is from a kidney transplant," he muttered.

Puzzle pieces moved around in her head, a couple of them clicking together. She was starting to get some of it, but not everything.

Vivian? You getting this?

"I was on dialysis for almost seven years. Then I got the

call that they'd found a kidney. Within days, I would be under the knife, my life saved. And that's where the problems started."

"What problems?"

"I couldn't afford the procedure."

She pointed at his abdomen. "But you're alive and with the scars to prove it. How was it paid for?"

His right leg bobbed incessantly. "Because they offered me a way out."

More pieces fit together.

"They said they'd save my life and give me the kidney. They'd cover all the expenses, and all I had to do was one favor when they called upon me later. One task, and that was it, debt paid."

"And you agreed," she said, stating the obvious.

"I agreed."

"And you sabotaged the plane for them. Did they tell you why they wanted you to do it?"

He shook his head. "No, just that I was to cut the landing gear. That would clean the slate with them. No debt, free and clear."

Sarah considered everything she'd seen and learned over the past few days and thought hard about the details. However, she couldn't come up with anyone with that kind of money and resolve than an organization like the mafia or a cartel. But this wasn't a cartel. Could there be a mafia that entrenched in organ donations to be setting up assassinations? Who was on that plane? Who was important enough to kill that they would go to all this trouble? And why would they leave Luke Roland alive to tell the tale?

Organ donor? The thought raced through her mind again. Vivian had asked her to complete the organ donor application online for the state of Texas.

Vivian?

She refocused on Luke. He seemed lighter for having told someone of the burden he held solely on his shoulders.

"Did you ever meet them?"

He shook his head.

"How did they contact you?"

"My cell phone."

"How powerful are these people?" She held up a hand. "No, wait, just tell me who they are."

"I don't know who they are. I know the hospital was reimbursed properly as I never got a bill, and the human tissue procurement company also got paid."

"The what? Human tissue procurement company?"

He nodded.

"What's their name?"

"True Legacy."

The rest of the puzzle slipped into place. Those two words were on the torn-up piece of paper in her kitchen garbage.

True Legacy.

Vivian had told her everything already.

Chapter 21

Outside the house, Sarah hurried to the car. Bruno stayed close behind. Both doors opened, then closed. Bruno started the car and pulled away from the curb without hesitation.

Sarah withdrew her phone and called Wilson.

As she hoped, he picked up right away.

"Wilson here."

"I'm ready to deal."

"Sarah, there's no deal."

"You talked with that FBI woman?"

"Yes, and her name is Special Agent Melanie Sullivan. And there's no deal."

"That's it? That's all she said? No deal?"

"Pretty much."

"Pretty much implies there's more. What else did she say?"

"You'd have to have irrefutable proof on where Hoffa's buried, or maybe it was a Marcello hit on the Kennedys on that fateful twenty-second day of November 1963 since you're in Dallas. Or maybe you know if there was collusion in the 2016 election."

"What the fuck?" Sarah gasped, thinking Wilson had lost his mind.

"Look, what I'm trying to say is, to turn Sullivan's head in any direction, you'd have to be selling some prime rib, and I don't mean just any prime rib. I'm talking about the prime of the prime."

"The prime of the prime, eh?"

"Yes, Miss Canada. The primest."

"Well, how about I hand her the man who sabotaged that plane? He's agreed to testify to what he did and give up the names of the people who made him do it. He'll even go so far as to explain how the deal was arranged in the first place. He's ready to talk."

"Hmm, well, you might have something there, but I doubt it."

Something playful in his tone caused anger to surface. She sat up straighter, her grip on the phone tightening.

Bruno got on the interstate, heading back to their motel.

"It isn't your place to doubt it, Wilson. Make the call to Sullivan. Maybe she wants to talk."

"Sarah Roberts, you still don't get it, do you?"

"Then fill me in. Help me get it."

"You're a civilian. You're running around kidnapping people and stealing spike belts and doing whatever the hell you think you're doing, and then when the heat comes down on you, you want to make a deal. Doesn't work like that."

"If Parkman didn't call you, what would have happened to those people in that truck? Where would those people be now if that plane wasn't stopped at Gate A12?"

"Fair enough, but now you have to stop. Turn yourself in, and bring that big guy with you." Of course, they'd know about Bruno by now. The cop who had her in custody had seen Bruno before he was yanked out of his cruiser. "Tell Agent Sullivan everything you have, and maybe the judge will go easy on you. Like two years, or maybe five instead of the twenty years you're heading for. Oh, and that's provided no one gets killed while you're out gallivanting around Dallas. If they get a murder on you, Sarah, you'll never see the light of day."

She set her head back on the headrest and stared at the ceiling of the rental car. Bruno was turning off the interstate. They were minutes from the motel.

"You're right, Wilson. I can see that now. This isn't working."

"I'm happy to hear you say that, Sarah."

"I can't do it this way anymore." She looked out the windshield, watching the road now. "Tell Sullivan …"

"Yes? Tell Sullivan what?"

"Tell Sullivan the deal is off. There's no deal. There probably never was a deal. Just like you said, she's probably not in the mood to deal. I will finish this my way. And when it's done, let her know that I'll head home, and she can clean up the mess I've left behind."

"Unwise Sarah, very unwise. Don't do this."

"Consider it done. I won't be calling again."

"Sarah, every law enforcement agency and member is currently looking for you. In the morning, your face and name will be blasted—"

"I know all about it. Sullivan even posted a reward for aiding in the capture and arrest of one, Sarah Roberts, armed and dangerous. I know, I know. Spare me the bullshit. I'm tired and getting irritated, and I'm not in the mood for FBI power plays. How do you think I knew about the truck we stopped? How did I know about the plane at Gate A12? You don't think I'll know where to hide and for how long? I'm going off the grid. Goodbye, Wilson. I actually thought we could work this out together."

"Wait, Sarah—"

She ended the call, stomped on the phone, and then tossed it out the window into the thick foliage lining the road. Five minutes later, Bruno pulled into the parking lot of the motel.

Sarah placed a hat on her head, exited the car, and strode for the room.

Once inside, Bruno shut and locked the door, then checked through the drapes.

"We good?" she asked.

Bruno turned to her and nodded.

She yanked off the cap and tossed it on the bed. After she used the washroom, she called Parkman's room.

"Come over in five minutes. We need to talk."

She hung up and pulled out her laptop. After turning it on, she logged on to the motel's shitty WiFi and typed *True Legacy* into the search bar.

She scanned the pages, typed in another search, and read

more.

About ten minutes later, Parkman and the four boys entered the room, with Bruno shutting the door behind them.

They all took seats and waited for her to speak. She tapped on the keys a couple of more times, raised a finger for everyone to give her another moment, and then used the trackpad to click open a page.

When she looked up, her gaze stopped on Aaron's face, knowing this would be one of the last times she'd see him without him violently angry at her.

She nodded toward Bruno. "Tonight, we found the man who sabotaged the plane at the airport."

"Wow, that's great news," Aaron said.

"Yeah, maybe they'll listen to you now," Parkman added.

Sarah was shaking her head. "Tried that. Called Wilson. No go."

"Don't talk to Wilson. Call the FBI."

"Wilson called Special Agent Melanie Sullivan for me. She told him there would be no deal. Turn myself in for kidnapping charges, and a dozen more is the only deal."

"Have you called him since you got this saboteur?"

She nodded. "Luke Roland, the aircraft mechanic who fucked with the landing gear, said he'd even testify. He'd tell them everything."

"And?" Parkman shot his hands out in a *c'mon* gesture.

"No go. They want me. It's probably because they think this landing gear-sabotaging thing is a farce. They're going with the bomb scare scenario with me as a kidnapper. Probably orchestrated to make that pilot fly me out of the States. Makes their story have more flair, pizzazz."

"What are you going to do?"

"First, I'm sending an email to Rosina. I need everything she can find on a certain human tissue procurement company."

"A human tissue what?" Aaron asked.

"Procurement company."

"Do they do what I think they do?" Benjamin asked.

Sarah nodded. "These companies harvest human organs, tissues, ligaments, skin, you name it, they slice it."

"Interesting description," Parkman said.

"All legal, too. Except, perhaps, one small detail."

"What's that?"

"They're *creating* procurements."

She tapped on the screen, pushed open the screen farther, and swung the computer around to face everyone.

"I didn't know it at the time, but the small plane using Gate A12 at the airport that was evacuated was chartered by a numbered company to fly a group of people to Los Angeles, where they were to participate in a parade to raise awareness for organ donation. Everyone on that plane was a registered organ donor in the State of Texas. That plane was never going to make it to Los Angeles."

"That doesn't make sense," Parkman said. "If the plane was sabotaged and meant to crash, they burn up in the explosion."

"Not if the landing gear failed. Luke explained that upon takeoff, they would register the problem. After radioing down the issue, they would circle to use up fuel and then attempt to land. Upon landing, anything could happen. But with emergency services close by, sure, some people would live.

But many could die on the scene, with others dying in hospital."

"And how would these procurement guys get the bodies?" Aaron asked. "They can't just swoop in with vans and load bodies and drive away, slicing off what they want."

"They pretty much can." Sarah flipped to another page. "On the website for this company, it says they have a contract with the local hospital and a contract with the coroner's office. They have to work fast when someone dies in order to harvest items that can be reused immediately. There're wait lists for kidneys, hearts, lungs, you name it, like the one Luke Roland was on. As soon as a kidney pops up as a match, you're called in and prepped for surgery."

"And this is all legal?" Benjamin asked.

"As far as I can tell, but I have to look into it more. And as I said a moment ago, I want to see what Rosina can dig up, too."

"Chances are that truck we stopped by Laredo was connected somehow," Parkman added.

"Shit," Sarah said, meeting Parkman's gaze. "I didn't even think about that."

"What's Vivian saying?" Aaron asked. "Anything?"

Sarah shook her head. "Nothing. She's gone right now."

"Great time for her to take off, with you in the thick of things."

Aaron respected what she and her sister had done over the years, but he hated it when Vivian vanished. For Aaron, it felt like Vivian was leaving Sarah unprotected, which Sarah understood. But he didn't understand that Vivian came when needed, and perhaps, at that moment, Sarah didn't need her sister. Maybe, just maybe, she could hunt down True Legacy on her own.

Sarah went on to tell them about Luke Roland and his free kidney transplant, with the arrangement of a favor at a later date.

"And he's willing to testify."

"He'd better be careful who he speaks with," Parkman said. "If they're that powerful, organized crime powerful, to be calling in favors to down planes filled with organ donors, then they're powerful enough to remove him from the equation."

Sarah glanced at Bruno, a shared understanding between them. They should've brought Luke with them and offered him protection.

"Shit." Sarah closed her laptop and got to her feet. "We should go back and pick him up."

"Sarah, it's late," Aaron said, getting to his feet. "Nothing will happen tonight. I'm sure he isn't calling these people and taunting them. No one will know he'd testify, but that guy you called about a deal. We can go in the morning and check on him. Besides, Darwin is here tomorrow morning. We'll all sit down, see what Rosina finds out, and decide what to do next."

She shot a glance at Parkman. He offered her a slight nod, assuring her he was behind her plan to remove Aaron and the three teachers from their presence.

She yawned, covered her mouth, then eased into Aaron's arms. Tomorrow, everything will be clearer. Aaron would be safely away from them tomorrow, and Bruno, Darwin, Parkman, and herself could finish what they came to Dallas to do.

Tomorrow would see a bounty on her head, but she could work around that.

The boys stood, and Parkman headed for the door. Bruno checked through the drapes, then nodded to Parkman and stepped aside.

"Oh, one more thing," Parkman said. "Did this Luke Roland guy give you anyone's name?"

"He went one better. He gave us the name of the human harvesting company."

"Which is?" Aaron asked.

"True Legacy."

He stepped back, his eyes widening. "You've got to be fucking kidding me."

Sarah shook her head, knowing she had a smug look on her face. "I didn't know what it meant when I wrote it over two weeks ago."

"Well shit, now you do."

"Now I do."

"What are you two talking about?" Benjamin asked.

"We're discussing bedtime." She gestured with both hands in a shooing motion. "Everyone out. You too, Bruno. Tonight, this room is mine and Aaron's."

Without much protest, everyone filed out, leaving them alone for the first time in over two weeks.

She strode over to him, shoved him onto the bed, and landed on top of him before the bed stopped shaking from his impact.

"Shhh," she whispered when he opened his mouth to protest. "Tonight, you're mine. Just shut up and love me.

Love me like there's no tomorrow because, who knows, there may not be." She giggled, which was something she rarely did. "Aaron, my love, *show* me how you feel about me. Then hold me until the sun rises again. Make it memorable."

When you hate me tomorrow, you might remember these moments ...

"I love you, Aaron—"

His lips silenced her.

For the rest of the night.

Chapter 22

ONLINE, THE MORNING BROUGHT an assault of emails and messages. Everyone and their neighbor had seen the FBI notice posted all over social media that they were looking for Sarah Roberts for unlawful flight from custody and kidnapping charges, among other things.

Caleb and Amelia, Sarah's parents, had emailed her twice, hoping she was okay.

Sarah closed her laptop after reading the lengthy response from Rosina, Darwin's wife. Rosina understood what was to be done and said she would do it as Sarah asked. Darwin was landing at the airport in less than two hours.

She hopped in the shower while Aaron still dozed, applied a mountain of makeup to cover her features, and let her long dark hair fall over her shoulders—which she hardly ever did because it was so much work to keep clean and in a pinch she'd rather just keep it tied up, not to mention the heat of August in Dallas—and dressed lightly.

When she exited the bathroom, Aaron was sitting up on the bed, staring at his cell phone.

"Morning," he whispered.

"Morning. Why are we whispering?" she asked, emulating his soft tone.

He spun around to look at her. "Sorry, just shocked at what I'm seeing online."

She shrugged. "So, I'm used to it, and you should be, too. Every time we get involved in something, the authorities want to stop me. They blame me for everything, and then—"

"No, not that." He held out his phone. "We expected that. I'm talking about this."

She frowned and reached for the phone. On the screen was a picture of Luke Roland. The authorities found Luke in his house, dead from a single shot behind the ear, execution style. The investigative journalist went on to talk about Luke's job at the airport and how he worked in the area where the Sarah Roberts attempted kidnapping took place the day before.

She skimmed to the bottom of the piece and saw her picture. It was added with the award offered by Agent Sullivan.

The authorities were now looking for Sarah Roberts as a suspect in the slaying of Luke Roland, as a neighbor's doorbell camera recorded her watching Luke's house the night before. The journalist went on to add that the camera videoed Sarah and an as-yet-unidentified large male approaching Luke's house within hours of his death.

Her hand was shaking when she handed Aaron's phone back to him. She couldn't deny how bad that looked. The last two people to see him alive. After everything that had happened, of course, Agent Sullivan would assume she'd killed Luke for some unknown reason. Assume is the wrong word. Sullivan would be *confident* Sarah killed him. Hence, she wasn't a person of interest. Sarah had elevated her status to suspect.

"And so it goes," she said, the weight pressing on her shoulders. She'd just lost her witness, Luke's testimony. Her side just suffered a fatal blow, not to mention Luke lost his life, and True Legacy just raised the stakes.

"You okay?" Aaron asked, taking his phone back from her.

"Yeah," she lied. "We haven't done this for almost two years. Just feeling it again. My nerves are having to get used to these waters."

"Well, don't get too used to them. We need to fix this and get the hell out of Texas."

She patted his arm. "We will."

"Like today," he added, his tone a higher pitch.

"Stay calm, Aaron. We got this."

"There's a fucking number on your head. Everyone and their dog will be watching for you."

"Hence the disguise." She tapped the side of her head, pressing in on her hair.

"This isn't a joke."

She let her hands fall to her sides, her face falling, too. "Don't you think I know that? Of course, it's not a joke. I don't have this sort of sense of humor."

Someone knocked on the door. Aaron shot up from the bed, but before he could protest and stop her, she grabbed the door and flung it open.

Parkman stood there, Bruno behind him.

"Well, get in here," she said.

They entered, and Sarah shut the door.

"Let me get some pants on," Aaron said. He was still in his boxers.

Sarah caught Bruno looking at the scars from Aaron's gunshot wounds. Aaron probably went up the respect ladder for Bruno with those scars and a missing finger, although his face remained unreadable.

"You saw what happened?" Parkman asked.

Sarah glanced up at Bruno. He was watching her now.

She nodded. "Yeah. We were filmed entering Luke's house. Then he was found murdered. Doesn't bode well."

"No, it doesn't." Parkman leaned against the door. "What's next?"

"Plans stay the same. Pick up Darwin in just over an hour and strategize." She jerked her head toward Aaron, who had his back to them. Parkman nodded his understanding. "Today, we make headway." She glanced at Bruno. "But there is one change. You, my dear friend, will need to leave. I emailed Rosina. She's arranging transportation out of the city and then a plane back to Europe. I'd love for you to stick around until the end, but unfortunately, you're too noticeable. And, after that camera footage, the FBI will have a solid idea of what you look like."

"Understood," he grunted.

She wished everyone she worked with were that easy.

Aaron moved up beside her, climbing into a T-shirt. "What am I doing?"

She faced him. "Nothing."

"What?" He stopped moving. "No one knows what I look like. I could help pick up Darwin. I could stake out a house or something."

Sarah was shaking her head. "Sorry, after what Vivian showed me, I need you to stay here all day, in this motel room, with Daniel, Benjamin, and Alex, safe and sound."

"That's bullshit. We can take care of ourselves."

Another knock sounded at the door. Her stomach dropped thinking it was Agent Sullivan. Bruno peeked through the curtain, then opened the door.

Benjamin, Daniel, and Alex moved inside. Bruno shut the door, then took up his position by the window. Alex scrutinized every move Bruno made. Between the two of them, Bruno, a three-hundred-pound muscle machine, and Alex, a hundred-ten-pound fighter, they could destroy so much, both matched on every level but size.

"What's bullshit?" Benjamin asked. "We overheard you, Aaron, as we stepped up to the door."

"Sarah wants all four of us to stay in the motel all day while they go out and do whatever it is they're doing."

It hurt Sarah to hear him whine, but it was also starting to annoy her. Everyone could leave, and she'd be better off. Even without Vivian's warning, she risked Parkman's life by involving him every time.

"Sounds good to me," Benjamin said, his voice cheerful. "I think that's a fine idea." He nodded at Sarah, then smiled wide. "Smart plan. I like to help, I mean, if that's helping. By staying here."

Sarah slapped his shoulder. "Then it's set. Parkman, you're with me. Bruno, a ride is coming for you soon. The rest of you, please stay here."

"And do what?" Aaron asked.

Sarah grabbed her laptop and her last few burner phones and stopped at the door. A couple of snarky retorts edged to the roof of her mouth. She suppressed them all and instead said, "I was hoping you guys could research True Legacy for us while we get Darwin. By the time we return, it would be great to know as much as possible about them."

"Isn't Rosina already doing that?" Aaron asked.

The tension building in the room had to be felt by everyone. Last night was amazing. Aaron was a wonderful man, one she wanted to spend the rest of her life with. But sometimes, she also wanted to throat-punch the fucker.

In an even tone, one that said stop-fucking-with-me, Sarah spoke. "I'm sure you can learn shit she might miss as you're in Dallas, where their headquarters are stationed. We're dumping the other room, too. All of you stay here, in this room. Going back and forth will attract unnecessary attention to us."

She opened the door, slammed a baseball hat on her head, and started toward Parkman's rented Camry.

Once in the car, with Parkman edging out of the motel parking lot, he said, "Aaron's a little pissed, eh?"

"He didn't need to come. I'm getting the feeling this'll all be over today or tomorrow anyway. He's just being overprotective."

"Can't blame him. You're definitely someone we all want

to protect."

She shot him a glare, then softened. "I know, I get it, but he was warned. Darwin even tried to stop him. I just wish he'd listen sometimes."

Parkman nodded and, as wise as Parkman was, decided to say nothing more on the topic.

Five minutes later, he said, "So, is Rosina making the call?"

"Yes."

"And we're going to the airport?"

"Yes."

"You really think that's wise?" He adjusted the air conditioner. "You know, after yesterday."

She thought about it, knowing he was right. There weren't any more leads, nothing to go on. Luke's address was the last thing Vivian gave her, and she'd been silent since Aaron arrived. She had nothing left to do until she heard back from Rosina and collected Darwin at the airport or eventually heard from her sister. Although, as necessary as it was, what was about to happen to Aaron and the boys disturbed her.

"Drop me at a café close to the airport. One that has internet."

"That safe?"

"I don't know," she spurted, vexed by the whole situation. "Find me one that isn't too busy."

Parkman didn't respond. He just drove. And that was the reason she loved him.

Chapter 23

With an extra-large black coffee beside her, Sarah logged on to the café's WiFi and checked her email. The café Parkman dropped her at was small, with tables along the wall that led to the bathroom. Her back to the front of the store, she was obscured and able to work without too much attention. An older couple and a single man reading a book were the only other three people in the café, other than a couple of staff members chatting near the back door. When she bought her coffee, no one took a second look at her. The blond Hayden Panettiere she arrived in Dallas looking like was now a dark-haired Mila Kunis. Unless they stared at her eyes, which were covered by sunglasses, no one would be able to see it was Sarah Roberts, the girl in the pictures Agent Sullivan had published everywhere.

She logged on to her email and saw several dozen more

waiting for her attention. Scrolling through them, she saw the one from Rosina she hoped had come in.

She clicked on it.

The FBI, namely Special Agent Melanie Sullivan, had been anonymously notified of Sarah Robert's whereabouts at a motel just south of Dallas.

Good!

Rosina did exactly as Sarah wanted her to do by telling the FBI that Sarah was being guarded in her motel room by her boyfriend and his friends from Canada. They were protecting her until they could get her out of the country. Rosina said in her email that the FBI would take less than an hour to put together a strike team of some sort and storm the motel, which would be happening any minute.

It would happen peacefully, she wrote, trying to assure Sarah. No one would get shot—not even Benjamin—at least, she hoped not.

Aaron wasn't stupid. If the gig was up and they came for Sarah, he wouldn't die to protect her when she wasn't even there. In fact, having them waste resources on him and his boys when they'd done nothing wrong should please Aaron.

In Rosina's research, she learned a ton about human procurement companies. Sarah began reading over ten paragraphs of notes Rosina made from her online searches.

Near the bottom, she read about court cases that went nowhere. When procurement companies removed tissue, organs, and ligaments before the coroner determined the cause of death, questions were raised. Rosina said dozens of cases were being investigated in almost every major city across America. Forensic pathologists have questioned the practice of these human harvesters for years, but they're protected by so many laws that cases have died in the court system.

One family in particular, Amanda and Brian Glenmark, sued after their eighteen-year-old daughter, Jane, had died. These parents still had no idea how their daughter died and would likely never know as True Legacy harvested her body before the coroner could determine the cause of death.

Someone bumped Sarah's shoulder as they strode past, heading for the toilets at the back.

She opened her mouth to mumble something, then decided against it, not wanting to attract unwanted attention.

Her email dinged.

Aaron.

She quickly opened it.

I'm sorry, Sarah. Just don't like this. Want our calm life back in Toronto. Also, I need the dojo to let off a little steam.

See you when you get back.

Love Aaron

The FBI hadn't gotten there yet. She checked her watch. Almost noon. It wouldn't be long now.

She reread the email and whispered a silent love you back at the screen but didn't type a response. She was supposed to be picking up Darwin and not answering emails, so she left it unanswered.

She'd almost forgotten about her coffee. After two long pulls on it, she placed it near the wall in case someone strolling by bumped it into her computer. Then, she reopened Rosina's email and continued reading where she left off.

Near the bottom, she got a surprise she didn't see

coming.

Rosina had scheduled an appointment at two p.m. for her with the Glenmarks as they lived in Dallas.

She had two hours to get there. Darwin was landing slightly after one in the afternoon. She couldn't wait for Parkman to return with him. The appointment was too important.

She mapped out the area where she was, then typed in the address where she was going.

The bathroom door opened, and the man who bumped her headed toward the front. When he passed her, he glanced down and was gone without making contact again. Did he recognize her? Was he making eye contact as a way to show interest?

It was the man who'd been reading the book. Or was he reading? Was he just pretending to read while watching her?

Paranoid but unwilling to turn around and look, she faced her computer.

The address was in a residential area. Amanda and Brian Glenmark lived in a small home on Castle Court in an area called Southlake, about a fifteen-minute drive from where she was, and they were expecting a journalist who had a few questions for them.

A journalist?

Why hadn't she thought of that before? She needed to call the guy who wrote the article with the Dallas Morning Newspaper.

It was time for the world to hear her side of the story instead of just the FBI's side.

But not before she met with the Glenmark family. Rosina

had outdone herself. Sarah was about to meet people who True Legacy had wronged, and no one would be watching their house on Castle Court. Since Sarah was alone, no one would see her meet with them, either. After losing their daughter, Sarah wanted no more harm to come to the Glenmark family.

Parkman knew where he had dropped her off, and by the time he grabbed Darwin and returned to the café, she could call him and give him a new address to pick her up.

She had to make sure what happened to Luke Roland was a one-time event.

After closing her computer and drinking from her coffee, she stole a glance over her shoulder.

The man reading the book held it high, but she was sure his eyes had been on her until she turned around. She watched him for several seconds until he slowly turned to look at her again. Then he smiled, and it was creepy.

Shit, he thinks I'm checking him out.

She slipped her laptop under her arm as the Glenmarks' address was memorized. On the way out the door, she consoled herself. As creepy as his smile was, at least Book Reading Man wasn't watching her because he thought he was staring at an FBI fugitive.

Using one of the burn phones, she called a cab. She would arrive forty-five minutes early for the interview Rosina had set up for her, but that was fine.

It was always good to keep people on their toes.

Chapter 24

AARON HAD KEPT HIS nose glued to the screen of his iPad as he researched True Legacy. While doing so, Benjamin and Daniel played games on their iPads, and Alex kept an eye on the parking lot and street while chewing gum.

"You guys might be surprised with some of the shit I've found here." He glanced up when he didn't get a response from any of them. "Guys, this True Legacy human procurement company is harvesting humans."

Daniel nodded at him.

Benjamin shivered. "Harvesting humans. Doesn't sound good." He pressed something on his iPad. "Anyone hungry?" he asked.

Alex moved away from the window and sat on the edge of one of the two beds.

"I could eat," Daniel said. "Order something?"

"That's what I was thinking. It wouldn't attract unwanted attention. No one's looking for us."

Aaron glared at Benjamin for a second, then focused on his computer again, partly watching them all from the corner of his eye.

"What?" Benjamin sounded wounded. "I'm just saying."

Daniel slapped his leg. "Well, I'm just saying order something. Think of this trip to Dallas as a holiday. Order four large pizzas."

"Deal."

Benjamin grabbed the motel phone and used his iPad to browse menus. Aaron watched it all, taking it all in, wasting their time in the motel while Sarah and Parkman were out there doing whatever the hell they were doing.

It made no sense to him. They could help. Even menial tasks. Something to get whatever Sarah was working on done so they could head home.

He scrolled to the next screen and was about to read a new article when Alex got up from the bed and headed for the bathroom.

"Hey, you gonna be a while back there?" Benjamin asked.

Alex shook his head.

"What's that mean? Yes or no?"

The bathroom door closed. Aaron heard the lock snick into place.

"Shit," Benjamin mumbled. "I needed to go."

"No," Daniel pointed at him. "You needed to order food. Take a piss later."

Benjamin grunted, pulling the phone to his ear. "Hey, the

line's dead."

Aaron frowned. "No dial tone?"

Benjamin shook his head. "Maybe I have to press something first." He tapped a couple of buttons and held the phone to his ear. "Nothing."

"It's an old motel," Daniel added, setting his iPad down and getting to his feet. "Who uses phones any more, anyway? Everyone's got a cell phone nowadays."

"If it doesn't work, why have it here then?" Aaron asked, setting down his iPad, concern mixing in his abdomen. "You don't think they—"

The motel room door slammed open, cutting him off mid-sentence. Whatever hit the door was so violent that the top hinge severed as the door swung inward. The door banged against the wall and canted at an ugly angle.

Aaron launched sideways, landing on the carpet behind the bed. Heavy pounding assaulted his ears. Daniel and Benjamin landed on the floor as well. Boots stomped around his head before he could scramble anywhere as men entered the room shouting orders.

FBI agents, clearly labeled and completely covered in combat gear, surrounded his position on the floor, weapons up and aimed, shouting for everyone to stay down.

Benjamin shouted over the din, telling them not to shoot, hands raised above his head where he crouched on his knees beside the dead motel phone.

Daniel had barely jumped at the intrusion. He merely turned toward them, raised his hands, and then lowered slowly to his right knee, then the left.

Aaron stared at the group of FBI agents piling into the

small motel room. Four surrounded him where he lay on his stomach as one of them landed on his back. He summoned all the willpower he could muster not to spin the man off his back and break something he owned. The dirty motel carpet shoved its way into his mouth and nose as the man's knee pushed down on the back of his neck. His hands were wrenched behind him, cuffs slammed painfully over his wrists.

Men barked orders. Several of them ran for the closed bathroom door. As Aaron was yanked to his feet, he was able to catch a glimpse of them slamming their shoulders into the flimsy door.

On the way out to the parking lot, Aaron hoped Alex wouldn't fight back. They'd done nothing wrong. It was Sarah they were looking for. Bruno, too, but he'd already left over thirty minutes before in a black SUV, headed somewhere he didn't reveal to them.

The agents lined the three of them up in the parking lot shoulder to shoulder. Tight-lipped, Aaron waited for the armed men in battle fatigues to come out with Alex, but after several minutes, the motel room emptied, and Alex was nowhere to be seen.

He exchanged a glance with Daniel, who nodded slightly.

Alex had disappeared.

"Special Agent Sullivan," one of the men said.

A woman stepped out of one of three dark-colored Suburbans. She closed the door, adjusted her black pants, then strode toward the man who had spoken.

"Go ahead," Sullivan said.

"That's it. Just the three of them."

Sullivan turned to appraise them, her eyes stopping on Aaron. "No Sarah?"

The man shook his head. "No Sarah, ma'am. But the bathroom window was open."

She looked away from Aaron and faced the man. "We have Rogers and Blacksmith back there. They see anything?"

The man shook his head. "They reported all clear back there."

Alex got away. Somehow, he was able to outwit two armed FBI agents stationed to watch the back of the motel. Did he use the roof? Was he able to clamber into an adjoining room? Some of the shit Alex did mystified Aaron because he'd never taught him half of it. When Alex came to him years ago, he could barely throw a punch. Now he was part ninja. He was probably watching them now, assessing, waiting to see if he could free them.

The Sullivan woman moved closer, stopping in front of Aaron. Sweat beaded on his forehead, pooled and dripped into his eyes. He blinked it away.

"You must be Aaron Stevens," she said.

He didn't respond.

"I don't know the names of these two yet, but I will shortly." She stepped back, watching them. "Harboring a fugitive will be one of the charges laid against you three, obstruction another." She pointed back toward the motel's front desk. "Clerk in there says you had a girl in that room earlier. A *dark*-haired girl." She smiled like she was in on some joke. "Sarah dye her hair?"

None of them spoke. The room had been air-conditioned, and now, standing out in the direct sunlight, he was soaking his shirt in sweat. His stomach was flipping, making him wish he'd eaten something earlier. That pizza would've gone down good. Beer too.

"You're going to tell me where she is, Aaron Stevens or more charges will be applied to you three." She leaned in close enough that he smelled mustard on her breath. "There will be so many charges, I'd consider you a flight risk. I'll certainly be recommending you're all held in custody until trial." She shrugged one shoulder. "Say, about a year or so. Investigations of this magnitude can take a long time."

"She serious?" Benjamin asked.

"We say nothing," Aaron said, his tone clipped, forced. "They've got nothing on us. We'll be out in a few hours. They haven't even read us our rights."

Sullivan stepped back, a smug look on her face. "Read these three men their rights and get them secured away. We head back to start the interviews immediately." She focused on Aaron again. "Lawyer up or not, I don't care. You lot aren't going anywhere for a long time."

It was his turn to smile. Darwin was landing at the airport, and Alex was still free. He was probably watching and listening at that very moment. This would be fixed within a day.

"A long time," Sullivan repeated.

Aaron snorted as they were dragged away toward one of the waiting SUVs.

"We'll see about that," he said under his breath.

Chapter 25

Sarah got out of the taxi four blocks from the Glenmarks' home. A large grassy field was to her right, and a building that was probably a school sat at the other end of the field. Still somewhat early for the interview, she dawdled, wondering how she'd pull off being a journalist. These people lost their daughter, and she wanted to talk to them about it under false pretenses. Doing and saying whatever she wanted when it wasn't hurting anyone left no mark on her conscience, but this was different.

Would they talk to her if they knew the truth? She could just tell them her name and that she was *that* Sarah Roberts the FBI was looking for. Sure, and everything Rosina had done to set this up would be for nothing.

She wasn't a journalist and had no idea how they routinely interviewed people, but she would surely try to pull it off.

She marveled at how calm and peaceful the neighborhood felt as she turned up their street. Their daughter probably loved growing up in this clean residential area.

Once she was standing in front of the house, she inhaled deeply to remain calm, then decided on a couple of opening questions.

"Hello?" a woman said.

Sarah started and turned around. A middle-aged woman with beautiful hair cascading over her shoulders was out doing yard work. She wore thick gardening gloves, and a rash of soil creased her forehead.

"You must be our two o'clock appointment," the woman said, stepping closer.

Sarah nodded, not sure what name Rosina gave her. "Yes, I am," she said, her right hand extended tentatively. "Sarah."

Amanda Glenmark held out her hand, and they did an air shake, not touching, as Amanda's hands were covered in dirt.

"I should clean up," Amanda said. "C'mon in." Amanda started for the front door with Sarah falling in behind her. "You're here a bit early. Wasn't expecting you for another hour."

"Hope that's okay."

"Of course." Amanda stopped at the door and glanced out at the street. "Where's your car?"

Sarah offered a warm smile. "Took a taxi. On the wages they pay us? Can't afford a car."

Amanda studied Sarah's face briefly, nodded, and said, "Well, come on in. I'll wash up and put on a pot for tea."

Once inside the foyer, she turned back to Sarah. "Unless you want lemonade or something cold. It's certainly a hot one out there."

"Something cold would be appreciated."

"Then cold it is." Amanda started for the kitchen. "Make yourself at home in the living room. I'll join you in a minute after I get Brian. He's in the back office."

She watched Amanda walk away. Then, her gaze drifted to the suitcases in the hallway. Beside them were two equally small carry-on cases. The Glenmarks were planning on going somewhere soon.

Sarah moved into the living room to the right of the foyer. A faux fireplace decorated the back wall, the hearth covered in knick-knacks. Amanda was a collector of stones, large and small. Sarah recognized cute pieces of slate that were set decoratively around the base of the fireplace. Family pictures adorned the mantle.

She moved closer, inspecting the photos. One picture was of the three of them when Jane appeared to be around twelve, a swimming medal dangling from her neck. Another picture of them had the Epcot Center sign in the background. San Diego SeaWorld graced a photo of them all when Jane looked to be fifteen or sixteen.

Before she could hold them back, tears started. Sarah wiped them away as fast as she could, not wanting to be found in their living room, bawling her eyes out. How could a parent lose a child? How could they live with that? How does one move on?

Sarah could barely function for the few months after she lost the baby growing inside her. How could these people raise such a lovely girl, and then she was gone in such a brutal fashion?

In this cruel, horrible world, parents who lost their children and kept moving forward, like Amanda and Brian Glenmark, were the true warriors. She would do well to be inspired by them. She backhanded the rest of the tears. It probably wasn't smart for her to be staring at family photos.

"Sarah?"

She jerked as if electrocuted. She clutched at her chest, letting out a short laugh. "Sorry, my nerves."

Brian Glenmark stepped into the room, hand thrust forward. A tall man, unafraid of the sun, his skin tanned to a dark leather, smiled wide, white teeth gleaming.

"Amanda said you'd be in here. I'm Brian, Jane's father."

They shook hands.

"Please, sit."

Sarah took a seat on the couch and slowly opened her laptop. She'd have to wing it without time to process questions in advance or buy journalist-like props. Although, how many times did a journalist call upon these people? How would they know what she was doing wasn't standard?

She set her open laptop on the couch beside her.

"You're going to type as we talk?" Brian asked.

Shit, they probably have been interviewed before.

"Only certain notes. Shorthand. It won't distract from our conversation."

"Oh, okay. You don't have one of those little recorder things?"

"Oh, Brian," Amanda said, entering the living room with a tray, three glasses, and a pitcher of a deep yellow liquid.

"Everyone's different. Let her do it her way."

At that moment, Sarah missed her own mother. Her parents had come to Toronto from Santa Rosa for a week-long visit after she'd lost the baby, but the visit was difficult. It was a strange time. Pain made Sarah irritable, whether it was physical or mental. Only Aaron truly understood that about her.

Amanda poured Sarah a glass and set it in front of her. After pouring one for her husband and herself, she sat in the plush chair beside Brian.

"You're planning a trip?" Sarah asked, gesturing toward the suitcases.

Amanda shook her head. "We just haven't unpacked yet. Yesterday's flight was canceled." She snuck a glance at Brian. "We were considering whether we'd even go at all."

"Somewhere south? An ocean, perhaps?" Sarah asked, hoping small talk would make them all comfortable with each other. "An extended family visit?"

Amanda shook her head again. "We were heading to Los Angeles for the organ donation events taking place there."

Sarah eased her computer closer. "Organ donation event?"

Brian watched her stoically while he sipped his beverage.

Amanda set her glass on the table. "Several of the companies that handle organ and tissue donation prepare events throughout the year to raise awareness. It educates others on the benefits and gets more people to agree to become an organ and tissue donor."

"I have to apologize in advance," Sarah said. "Some of the questions I may ask could be hurtful."

The Glenmarks looked at each, then back to Sarah.

"Ask away," Brian said.

"Well, what I wanted to know was why you're so active in that community after what happened to your daughter."

Amanda turned her attention to the pictures on the mantle. "You can say her name. Our daughter died, and that's not something we can change." She slowly turned back to face Sarah. "How Jane died is still a mystery."

"*How* she died? Wasn't an autopsy done?" Sarah placed the computer on her lap and typed some random words, her ears wide open.

"When Jane was taken to the hospital and pronounced dead, I pleaded with them to leave her body alone even though she was a registered donor."

"I'm assuming they didn't, then."

Amanda shook her head—it seemed she was fond of doing that. "No, they didn't. The harvesters, animals really, which are different from legitimate procurement companies, swooped in and took her bones, tissues, and heart valves. They even washed parts of her body, like her hands. The coroner could not determine the cause of death."

Sarah sank deeper into the couch's back, listening to what Amanda said. "How could that be possible?" The pitch of her own voice surprised her. "How could someone's loved one be violated in such a way? Don't they determine the cause of death and then perform the organ donation? What if she was murdered?"

"Our questions, too. That's why we hired a lawyer and went after True Legacy, the procurement company that stole our daughter's body parts, but nothing came of it."

Sarah set her laptop aside and reached for the lemonade. Her mouth had dried up. She took three full swallows, then set her glass down.

Brian watched her, his fingers steepled.

"Let's pretend I know nothing of organ donation," Sarah said, which was essentially true. "Please, tell me what happened to Jane from the beginning."

"She was found unresponsive several blocks from here," Brian said. "That afternoon, she'd taken her bike and gone riding with friends. Once they headed home, she took a trail through the woods back to our neighborhood. She never made it."

"And there's no official cause of death? For an eighteen-year-old?"

Brian nodded. "None."

"It's unlikely," Amanda started, "she had a heart attack, but it's possible. People have heart attacks at her age. It could've been a number of things, but we just don't know."

Amanda seemed quite composed for a woman talking about her dead daughter. Sarah guessed that took practice.

"And the coroner couldn't determine anything? Not even an educated guess?" Absolutely mystified, Sarah stared at the two of them, holding the glass of lemonade in her hand. It shook, so she set it down, not wanting them to see her nerves. This talk of losing a child was starting to overwhelm her.

Brian shook his head. "Nothing, even if she was murdered. We don't know."

"I'm so sorry. I just can't wrap my head around this. How the hell is this possible? How is it allowed?"

Amanda lost some of her composure. She snatched her

glass and sipped quickly. After setting it down, she grabbed a tissue and dabbed at the bottom of her eyes.

"It's like time has stopped, yet we still age, even faster than before Jane died." Amanda discarded the tissue and let her hands fall to the side, where she clenched them and unclenched them several times. "My mind races, thoughts always spinning around. I went through the stages of grief, sped through some, dawdled in others. Shock, disbelief, and rage, all to understand how we got here, to this place, without our daughter."

Now Sarah wasn't sure she could hold it together as Amanda spoke. Every emotion she endured when her baby left her body rose to the surface, like a thousand balloons of emotion ascended to the ceiling of her mental well, all threatening to pop at the same time.

"When you lose a child, you feel broken inside," Amanda said.

Sarah found herself nodding, wiping a tear from her cheek.

Brian watched Amanda as she spoke.

"When they harvested Jane, a desire for vengeance enveloped me, no matter the consequences. It was like she died twice. I was looking for a fight." Amanda pinched her lips together as if she did it to keep them from trembling. She lifted her chin defiantly, then stared at Sarah as if forcing herself to make eye contact, to be strong. "I wanted True Legacy to hurt. I wanted them to bleed, too." She patted Brian's arm. "He helped me through that. We hired a lawyer." She shrugged as if it was all no big deal. "And now we can see where that got us—"

She stopped talking, emotion closing her throat. Her shoulders were hunched, her head hung, and her hands twitchy. Amanda started to cry.

Sarah found herself clutching her abdomen, her hands pressing into her stomach. When she looked down, her vision blurred with tears, all the balloons popped, and embarrassed or not, she wailed for the loss of her own baby. She cried in front of these two strangers as Amanda wept for Jane, their children stolen from this horrible world, lost forever.

Sarah tried to control the tears, but they wouldn't abate.

Someone plunked down beside her. The realization that Amanda came to console her overwhelmed her at the moment, and they held each other, letting the floodgates open.

It was several minutes later when Amanda eased up and off Sarah. She stepped away from the couch, and then a ball of tissues was placed on Sarah's lap, which was now damp in the thigh area.

"I'm sorry," she was able to mutter.

"Don't." Brian's voice. Calm, controlled.

"It's okay, Sarah," Amanda whispered. "We've all suffered loss. We need to let it out."

Sarah shrugged, twirling the wet tissues in her hand. This wasn't supposed to happen. It's not supposed to be about her. Besides, she thought she'd dealt with it—mostly.

"I lost a baby," she said. "Earlier this year. Miscarriage."

"Oh, Sarah. I'm so sorry."

She dabbed at her eyes and looked up. "This isn't about me, though. I'm sorry our talk went in this direction. Please, let's get back to some of the facts."

She drank the rest of her lemonade, poured a little more, then inhaled deeply.

"Are you okay?" she asked Amanda.

Amanda nodded. "Please. Let's continue. I got this. We can do it."

Brian nodded. "I'll start then. Sarah, you'd asked how it was possible that procurement companies can do what they did to Jane. Let me explain a little about how it works. These procurement companies have contracts with hospitals and local morgues. True Legacy has teams embedded in government morgues with key cards to access the building at any hour. Sometimes, they've rented rooms and suites where surgical teams are hard at work harvesting. We believe in some of their practices, and we support organ donation, but not until the cause of death is determined." Brian shrugged nonchalantly. "How else are they expected to grab that heart or kidney and race it to the new recipient while it's still a viable option?"

Sarah licked her lips. She was back under control and feeling lighter. Maybe a good cry was all she needed. For now.

She took another drink. "You seem so ..."

"So what?" Brian asked.

"Okay with everything."

He clasped his hands together and looked at his wife. "We're firm believers in organ donation. It saves lives. Even after what happened to Jane, we still back it. All we want is for the cause of death to be determined. For instance, if they could have been able to see Jane was murdered, then True Legacy wouldn't have been able to touch her as an investigation would've had to be conducted. If it was a heart attack, tell us and then harvest away. Jane would've wanted to help others."

"So there are circumstances that are off limits for these people, these harvesters? They can't touch murder victims?"

"Absolutely. Famous people are mostly exempt. Otherwise, the media would catch wind of it. Victims of suspected child abuse and homicides where the police are involved." He shook his head. "The authorities do autopsies, toxicology reports, and on and on as bodies are often needed as evidence. In those cases, procurement companies can't show up and start cutting out pieces." He looked at Amanda, then back to Sarah. "But sometimes they still do."

"That's unbelievable."

"Sarah," Brian cleared his throat, "True Legacy has a computer database where they can log in to government files searching for potential procurement candidates. They donate iPads to all the morgues they work with, so the details of recent deaths can be uploaded immediately. With the help of our lawyer and our *dead* lawsuit, for want of a better word, we learned that under federal rules, hospitals are required to alert procurement companies they're contracted with when an organ donor dies while at their hospital. With iPads and access to morgues, True Legacy is also aware of deaths outside hospitals. And they have a huge list of needs all prepared. Kidneys, lungs, hearts, and even skin, too."

Sarah's eyebrows rose in surprise, an image of Ed Gein in her head. "Skin? Call me naïve. Why the hell would they want skin?"

"Skin is often used for cosmetic surgeries and wound

care, to name a few. An eight-by-ten inch square of skin can sell for over fifteen thousand dollars."

"What?" she shouted, rising from the couch. "You're fucking kidding me." She cleared her throat and settled back down onto the couch. "I'm sorry. That was unprofessional of me." Her eyes watered momentarily as she grabbed her glass to distract herself from her outburst. After emptying it, she eased back onto the couch. "I'm shocked. I can't believe what you're telling me."

Amanda was nodding. "It's all true. Brian, here is the numbers guy. He memorized the numbers during our year-long court case, which went nowhere."

"Then tell me another one." Sarah wanted them talking so she could calm herself. Every nerve in her body wanted to run out their door and find whoever ran True Legacy and harvest their heart valves using bullets as her tool of choice to make them pay for what they did to Jane.

"A jawbone, used for dental surgery, can net True Legacy over three grand. And the tip of your hip bone, the iliac crest, can go for about a thousand. It's used for spinal fusion. There's so much more."

"Okay." She took a deep breath. "I can see the benefits. Certainly, organ donation can be a good thing—"

"Hence why we still stand behind it," Amanda cut in. "Jane would have wanted us to stay with it."

"But if they're harvesting before the cause of death is determined, how do they not know there's a murderer still out there?"

Brian shrugged again. Sarah was starting to wonder if it was a nervous tick. The man shrugged at half of her questions.

"We don't know. When we got to court, we learned dozens of cases were being investigated in Los Angeles and dozens in New York, with most of the investigations here, in Dallas, Texas, where True Legacy has their head office. All of these investigations were due to body parts being taken before a coroner's autopsy report was completed. We learned that in many cases, coroners were left guessing the cause of death, leaving wrongful death and medical malpractice lawsuits dead in the water because of the tissue harvesting True Legacy does."

"Then why aren't there laws to stop the early harvesting of bodies?"

"Sarah, laws are there, but they're there to protect harvesters."

"You're kidding."

Another shrug. "I wish I was."

"What happened to your case?" She leaned forward and poured another drink from the pitcher without asking. Neither one of them reacted.

"Organ procurement before an investigation is legal. It's so they can grab organs quickly, as we just mentioned. To increase these numbers, many states passed laws forcing coroners and medical examiners to cooperate with companies like True Legacy. In some states, procurement companies have the power to stop an autopsy so they can get in there first."

"No, it can't be. *Stop* an autopsy?"

Amanda's hands were twitching. "It's true."

Brian took a sip of his beverage, then said, "Even though

they claim to just be taking tissue, bone, skin, fat, ligaments, and other tissues that are not life-threatening pieces, they aren't. They're actually taking much more than they claim. It's fueling a huge biotech market in which half a teaspoon of ground-up human skin is pricey. One human body can be turned into materials for products that'll sell for hundreds of thousands. Companies like True Legacy are extremely wealthy and protected by the laws of our state. They run roughshod over dead bodies."

"Protected by laws? How?"

"Well, we tried to sue them, but you can't. State laws protect coroners and procurement companies from lawsuits except in cases of extreme wrongdoing. And try to nail down a definition for that." He placed a hand on Amanda's knee. "In our case, True Legacy claimed to have no complaints or issues with autopsies from the people it works with. The law hasn't been helpful. When our lawyer jumped ship, we considered continuing on our own, but there was really nothing we could do. Even though we learned there are a lot of cases where the cause of death could not be determined due to True Legacy's meddling and greed. Even though they've screwed up suicide and murder investigations, the law still protects them. They hide behind federal laws, privacy laws, permissions granted for access to bodies by colleagues, and weak laws stopping anyone from suing them."

"Why?" Sarah asked. "I'm sorry. I keep asking why. Just trying to get my head wrapped around this." It felt like a hole had formed in her chest where her heart should've been. Maybe it was better that she hadn't brought a child into this sick world. "Help me understand. For my own sanity." If she was looking in a mirror, she suspected her face was as white as her computer's blank screen. "Why is any of this allowed on any rational level?"

"Sarah, they're saving lives, that's why." His tone dripped with sarcasm. "Someone's dead. That's over, that's final, they're gone. But someone else is dying, and they can be saved to live another dozen years or more. These harvesters are saving people's lives, one kidney and one heart at a time."

"Something in your tone isn't convincing me you're still on their Christmas card list."

The Glenmarks exchanged a glance again. Amanda sipped from her glass. Sarah did the same.

"We stay close," Brian said. "We'll support them. But we're watching."

"For what?"

He pulled his hand away from Amanda's leg and leaned forward, his elbows resting on his knees. "For anything that'll nail them to the wall. There are over twelve million registered donors in Texas alone. They can't keep waiting for them all to die. True Legacy is a supply-and-demand company, like most. Their demand is high. Their supply is low. Especially for young people. They're the demographic dying the least these days. Unless someone *helps* them along."

Something clicked for Sarah. "And you think they're working on ways to increase their supply?" Her voice was barely above a whisper.

They both nodded.

"We have evidence True Legacy has hired hackers to log on to the DMV database and search out organ donors. They're hunting for matches because they have long lists of people waiting for organs and tissues. Then some arm of True Legacy, like black ops with the military, systematically kills these people and harvests their bodies before anyone's the wiser."

"You're kidding, right? This has got to be a joke. You're not just talking about murder, but *legalized* murder. One where crime does pay."

"Sarah, they've been executing matches and making sure deaths are done in a way to save the organs needed to be harvested for years. We think Jane was part of it. Jane, our daughter, was murdered several blocks from here so someone else could live, someone with a lot of money. We just can't prove it."

Stunned into silence, Sarah stared at them. Forcing her mouth to obey, she said, "Knowing this might put your lives at risk, you continue?"

"Well, thanks to you," Amanda said, "we're alive today."

Sarah scratched her right temple and rubbed the back of her soaked neck as she sat forward. "I saved your lives?" she asked. "How did I do that?"

Amanda got to her feet and checked her watch. She looked over Sarah's shoulder through the living room window. When Sarah turned around, a black Subaru was pulling up to the curb out front.

"Right on time," Amanda said. "I'll let her in."

Amanda exited the room and headed to the front foyer.

"Expecting guests?" Sarah asked.

Brian nodded. "You'll see."

You'll see was never good for Sarah, but she felt she could trust these people. Also, Alejandro's gun was still at the back of her pants. If True Legacy representatives were showing up, her weapon would be emptied. So she waited on the couch, rocking back and forth, feeling submerged in murky water at everything she'd just heard, her emotions running amok. Moments later, Amanda stepped back into the living room, followed by a woman in her mid to late forties, possibly early fifties.

"Sarah, I'd like you to meet Rose Marie Van Dee."

Sarah got to her feet, her legs wobbly, and shook Rose's hand.

"Just call me Rose. All my friends do."

Amanda gestured at the couch. "Rose is an investigative journalist with the Dallas morning paper. She documented our story when it happened and wrote about it."

Sarah bit her bottom lip and turned to Amanda and Brian as she sat back down. They had to know she wasn't a journalist after all. The ruse was up.

"When Rosina called yesterday from Italy," Amanda continued, "we talked for an hour at least."

"Rosina called," Sarah said, more a statement than a question. Of course, Rosina called. How else could she make the appointment for her?

"Remember when you asked if we were going on a trip?"

Sarah nodded, not sure she wanted to speak. Lying to these people after all the truth they had offered filled her with shame.

"We were sitting on that plane yesterday at Gate A12."

It was like someone punched her in the gut. There wasn't enough air in the room.

"After they took us off the plane, Rosina was able to find out they searched it for a bomb but didn't find one."

Sarah nodded for Amanda to go on as she wasn't ready to open her mouth yet, not sure what she'd say.

"What they found was someone had cut the landing gear. I don't know how Rosina discovered this, but she was able to get a report on it before the FBI sealed the records." Amanda snatched a piece of paper from the table to her right and looked at it. "Here it is, in black and white." She leaned forward, extending the paper to Sarah.

She took it and could see the report on the landing gear, just as Luke told her last night. He had sabotaged the plane, and here was her black-and-white proof on FBI letterhead.

Got you, Sullivan.

"Organ donors chartered that entire plane for the event in Los Angeles. If we'd crashed and True Legacy could get there in time, which we suspect was their plan, they would've profited from all the people on board that flight. Do you see what we mean?"

Her cogs and gears clicked into place. She was able to trust her voice again. "And they would've silenced you at the same time." She was thinking of Luke Roland and how fast they were able to silence him.

"Exactly," Brian said.

"So you know who I am?" Sarah asked.

They both nodded.

"You've known all this time?" she asked, heat rising to her face.

They nodded again.

"We know you're here to stop True Legacy because no one else can or is willing to. From Rosina and what we learned about you online, we understand that you can do special things, like find murderers when the police can't. And so, that's why we asked Rose Dee to join us. She's going to write whatever you want in tomorrow's paper. The FBI is after you and posting rewards. That poor man, Luke Roland, was in the news this morning. True Legacy must be stopped, and we think you are our only chance."

Sarah looked at her empty glass. "Do you have anything stronger? Like whiskey?"

Chapter 26

THE AGENTS HAD DRIVEN them to the FBI field office in the J. Gordon Shanklin Building. After separating them, Aaron was photographed and fingerprinted without ink while still in cuffs. Technology had advanced in the fingerprinting business. He had to assume Daniel and Benjamin were also being fingerprinted and photographed.

They'd shown him to a room where he'd waited alone for over an hour. It was a small rectangle with a desk and three chairs. He took the single chair farthest from the door where his back could be to the wall. There had been no washroom breaks, no offer of coffee or even water, nothing.

Agent Sullivan couldn't charge him, Daniel, or Benjamin with anything. They were looking for Sarah, but there was no proof the dark-haired girl seen in their room was Sarah. Sure, they had camera footage from Luke Roland's home, but going solely on the motel clerk's word, they didn't have much.

Although they knew who he was. And the likelihood of the dark-haired girl being Sarah—which it was—had to be good.

The lock clicked, and the door opened. The woman from the motel ambush, Agent Sullivan, entered the small room, followed by another agent dressed in a suit.

"Hello, Aaron," she said, closing the door.

The other agent sat in the chair beside the door. Sullivan edged around the desk and sat in front of him.

"I think we got off on the wrong foot at the motel."

He squinted at her, then relaxed his eyes.

"I'd understand if you were upset with me."

He just stared.

She looked at her colleague, then back to Aaron. "I'd love to start again."

What was she playing at? Start again?

"The cuffs have to stay, though." She offered him a smile. "I respect your capabilities. You and your little posse are extremely talented in the martial arts, no?"

Aaron waited. That wasn't a question he was willing to answer.

"You've pulled through a lot of scrapes over the years. Tell me something, you've actually killed people." She pointed at the wall where the corridor lay beyond. "So have those boys. And yet, you're all free to roam. Aren't there laws regarding murder in Canada?"

"You know there are," he said. "Is that why you arrested us? To discuss Canadian laws?"

"Right to business, eh, as they say in Canada." She checked something on her phone and then placed it back in her pocket. "Are you comfortable? Need some water or something?"

The nice part. Easy questions. Working on his trust and his level of comfort.

"Let's just talk," Aaron said. "If you've got charges, list them. If you don't, I'll be leaving."

"Whoa, not so fast, Shotokan man." Sullivan leaned back in her chair as if blown back by a heavy wind. "We're just talking."

"No. We're not. You're interrogating me without a lawyer."

"Is that what you want? A lawyer?"

"Depends on your questions. Depends on the charges."

"Well, it seems you were harboring a fugitive."

Aaron remained silent.

"Your friends claim Sarah Roberts was in that room with you."

Daniel and Benjamin would never tell Sullivan something like that. He let a smile play across his mouth to show her he knew she was lying.

"Caught lying in an interview," he said. "Or bluffing, whichever, causes you to lose all credibility, Sullivan. Neither one of those boys would tell you shit."

"Then tell me this. Where's Alex? He flew in with you yesterday. That's not a lie. I checked."

Aaron couldn't answer because he had no idea. "Alex has disappeared. I have no knowledge of his whereabouts."

"And a man called Parkman? Do you know where he

is?"

Aaron shook his head back and forth.

"What's Parkman anyway? A last name? His first name? Tell me his whole name."

Aaron let a short laugh slip. "I've never asked. Everyone knows him as Parkman."

"Does he have another name?"

"I'm sure he does. Just don't know."

She seemed bothered by that. "What about a huge guy named Bruno? Does he have another name? Or do all of your hired help just use fake names?"

He shook his head again, adding a shrug this time.

"Well, you don't know much, now do you?"

"Apparently so."

She got up from her chair and stopped by the door. "Last chance before the charges are filed against all three of you. Interested in helping me? It will go a long way for you when this gets to trial. Shit, I'll even put in a good word for you."

Aaron looked away from her and stared at the wall.

The door opened, and Sullivan hesitated.

"Agent Gigi Walentiny, process these jerks. List all the charges we discussed and ensure the pretrial services officer gets in this room immediately."

Walentiny nodded, staring intently at Sullivan's face.

"Tell him I'll recommend no bail and no signature bond." She pivoted back to face Aaron. "I think you call that 'promise to appear' in Canada, although I'm not entirely sure." She refocused on Walentiny. "No signature bond," she repeated, "and since they're Canadians, I want passports seized because these bastards will run. And tell the prosecutor to argue to the magistrate they sit in front of," she checked her watch, "which can still happen today, that if a bail number is set, make sure it's in the millions." One last look over her shoulder. "You're going to enjoy Dallas on my terms." It was her turn to shrug. "For several years if I have my way. All of you are."

Sullivan moved away from the door with Agent Walentiny right behind her. The door closed and clicked locked with such finality. It was the first time since he'd left Toronto that he doubted his decision to come.

They were in a lot of trouble, and no one knew where they were.

Unless Alex did.

Alex was their only hope.

Chapter 27

Amanda had opened a bottle of Scotch even though it was mid-afternoon. They'd all taken a shot, then settled back down to talk. Rose Dee explained her role and what she wanted to accomplish for Sarah.

"I've already cleared it with my editor. As long as I can write it fast enough, this story will be on our online paper tonight and the printed one tomorrow morning."

"Aren't you worried about repercussions?" Sarah asked.

Rose set her empty glass down. "For one, I haven't signed a donor card, and two, it would be reckless to silence all their critics. They'd be exposing themselves."

"Donor card or not, it's starting to sound like these people at True Legacy operate much like organized crime. I mean, look what happened to Luke Roland shortly after talking to me."

"And we were almost killed yesterday," Amanda added.

Sarah tilted her head sideways. "By the way, did Rosina tell you how she knew to call you? I mean, how did she find you?"

Brian nodded. "Apparently, she had looked into the plane at Gate A12 and saw it was a chartered flight. When she looked up who had chartered it, she saw the plane was full of registered organ and tissue donors. She got the list of people flying on that plane somehow and started calling them. She said we were the third number she tried who answered. I guess others just booked another flight. We saw it as karma and decided we'd go another time."

Amanda chimed in. "I was the one who answered the phone, actually. Once we exchanged information, Brian came out of his office, and I put Rosina on speakerphone. She said her husband, Darwin, was arriving today to help you deal with these harvesting murderers. It was then that we learned all about you."

"So when Rosina emailed me and told me about you and that I should come pretending to be a journalist, she was just screwing with me."

They all laughed, but Sarah. She didn't see the humor.

"That was Brian's idea, seeing as we were going to have a journalist already here." She pointed at Rose. "But you showed up early." She cleared her throat. "Which was probably a good thing. Seems like we needed time to get to know one another."

Sarah nodded, then focused her gaze on Brian. "That's where the tape recorder question came from."

He raised his hands in supplication. "Caught red-handed.

I admit it." He was laughing again. Actually, it was good to hear them laugh. "I was having a little fun at your expense. With all this seriousness, and with me being a prankster most of my life, I was happy to let you think you had to act like a reporter."

Sarah downed the last of her Scotch. "I might need a lot of that when this is all over."

Amanda cleared away some of the cups while Rose wrote furiously in her notebook. Sarah filled them in on what happened at the airport and how she had to stop that plane from leaving. She handed the paper that Amanda had shown her to Rose.

"Proof the plane was sabotaged, and you can go on record about Luke admitting to my colleague and me that he did it and that he was willing to testify about his free transplant in exchange for a favor."

"That'll go in the article for sure," Rose said.

"What angers me," Sarah continued, "is the FBI's keeping that information sealed to make it look like I'm the bad guy when I actually took part in saving that plane from an accident."

"You don't think they're working with True Legacy in any capacity, do you?" Amanda asked.

"No, I don't. To think that would put me over the edge. There'd be no stopping these people in that case. I'd end up dead or in a federal lockup for years." She hesitated a moment, thinking about Aaron and where he might be. "Look, there are a lot of things happening right now behind the scenes." She checked the time on her computer. "By now, the FBI has raided my motel and arrested my boyfriend and his three friends he brought with him from Toronto yesterday."

"They've arrested them?" Rose asked without looking up, her hand still scribbling away.

"In their search for me, they have taken them into custody. That said, I don't mind at the moment. I can get them out in a few days when this is all over. They'll be safe inside." She didn't want to discuss Vivian's prophecy of Aaron's death. "Darwin has already landed, and Parkman will be on the way back to the café where he dropped me off."

"What's your plan?" Brian asked. "What's next?"

"I was hoping to strategize with Darwin and see what else Rosina had come up with. She emailed a huge amount of information on True Legacy. I still have to go through some of it."

"Okay, how can we help?"

"By staying safe, staying alive. We may have our day in court after all." She considered things a moment more. "Maybe you two should grab those suitcases and get a hotel for the night, perhaps two nights."

Amanda and Brian exchanged another glance, then nodded at each other.

Rose looked up from her note-taking. "I'll help by exposing them for what they are in tonight's internet news blast. Sarah, are you sure you want to go on record calling out the FBI as bungling the memories of the dead by coming after you when the enemy is True Legacy? You know, calling this company organized crime and speaking about the FBI Dallas field office the way you are, if I am to quote you, could land you in legal hot water."

"It's not slanderous if it's true."

"At this point, it would be considered slanderous as these are alleged crimes, allegations of criminal activity. It isn't true because you say it is. At least, that'll be their retort. Or expect something akin to it. Come to think of it, my editor might change some of this."

"It'll be proven soon enough, or they'll be harvesting my bones—" She stopped, her face hardening. "Shit."

"What, Sarah?" Amanda asked. "What is it?"

"Before coming here, my sister got me to fill out an organ donor application for the State of Texas."

"You're American?"

Sarah nodded. "Born and bred. I live in Canada with my boyfriend. I've grown fond of Toronto. But I have an American passport."

"Why would she do that?" Brian asked.

It was Sarah's turn to shrug. "I have no idea, but I'm guessing I'll find out soon. I just hope I'm alive when I find out."

The phone in the kitchen rang. Amanda jumped up and started that way.

"Expecting any calls, Brian?" Sarah asked.

He gave a slight shake of his head.

"Hello?" Amanda said in the kitchen. "Okay," she added, her voice hesitant. "One second."

She peeked around the corner. "Sarah, a man said he wants to talk to you."

Sarah didn't move right away. "Who would know I was here?" she said out loud. Then it dawned on her. Rosina knew, and she'd called yesterday. Parkman and Darwin would be at the café, and Sarah was gone. Yesterday's burn phone was broken, so Parkman had no way to reach her. So they contacted Rosina, and she gave them this number. That had to be it.

She rose from the couch on shaky legs. Partly from the Scotch and partly from what they'd been discussing for the past hour.

"It's probably Rosina's husband, Darwin, wondering when I'll be done."

She took the phone from Amanda.

"Hello? Darwin?"

"Sarah Roberts," a man's voice said.

It wasn't Darwin, and it wasn't Parkman.

"You're creating quite a lot of bodies to be disposed of in Dallas."

"Who is this?" she said, seething on the inside that they would call here.

The man's voice had steel in it. Like she was talking to someone who had no emotion, someone apathetic. It fit as only that kind of person could orchestrate, on purpose, multiple deaths to save the lives of others and feel what they were doing was noble.

"Luke Roland was a favor. One professional to another. That truck you stopped by Laredo was bound for the morgue. Do you have any idea of the huge demand for Mexican donors? We even had people in pre-op being readied for surgery as soon as that truck arrived. You've cost me a considerable amount of money. And now you're with the Glenmarks. You're becoming a royal pain in the ass."

All kinds of puzzle pieces were fitting together.

"You're finished in Dallas, whoever you are. True Legacy is closing down across the United States."

The man laughed, and its sound grated on her nerves. She detected Amanda, Brian, and Rose gathering around her, but she could only tighten her grip on the phone until her hand was slippery with sweat.

"Your tiny threats hold no weight, little one. By this time tomorrow, your boyfriend and his colleagues will be dead. Leave it at that. One for one. You hurt us, we hurt you. Then, walk away, and we can forget one another. Agree to disagree, shall we? I'd be more than happy to let you live, just not in Texas. Bury Aaron Stevens, then leave the state. Sarah, you took a gamble, a bet, and you lost. Collect yourself, accept your losses, and run home, little one, tail between your filthy legs."

The kitchen spun around her, and she bumped into the wall before Brian's hands righted her.

"You can't get to him, and even if you—"

"Please, spare me more threats. You're like a tiny kitten, all mouth and small claws. In your own head, you're vicious, but in reality, you're just a nuisance who should be drowned in a river. I'll email you tomorrow with a task for you to complete. It might save Aaron. Who knows? I'm assuming you aren't staying at the Glenmarks' house overnight, even though your motel was raided. That would put their lives at risk. Or are we having a *Final Destination* party? They were supposed to die on that plane yesterday. Finding unique ways to kill all the passengers could prove delightful."

He knows too much. He must have someone on the

inside at the FBI. This was too big. What had she gotten the Glenmarks into? Why the *fuck* had Aaron come to Texas when she explicitly told him to stay home?

Her mouth opened, but for the first time since she was an adult, nothing came out. Emotion was taking her over, and she just couldn't find words through her fury and remorse.

"Tomorrow it is," he continued. "One task, then off to home you go. Alone …" He grunted the last word in a deeper voice.

The line went dead.

Chapter 28

THE PHONE DROPPED FROM her hands, and Brian caught her before she hit the floor. He guided her to a kitchen chair.

After a few moments, to calm her racing heart, her hand on her chest, she told them what the man said.

"I have to call the FBI and warn them to keep a close eye on Aaron."

"You think that's wise?" Brian asked. "I mean, what if there's weight to the notion someone there is feeding True Legacy information."

"He's right," Rose said. "This'll run tonight." She held up her notepad. "They couldn't afford to let anything happen to them. And you told us the guy has some task for you for tomorrow. To save Aaron." She shook her head. "They're not coming after you or Aaron today. You've got twenty-four hours to figure it all out."

Sarah bent over, holding her stomach. "I feel sick."

"You need to move to the bathroom?" Brian asked.

"No, I'll be fine. Just give me a moment. I just need to breathe and clear my head."

They eased back, giving her room. She closed her eyes and focused on breathing. She hadn't felt this weak since she was eighteen and held captive by Curt. Or maybe his name was Gert. It had been so long that she had forgotten his name. But how did she get out of that? She was strong, she fought back, and she had a lot of support from the FBI. Not like this. Now, she was weak, and the FBI was after her.

Oh, how things change.

She started this and would see it through to the end, even if it killed her.

She got up from the table, and they reconvened in the living room.

Sarah looked from Brian to Amanda, then back to Brian again. "You two can't stay here until this is over."

"I agree," Rose said.

Brian nodded. "We thought so, too."

Once Amanda and Brian decided where to spend the night, Rose said she'd drive Sarah back to the café. After a lot of hugs and wishes of Godspeed, they said their goodbyes, promised to fix this, and said they'd stay in touch.

Amanda and Brian swore they'd leave their home within a half hour. They had a few things to clean up first. Sarah agreed thirty minutes more wouldn't be a problem.

Sarah followed Rose out to her Subaru. Once she cleaned off the passenger seat, Sarah got in gingerly. She needed food. She needed energy. A nap, a good night's sleep—she didn't get a lot last night. That made her think of Aaron, how he held her all night, warm and gentle. Where was he now? And it was all her fault.

Tears threatened again. She stamped her foot into the floorboards. She'd have to find a way to be stronger. This was getting ridiculous.

Rose started the car. "You okay?"

"No."

"Okay."

Rose edged the car forward and stopped at the stop sign half a block up.

Tires screeched beside them. When Rose jumped, her foot lifted off the clutch, and the Subaru jerked in place and stalled.

Rose screamed as a van pulled up so close to her door that she couldn't get out.

Sarah slammed her shoulder into her door and dropped out onto the pavement, rolling away from the car, already pulling the weapon out of her pants.

A man landed on her, wrenching the weapon from her with speed and strength. She rolled onto her back and raised her hands to grab at anything she could break.

"Sarah!" Parkman yelled. "It's us. You don't need a weapon."

She screamed a short burst to release her frustration. "What the hell!" she shouted.

Parkman grabbed her behind her arms and lifted her to her feet. Then he was half dragging her to the van. Adrenaline had rendered her a shaking mess.

"Who's the driver of the Subaru?" Parkman asked.

"A friend."

Parkman stopped at the van's door. "A friend?"

"Yes."

"Oh, okay. Rosina said …" He cleared his throat. "We thought …"

"Thought what?"

"Thought there was trouble," a man said.

Sarah turned toward the voice. Darwin sat in the front seat of the van.

"We'll explain. Get in."

Sarah shrugged out of Parkman's grasp and headed back to Rose, who was in the driver's seat of her Subaru, her face a mask of white, her breathing like she'd just finished a marathon.

"These are my friends," Sarah said.

"What?" Rose managed.

"They thought I was in trouble."

Rose's eyes focused on Parkman. Then she lowered her gaze. Sarah turned to see what Rose was looking at.

Parkman stood at the van's side door, holding Alejandro's gun. He saw what they were staring at, then tossed it inside the van.

"Sorry," he said.

Sarah refocused on Rose. "It's okay. Go to your paper. Write your article. Everything stays the same."

Rose nodded, big, long nods. She shoved the clutch down, turned the engine over, and jerked the car forward. After a couple of tries, the gears grinding, Rose got it into second gear, and then she was gone.

"You guys scared the shit out of her."

Darwin mouthed *sorry* through the windshield.

"Scared the shit out of you, too," Parkman said. She detected a laugh in his voice.

"How did you guys know where I was?" She considered her question a moment. "Wait, you spoke with Rosina. She offered the address."

Parkman nodded.

Sarah entered the van, and Parkman slammed the side door shut.

"We've got a lot of planning to do," Sarah told them, her heart finally settling into a regular rhythm.

Darwin started away from the stop sign. "That's what I'm here for. Planning."

"We have to stop True Legacy."

Darwin glanced at her in the rearview mirror. "From what Rosina told me, that's exactly what we will do while visiting Dallas, Texas. We're going to end them."

Parkman clapped his hands together. "Exciting," he said. "But first, I need toothpicks."

Chapter 29

Sarah spent a sleepless night, wrestling with dreams of Aaron dead, waking to speak to Vivian, who was still vacant from her consciousness. At one point, she awoke to find the second pillow on the bed wrapped between her legs and arms as if she was cuddling it.

Aaron should be there. She knew he couldn't be, but she needed him.

She rolled onto her back and stared through the darkness at nothing, thinking how all that was wrong. Aaron should be in their apartment in Mississauga. The three teachers had classes they could be teaching. All three, in Toronto, still breathing, their lives ahead of them. Instead, they were in some kind of federal lockup.

And it was all due to her actions.

She kicked off the covers at five in the morning and

powered up her laptop, already aching for two or three large coffees.

"Can't sleep either?" Parkman said.

She started, then turned toward him. He was sitting up on the small couch he'd taken as a bed, the early morning sun painting a fine line across his face where it crept through the drapes.

She shook her head.

"Me neither," Darwin said as he sat up.

"Who's going for coffee?" Sarah asked.

"I will," Darwin said. "Better you two stay indoors."

"Buy four," Sarah muttered.

"Four?"

"Yeah, I want two. Don't worry, I'll pay."

Ten minutes later, Darwin was gone for coffee, and Parkman was reading something on his phone.

"Did you see this article on the Dallas morning newspaper website?" he asked.

"Yeah. I was just starting to read it."

"You and that reporter went all out. This'll make waves."

"That was the intention." Sarah looked up. "By the way, if we ever have the pleasure of meeting Rose Marie Van Dee again, I want you and Darwin to apologize for making her shit her pants yesterday."

Parkman glanced up at her. "Of course. Shit, I'll even send her a bouquet of some kind of flowers. After what she wrote about True Legacy here, I can see how she'd get fucked up when a van screeches to a halt at her car door, and you're basically being attacked. I mean, that's probably how she saw it."

"And the gun. Don't forget the gun."

"Right, she saw the gun." He looked at his phone. "I can't believe she even printed the proof about the sabotage. You're looking pretty clean here."

"That and True Legacy probably won't stop until I'm dead now."

"After what they told you on the phone, I'm surprised they were willing to let you leave Dallas."

"They probably don't want that, but killing me might be something that'll bring too much heat. Who knows."

They read on in silence. Darwin returned with coffee, bagels, cream cheese, and a small variety of cherry tomatoes, grapes, and bananas.

"Wasn't sure when we'd all be able to hang in a restaurant, so I thought this would do in a pinch."

Sarah was half done with one of her coffees when she said, "It'll absolutely do in a pinch. Prefer this over a restaurant anyway."

She checked the time. It was after seven. The morning was already heating up, and she had no idea what the man who had phoned her the day before had in store for her.

"I wonder how he will reach out to me," Sarah mumbled to herself. "He said email, but that's traceable."

"What's that?" Parkman asked, his mouth full of bagel.

"Yesterday, the guy who phoned the Glenmarks' house. He said he'd be in touch today. I wonder how. He doesn't have my phone number."

Parkman shrugged, swallowed what was in his mouth, then said, "Probably email. Like he said."

She gave her head a shake. "Of course, but that can be

traced."

"Sometimes, not so easily," Darwin said. "What about Aaron and the boys? Want me to check in on them today? See how that Sullivan woman is treating them?"

"Probably a good idea," Parkman said as he popped a tomato in his mouth.

They both looked at him.

He stopped chewing. "What?" He swallowed. "Fueling up for the long hot day ahead."

They laughed, making Sarah feel slightly better. Moderately.

In a low voice, Darwin asked, "How are you feeling? Getting through this, you know, with Aaron where he is?"

Sarah nodded and looked at the floor, hoping he wouldn't see the shame in her eyes. Getting Rosina to call the Dallas FBI anonymously to give them the motel address Sarah had sent her still rankled her. Was it the right thing to do? Sure, it got them off the street and into protective custody, but the man on the phone said he could get to them. That had to imply the FBI was infiltrated in some way. And if so, and something happened to Aaron, how the hell would she ever figure this all out, end it all? She'd be an absolute wreck, useless, in a ball of grief, remorse, regret, and shame. For the rest of her life, and she hoped it wasn't long, she would be reminded daily that she had her boyfriend killed, the future father of her baby, her future husband.

"I'll be okay. We just have to keep going."

"Checked your email yet?"

She tossed her empty coffee cup into the tiny motel room trash can, snatched the other off the table, popped the lid, and sipped from it.

"I'll check now."

Darwin moved back to the bed and propped up pillows so he could sit with his back against the wall. A few moments later, he was on his phone as well.

When her email opened, there were one hundred and seventy-two unread messages. By the time she cut it down by twenty-five, fifteen more had popped up. Friends from all over the world, people she'd saved and worked with in the past, detectives from Los Angeles, Toronto, and even a cop in Italy when she was there sorting out a GMO issue years ago, had messaged her, asking if she was okay.

There was a message from Detective Marina Diner, but she skipped that one. Probably just more advice to turn herself in.

Farther down the list was what she was looking for. It was an email from the FBI. Before clicking on it, she read the subject line.

CONTACT ME. IMPORTANT

The sender was Special Agent Melanie Sullivan.

Sarah took a deep breath and opened it.

Besides the *Sarah* written at the top, Melanie wrote one line and her direct cell number below.

Please call me, Sarah. Allow me to bring you in. We can protect you.

Melanie

That wasn't much of a plea. There was no bargaining chip, no mention of a deal. But Sarah knew what cards Melanie held. She held Aaron, the ace of spades, in the royal flush.

She kept scrolling but couldn't find any emails from True Legacy or anyone purporting to be from them.

After a half hour, she closed her computer and lay down again. She was starting to feel the effects of not sleeping enough. She closed her eyes.

"You going back to sleep?" Parkman asked.

"Possibly. For a little bit."

"No emails?"

"Dozens. But none that were important enough to discuss." She waited a moment, then added, "Well, there was one from the FBI."

"What?" Darwin said, his bed groaning when he moved on it.

"That Sullivan agent. She just told me to turn myself in. That she can protect me."

"Hmph," Parkman grunted. "Protect you? Does she know something about someone coming after you? What makes her think you need protection?"

Sarah lay with her eyes closed and considered the email. Maybe she would call her. But not until after a half hour or so. She could use a little rest.

"You gonna call her?" Darwin asked.

She knew both of them were anxious to know what came next. She wanted to know that, too. So much went wrong, and so much was going wrong. Luke Roland was murdered. Sarah had broken out of custody. The FBI was holding Aaron and his teachers, and Sarah was taking a nap, while Vivian was nowhere to be found.

"I'll call her. I just have to think. This all seems to be falling apart, and Vivian's gone, and I feel directionless."

"It's okay," Parkman said, empathy in his voice. "We know. Take the time you need."

She loved these men. They were family, blood. Each one would die for the other. They'd been tested in the past, and for some crazy reason, they were all still alive. Even after Sarah had the insane notion that Parkman had tried to kill her once and she'd held a gun to his face, made him get on his knees, was squeezing the trigger, even then, they all got past it. She redeemed herself later and saved his life but still didn't feel she deserved his love.

The time of playing with other people's lives was over. Her friends and family weren't puppets Vivian could use to further her aims. Maybe a new pact was needed. Maybe Vivian and Sarah needed to work alone. Fewer deaths, fewer injuries, and fewer arrests of the men she loved in her life would take place.

When she opened her eyes, the sun played across the room from a different angle.

And the room was empty.

"Guys?" she called out, leaning up on her elbow.

She turned and looked at the bathroom door. It hung open.

Darwin and Parkman were gone.

She hopped off the bed and checked the time. It was just past noon.

"Shit, I've slept another three hours. What the hell?"

She opened her laptop and saw a handwritten note.

Be back around one p.m. Gone for lunch. Will bring you some.

She crumpled up the note and powered up her computer.

Emails totaled over two-hundred-fifty now. She scrolled past two emails from Rose, one from her mom and dad and one from the Glenmarks, looking for anything from True Legacy.

Nothing.

Then she saw another one from the FBI.

She grabbed a burner phone, one of two left, and typed in Melanie's number. On the first ring, she spied her leftover coffee from the morning. Cold as it was, she swallowed half of it, gagged, then set the cup down.

The phone wasn't ringing. Agent Sullivan had already picked up.

"Hello?" Sarah whispered.

"You okay?" Sullivan asked. "That sounded like gagging."

"Yeah. Coffee. It's cold."

"Don't like cold coffee?"

Sarah hadn't called to chit-chat. "I'm not coming in."

"Sarah, you have to. Our problems just got bigger."

"Why? Because of what the media is saying?"

"Well, that, sure, but there's more. And now I'm scared."

She frowned. This didn't sound like the agent who was all gung ho to nail Sarah Roberts.

"Why are you scared?" Then it dawned on her. "Oh, I get it. You're going to lose your job."

"Sarah, Aaron, Benjamin, and Daniel are being processed and—"

"I know. You arrested them yesterday. Is that why you wanted me to call? To tell me shit I already know?"

"Sarah Roberts," Sullivan said, her voice rising in anger. "Listen to me. Your boys are being processed to be released."

"Released!" Sarah gasped the word. That couldn't be. She needed them on the inside, safe in a federal building until this was all over. "Why? Can't you keep them for now?"

"Bail was set at three million, one for each man."

"So, we're good then. Aaron doesn't have that kind of wealth. We don't even own a house, for fuck's sake."

"A local *anonymous* company posted the bail. The money was placed in a separate account to show the court that it was there."

Sarah shot to her feet and ran to the window. They had to go pick them up. She would have to get Darwin to find mercenaries to ferry the boys out of town. She had so much to do with so little time.

"Wait, wait, what company?"

"Anonymous. And even if I knew, they've sealed everything with this case."

"*They've* sealed everything? It's not your case?"

"No, no, it's still my case, but I'm only the *assistant* special agent in charge at the Dallas field office. I'm not the *actual* special agent in charge. In short, I have a boss, someone I report to, and they're calling the shots."

"Okay, so where are they now? Where's Aaron?"

"In about half an hour, they will be walking out the front doors of this building, free to do what they want except leave the city. The company that bailed them out is sending someone to pick them up."

"Sullivan, you can't let that happen." She tightened her grip on the phone as she felt the world shift under her feet. How could this get any worse? "You *have* to keep them safe, keep them locked up." She grunted most of that last sentence through clenched teeth that didn't budge when she talked.

"I'm sorry, Sarah. I did all I could for you. I just wish you had've come in."

"Okay, deal. I'll come in. Just keep them there."

"Too late. I can't keep them here. Bail's been posted. It's out of my hands. However, I still need you to come in. But just know, your friends are free to go."

Then Sullivan did something that made Sarah scream until she ran out of breath.

Special Agent Melanie Sullivan hung up the phone in her ear.

Sarah dropped to her knees, her arms resting on the couch Parkman had slept on. The prophecy of Aaron being killed raced through her mind. Vivian had shown her the future. She'd tried to avert it, tried to stop Aaron. She'd done everything she could think of, but now someone posted three million dollars bail.

And that someone was picking them up.

Even if Darwin's van was outside this minute, the FBI building was more than a half hour's drive.

"Who could afford that kind of money, but a company like True Legacy—"

Something Sullivan said flitted to the forefront of her consciousness.

Bail was set at three million, one for each man.

One for each man? Three million? But there were four of them. Then she recalled what else Sullivan had said.

Aaron, Benjamin, and Daniel are being processed ...

What about Alex? Where was he?

Even though the light was small, a glimmer of hope

always started as a seed and grew from there. Sarah allowed that seed to grow. If Alex was free, he was on the outside, watching his brothers. He would be there for them.

That fuckin' guy, every time ...

She ran the conversation over in her head, sure Sullivan had said *three million* and three names. One hundred percent of Alex was not in custody.

She got up and ran to the computer, wiping her face, ready to fight.

Seventeen emails had come through since she'd called Sullivan.

Her breath stopped in her throat when she saw the third email that came in two minutes ago.

The subject line read,

YOUR TRUE LEGACY IS TO KILL CHILDREN.

It took two attempts to open the email as her hands were shaking too much.

Then, she read the few sentences in the email's body.

The nightmare was just starting, and she had no idea what to do. Vivian had to show up. There was no way out of this, no way at all. She was doomed from the start.

This was Hell, and she was stuck there, rooted to the spot for eternity, for she would surely burn with the best of them for the decision she was poised to make.

She reread the email:

There's a white Buick parked in front of the Glenmarks' house. The keys are under the seat. Inside the Buick, you will find an iPad with GPS coordinates locked onto two vehicles.

They are identical gray passenger vans.

Van #1 is heading north out of the city on the Sam

Johnson Hwy U.S. 75. Inside are six preschoolers and little kids on a field trip courtesy of my company.

Van #2 is heading south on the Sam Johnson Hwy U.S. 75. Inside is Aaron Stevens and the two men he brought with him from Canada. We have gracefully posted their bail.

Both vans are loaded with explosives.

Choose one van to stop. Choose wisely. To defuse the bomb in the black bag under the passenger seat of either van, simply type 187 on the screen.

I have cameras in each van. I will know if you send someone to save the other one. I also have access to the iPad in the Buick. With one button, I can remotely shut it down, and no one will know where the vans are until someone calls about a wreckage on the highway.

Go, Sarah, to the Buick. Go now.

When I see the Buick moving toward U.S. 75, both vans will start in opposite directions. That'll give you ample time to catch up to whichever one you have chosen to defuse.

Who dies today is on your shoulders.

Whether it's random kids or the adults, men in your life, I have use for their parts regardless.

Happy hunting.

P.S. Do not contact the authorities, or this ends with everyone dead.

Sarah wailed until her throat was raw.

Chapter 30

Sullivan stopped Aaron in the corridor and motioned for Agent Walentiny to let her speak with Aaron momentarily. She led Aaron to an interview room, stepped inside, and closed the door behind him.

"What's this?" he asked. "More questions? Bit late for that, isn't it?"

Sullivan eyed him, looking up and down. The handcuffs had been removed, and they had been allowed time to prepare to leave. A gray passenger van had pulled up about ten minutes before, one more perk from the anonymous company paying their way out of custody.

"You have a lot of friends with money," she said. She couldn't help the sarcasm in her tone. It pissed her off the boys were free to go. She thought they were the honey to Sarah's bee. Once Sullivan got the tip on the motel they were staying at, she was sure she could get them all off the street.

"Well," Aaron said, studying her face. "Whoever it was, I'm grateful to be out of here."

"Don't speak too fast."

He frowned. "What's that supposed to mean?"

Someone knocked. "Let's go," Walentiny shouted through the door. "They're asking where he is now."

"Look, I'm not the enemy here," Sullivan said, wondering how much she should tell him.

"Sure looked that way to me." Aaron moved to step around her.

She edged in front of him. "A lot is going on that you don't know."

"Well, great, but none of that involves me anymore, does it? We're out of here."

"Wait," Sullivan said, grabbing his forearm. After a second, she released it.

Aaron stared into her eyes. "Something's actually bothering you, and it's something bigger than us getting a free ride out of this place. What's going on, Sullivan?"

The knock on the door again.

"Coming," she shouted, then refocused on Aaron and leaned in close. "I think your life is in danger."

He laughed a short, clipped burst. "Yeah, right. Okay, Special Agent, thanks for the tip."

"I'm serious," she said, changing her body language to match her tone, hardening in a rigid military stance. "The people who orchestrated the sabotaging of that plane are powerful. As soon as Sarah spoke with Luke Roland, he was murdered. I don't want that to happen to you." She paused.

"Or Sarah."

"Sabotage, eh? Thought Sarah was in trouble for that kidnapping thing and bomb threat." Aaron was so close to her that he felt her exhale on his cheek. "You've been lying this entire time. Tell me the truth for once. Make me believe you."

Sullivan crossed her arms and stepped back, feeling uncomfortable that close to him. "Okay, you want the truth, here's the truth. When Sarah arrived a few weeks back, we became aware of her presence in the area. We weren't the only ones paying attention. True Legacy did as well." Something flickered across Aaron's eyes. He knew the name well. "Without looking to make waves, I called up to Toronto to see if anyone there knew Sarah. I was put in touch with—"

A knock on the door interrupted her.

"In a *fucking* minute," she shouted at it, then turned back to Aaron. "I was put in touch with Detective Marina Diner. She agreed to fly down here and meet with Sarah to find out what was going on. A lot of people in Toronto said many great things about Sarah, so I wasn't too worried. Also, she was mostly dealing with border patrol guys down near Laredo. Anyway, Detective Diner was just showing up at the airport with her friend, that Suzann woman, when they bumped into Sarah, coincidentally. There's not enough time to tell you the rest other than to say we've had a three-year investigation regarding True Legacy, and Sarah could jeopardize that. I wanted to arrest"—she used air quotes on that word—"her so I could keep her safe. Almost anyone who goes against True Legacy seems to die early."

"Why not tell us all this yesterday? Or the day before?"

"Because Luke hadn't been killed, and that plane thing hadn't happened, and, well, shit, it's just getting out of hand now."

"Okay, what you've been doing makes sense. Thank you for your honesty. I'll meet Sarah and tell her what you've told me. Your truth will go a long way with us."

She grabbed his arm again. "Aaron, just stay safe and trust no one. I don't know what is here to pick you up, but I'm told I can't stop it."

He patted her hand. "Don't worry. We got this."

The door shot open. "Sullivan, they're waiting." Walentiny stepped inside. "I can't stall them anymore."

"Aaron," Sullivan whispered, jerking him back close to her. Near his ear, she whispered, "If that's True Legacy out there in that van, you may be walking into some kind of trap." She eased a cell phone into the front pocket of his jeans. "Take this. I'm the only number programmed into it. Call if you need me." She released him.

Aaron nodded at her and left the room. Seconds later, he hurried back.

"I need a favor. We've got two more minutes, right? They can wait."

"What do you need?"

Aaron told her.

She nodded. "I can do that."

Once she completed Aaron's request and let him head back out to the waiting passenger van, she fumbled around in her pocket for a second and then found her car keys.

An idea struck her that was so brilliant she had no idea why she hadn't thought of it before. She ran from the room, heading to the garage where her FBI-issued sedan was parked.

251

heading to the garage where her FBI-issued sedan was parked.

Chapter 31

Sarah fumbled with the motel's door knob. She couldn't focus on it. Her eyes had glazed over until the room was a blur. Her head pounded in rhythm with her racing heart as the room spun.

Am I fainting?

She found purchase on the knob and held tight, righting herself, breathing in gasps, then closing her eyes on the room to calm it. Her breath was short, her throat tightening, and she opened her eyes again. The room had stopped wavering, but she'd broken out in a sweat even though she was shaking all over as a sudden chill enveloped her body.

Is this what a panic attack feels like?

"I don't have time for *panic* attacks," she muttered to herself and ripped open the motel room door.

When Darwin and Parkman had picked her up at the

Glenmarks' the day before, they had driven thirty minutes north of Dallas to get away from the large population of cops. Now, she saw that was to her disadvantage. She had to get back to the Glenmarks and get inside that Buick. There was a van to catch, a bomb to defuse.

She stumbled outside into the sun but could only see two vehicles. Darwin and Parkman were still out getting lunch.

"Lunch," she whispered, her appetite replaced by an acid stew toiling in her gut.

How would she get through the day knowing she murdered the people in the van she didn't chase? How could she—

Sarah lumbered toward the motel's front desk, the sun blinding her. The fear of having lost control, impending doom, and Hell's fires used to ignite her make her mad. But after February happened, she just couldn't find the right amount of coal to fuel her internal flames anymore.

She needed the old Sarah back. She had to find herself.

Coming to Dallas and getting back into her pact with Vivian to help people shouldn't have been something she entertained unless she could follow through. Moments of doubt and indecision weren't an option. When committed, she was fully committed.

And with each step toward the motel's front desk, she confirmed to herself she was in. All the way.

Yet, the full-body sweat said something else to her. She shook as the chills increased. Her breathing hadn't improved much, but at least the tightening in her throat had eased.

A pain shot through her chest.

And that was when she'd had enough.

Sarah dropped to her knees, lowered her head to the pavement, clenched her fists, and screamed out all the anguish, the pain. She screamed for her lost baby. She screamed for Aaron. But most of all, she screamed in that empty motel parking lot at the evil she faced and resolved to die before letting anything happen to those children or Aaron.

When she had let it all out, she hopped to her feet and ran to the front desk, looking as crazed and demented as she felt.

The door banged hard against the back when she tore it open.

A young woman behind the desk jumped and tossed her coffee all over her face, and the papers scattered across the flat surface in front of her. Sarah had seen her watching, no doubt wondering why one of her tenants was on the concrete, curled up on her knees and screaming.

"Can I," the clerk said, wiping at her face, "help you?"

"Where's your car?" Sarah stammered.

"My car?"

Sarah launched onto the countertop and, in plank formation, pivoted around and dropped onto her feet behind the counter.

"You can't come over—"

"Key," Sarah shouted, jamming her hands into the woman's pockets.

"Hey," the clerk said, trying to move away from Sarah. "I'm calling the police."

The pocket yielded a set of keys for a Nissan. The black one in the parking lot she'd spied.

Sarah launched over the counter again. "Call the police. Tell them Sarah Roberts stole your car."

"Sarah Roberts?" The woman barely got the name out. "Aren't you the one—"

The door closed behind Sarah as she ran for the Nissan.

She was still sweating profusely. But the chills had stopped, her stomach had settled a notch, and her headache was abating.

She was in the car, had it turned on, and was racing out of the motel parking lot in under a minute.

Ten minutes later, she was calling the FBI to have them patch her through to Sullivan.

The race was on to save lives, and she would do just that or die trying.

If her blackened and bruised heart stopped beating, then she'd stop.

Nothing else could do it. Nothing else could stop her now.

Chapter 32

SPECIAL AGENT MELANIE SULLIVAN got to her sedan, exited the garage, and drove around to the front of the Shanklin Building that housed the FBI field office before the gray van departed.

Usually going everywhere with her partner, Agent Walentiny, this last-minute decision found her alone in the car.

To do what exactly? Follow them? Where? To a hotel, someone's residence? And then what?

She had no idea. But she knew something wasn't adding up, and lives were in danger. She had no recent leads and nothing to go on but a gray passenger van carrying three Canadians linked to the case. Out of options, she had to follow it.

The van pulled away from the curb. She eased into traffic

as the van headed onto Northwest Highway 12 toward U.S. 75. Following at a safe distance—she decided to stay back at least six vehicles as FBI sedans were often recognized by those seeking to evade FBI attention—she drove calmly holding her phone as she considered calling Walentiny. Was it necessary to have backup? Should Walentiny know where she was headed?

The vehicle was signed out to her, and it had GPS tracking. In the event an investigation was ever launched, they could see where she was headed.

The van maintained an even speed until it turned onto the Sam Johnson Highway U.S. 75, heading south. Due to construction, traffic thickened, but she could still keep a close eye on the van.

Maybe it was nothing. Maybe she was paranoid. Why bail them out and then kill them? It didn't make sense.

The FBI could certainly investigate an *anonymous* company after providing bail and then executing the men they freed. That would be stupid of them if it were True Legacy. One thing that the company prided itself on was staying out of the spotlight. They absolutely despised attention.

The driver signaled their intent to exit U.S. 75. Minutes later, she followed them into the parking lot of a McDonald's off Fitzhugh Ave.

Unobtrusively, she parked near the gas station connected to the parking lot of the McDonald's to watch them. There were several ways in and out of the parking area, so she couldn't just sit and watch one particular entrance. She had to keep her eyes on the van and the van alone.

A man in his thirties exited the driver's side, checked his phone, then headed into the McDonald's. All three men previously in her custody remained in the back.

Lunchtime? If so, why aren't the others going inside?

A taxi pulled into the gas station, stopped in front of her sedan, and didn't move.

She frowned. If the van's driver came back and they left before the taxi moved, she would be arresting the taxi driver for obstruction or something.

A slim man in the back seat was paying the driver. The backdoor opened, the man exited, and the taxi pulled away.

"What the fuck?" Sullivan whispered to herself. "Move along, man."

The taxi's occupant just stood there, staring away from her, looking at the McDonald's, she guessed.

Without provocation or reason, the slim man moved until he was in front of her car, came alongside the driver's window, and then knocked.

She made a shooing gesture with her hands and said, "Go away."

He glanced at the restaurant again, then back to her. Once more, he knocked.

She lifted her ID to the window and slapped it against the glass. "FBI business. Get lost."

He knocked again, this time with the knuckles of his clenched hand.

"Are you fucking kidding me?" she shouted inside the car. This idiot was going to blow her cover. The van driver would exit the restaurant at any time, and she'd be made.

She rolled the window down two inches. "I said get lost.

I'm the FBI, and I'm working right now. FBI business."

"Aaron's in that van. I'm watching, too. But my ride was a lot more money. I'll ride with you."

She refocused on the man's face. Could he be the one who got away at the motel? Was this the man named Alex, one of Aaron's dojo teachers?

"Alex?" she said tentatively.

He nodded. "I can help."

Sullivan jerked her head to the right. "Get in. Hurry."

Chapter 33

SARAH MADE IT TO the Glenmarks' house without having to rely on a map, having already found it once the day before. The FBI had given her the run-around. They kept putting her through to someone named Walentiny. So she hung up. Maybe she'd try again later. For now, her task was to secure the Buick and get on the road.

Even though she had surpassed the speed limit most of the way, she was fortunate not a single cop had tried to stop her.

She glanced up at the closed drapes of the Glenmarks' living room window and slowed for a second. It seemed a lifetime ago she was chatting on their couch, sipping lemonade, and crying with Amanda.

The white Buick was where the email said it would be. Sarah jerked the Nissan to a stop, bolted from the car, and ran to the Buick.

It was unlocked. She found the keys and the iPad inside, just as the email had claimed. Once the keys were in the ignition, the iPad affixed to the dash lit up, and a map of Dallas appeared. It zoomed in to show two red dots flashing by U.S. 75. One was in the Belmont Park area, and the other was in an area called Richardson. Belmont Park would be the van heading south, which meant Aaron was there. The Richardson one was farther north. The preschoolers out on a field trip.

A twist of the key and she would be on her way. But she stopped, her fingers holding the key in the ignition. What if this was the vehicle with the bomb? Wouldn't that remove their problem faster and easier? If Sarah were gone, Aaron would have no bearing on True Legacy. The authorities would investigate, but good luck tracing a bomb back to a human procurement company like True Legacy. They would've hired pros, the best of the best, to ensure nothing led back to them.

She didn't want to die, but what other option was she left with? She had to go after one of the two vans, at least try to stop this madness. She recalled what Plato once said: *Only the dead have seen the end of war.*

A quick wipe of her brow and her decision was made. She had already wasted another minute—although neither van had moved. It was time to turn on the Buick or walk away.

She twisted the key.

The engine started.

After it was in gear, the car moved forward. No problem,

no bomb. She exhaled, wiping at her face again. She had to stay alert and ready for anything. She had to decide which van. It was too much to deal with, too much weight.

The urge to pull the Buick to the curb and stop overwhelmed her. Let the world spin on its axis, and the chips drop where they may. But she couldn't.

Six preschoolers or three Canadian men? Death on her shoulders, the weight unbearable.

Even before she got to the Buick, she'd already made up her mind. She knew in her heart who she would choose to save. And when it was all done, and the bodies were shoveled up off the road, and the grieving started, she would hunt True Legacy and burn it all to the ground. Every member of their board, every person responsible for the lost lives, for people like Jane Glenmark who didn't get a cause of death, for all the lawsuits, for everything.

Accountability was a bitch, consequences worse, and she had no problem dispensing all the payments in full to True Legacy.

Perhaps that was *her* true legacy after all. Making people pay for their crimes when they acted above the law and were able to escape the judicial process.

She drove toward U.S. 75 without wavering in her intent. There was a gray van to stop and the code 187 to enter into a readout of some kind in a black bag under the passenger seat.

For now, she had a job to do. And it wasn't Vivian giving out the tasks. Her sister was still gone, and it infuriated Sarah to no end that she would send her to Dallas and then disappear.

"What, you don't want to see who dies in the van?" she

yelled in the empty car.

The signs for U.S. 75 were overhead. She stopped at a red light and saw both dots on the iPad had just started to move. The Belmont Park dot had started south on U.S. 75. The Richardson dot had started north.

Sarah looked up at the signs in front of her. To go southbound, after her man and his two teachers, she would access the highway to the right. To go north after a group of innocent preschoolers with no dog in this fight, she would cross the bridge spanning U.S. 75 and take a left.

The light above her changed to green. She started forward and turned on her blinker to indicate her intention.

Then she turned left and started north.

After the preschoolers.

And she cried.

So hard she had to furiously wipe at her face with one hand and steer with the other to stay in her lane.

"I'm so so sorry, baby. I didn't want this, but I have no choice—" Her throat closed, and she hitched a breath. "I'm sorry, baby."

A car horn blared to her left. She righted the Buick and wiped at her face again.

Then she shoved the pedal down and gave chase.

"Goodbye, Aaron," she wailed. "Please forgive me. You know I could never let anyone hurt these children." She gasped, screamed, and added, "Not after February. *Never* again! Children are life. My life."

If there was a God, she hoped he could forgive her, too.

She used to believe because Vivian told her so.

But lately, it seemed He'd turned his back on the human

race.

She gave chase and lost hope for her soul with every mile while whispering Aaron's name with each salty tear she tasted.

Chapter 34

THE FBI VEHICLE BARELY moved when Alex dropped in the passenger seat. The door was closed, and he was seat belted in before Sullivan looked away from the van.

"How did you do it?" she asked.

"Do what?"

"Evade us when we came to the motel?"

"How do you even know if I was there?"

She nodded. "You were there. We were watching."

He faced her. In his eyes, she saw something most people would fear. It stirred something in her she didn't like, something primal. He was dangerous or had the potential to be dangerous. At that moment, she decided she didn't want to ever piss him off. His small stature notwithstanding, the aura he gave off told her this man meant business in a deadly way.

"Bathroom window," he said, his voice monotone.

That was it. The man spoke without emotion. He used words as tools to convey his meaning. Emotion was trapped in this man's movements, his physical bearing, not his words.

She looked away to watch the van. "That window was too small. Besides, we had two guys back there."

"I can squeeze. I clambered to the roof. No one checked the roof. Then I watched all of you. Collected names."

She turned to him again, impressed. "Damn, that's good. We didn't look up on the roof."

"I know," Alex said, then nodded toward the van. "There."

The driver was headed back to the van, three large bags in his left hand, his right holding a cell phone to his ear. The driver nodded a couple of times, got behind the wheel, and the van was leaving the parking lot within seconds.

Sullivan eased out and followed as the van got back on U.S. 75 heading south.

"Where the hell are you going?" she asked the van driver, not expecting an answer.

Her cell phone dinged. A text.

She handed it to Alex and then got them underway. "Can you read that for me?"

Alex took the cell. "It's from your partner, Walentiny."

"What's she saying?"

"She asked where you are?"

"Tell her I'm out for lunch. Be back soon."

Alex typed beside her, then set the phone down.

Within a mile, it dinged again. Beside her, Alex picked up the cell.

"You won't like this," he said.

Without taking her eyes off the van, she said, "Read it."

"It says, stop what you're doing and return to the office."

Now she looked at Alex. "What I'm doing? Eating lunch?" She watched the van a moment more, then shot a quick glance at Alex. "Ask her why?"

Alex typed. Seconds later, the phone dinged.

"She says to let the van go. Cease the tail. We are not authorized to follow. She adds that harassment charges may be pending if you don't pull away now."

She slammed the wheel with her hand. "Fuck!"

Alex set the phone down on his lap. "You can't continue to pursue. But I can."

"Yeah, and how are you going to do that? Steal my car?"

He turned to her. That look was back in his eyes. She shivered.

"To stop whatever's happening, I will do as necessary."

"Well, you can't steal an FBI vehicle, tracked by GPS, while going sixty miles an hour."

"We will have to see." That tone, again, clipped monotone.

She suppressed a whole body shiver. Definitely, a man she wanted on her side or out of her life. Either worked just fine.

Her phone rang this time. She smashed a button on the dash that connected it to Bluetooth even before Alex had lifted it.

"Why?" she yelled. "Who's telling us to stop following them?"

"Who are you following?" a woman's voice came through the speakers.

"Sarah?" Alex said. "Are you okay?"

"Alex? Oh, thank God. Are *you* okay?"

"Of course. I'm with Agent Sullivan. We're following a gray van heading south on—"

"US 75," she finished for him.

"Vivian tell you?" he asked.

"No, they did." She sounded ragged, her voice cracking.

"Sarah," Sullivan said. "We need to talk. There are things you should know—"

"No," Sarah shouted through the speaker. It sounded like she gasped the word. "You need to listen, Agent Sullivan. I don't know how you came to be following that van, but I know there's a bomb on it."

Sullivan and Alex exchanged a quick glance. Then Alex was rolling his window down.

"What are you doing?" Sullivan shouted over the sudden sound of the incoming wind.

"Going to the hood. Drive closer."

Alex started to climb out of the car.

"Holy shit!" Sullivan screamed. "Get back in here." He was sitting on the door now.

"Alex!" Sarah bellowed through the speakers.

Alex stopped and looked back inside. "What, Sarah?"

"Sit down."

He waited a moment, then did as she told him.

"Roll up the window."

Alex obeyed.

"Listen first. There's still time."

Sullivan's phone dinged in the background.

"What was that?" Sarah asked.

"Another text from my partner, Agent Walentiny. They're ordering me off the van."

"Walentiny's being a dick. She wouldn't put me through to you. Had to find another way. Then I remembered you emailed me your direct phone number. Listen, there's a bomb under the passenger seat of the van in a black bag. The code to defuse it is 187. But you've only got about fifteen minutes to deal with it."

Sullivan watched the top of the van as it eased to the right, her stomach twisted with nerves as Sarah spoke.

"It looks like the driver's preparing to exit the highway."

"Sullivan, I can't ask you to do this, but if you go after them and you're able to stop that van and get to the bomb in time, they will be watching."

"Explain," Alex said.

"I'm following an identical van heading north on U.S. 75. Both have bombs planted. This van is full of preschoolers. They have cameras inside each vehicle. I was told that if anyone other than me tries to defuse the bomb, it will go off."

"I'll do it," Alex said. He lunged forward and slammed an open palm into the glove box, the tiny door rupturing under his flesh.

Those three words revealed all the pent-up emotion the man beside her seemed able to keep to himself. That one punch—or whatever that was—told her everything about Alex. He was a fighter, but the kind that fought righteous battles. He stuck up for the weak and went after those who hurt the innocent. Quite possibly, Sarah was like that, too. She was attempting to stop a van with people she didn't know when her boyfriend was probably as good as dead.

Who are these people? Sullivan thought.

"If you want to live," Sarah was saying, "pull over and let them go."

"*No!*" Alex shouted. "Get me close."

More emotion. A volcano of it.

"I will leave it with you," Sarah said. "But if there's a way, if you can find a way, please save my Aaron. He's all I've got left in my heart—" It sounded like she choked on something. "Please, I had no choice." Sarah was crying, bawling the words out now. It brought goosebumps to Sullivan's arms. "Save Aaron, Daniel, and Benjamin, my Alex. Please, do what you can, sweet, sweet, Alex."

Alex jerked both hands at the windshield, telling Sullivan to get closer. The man was so pent up that he was literally elevated off the seat now.

She pushed the sedan harder. Fuck the consequences and fuck orders to pull off the pursuit.

"Code 187," Sarah said again.

"I will find a way, Sarah."

The line died.

The van turned onto an exit ramp. Sullivan followed. Alex started systematically cracking his knuckles. After the twelfth crack, she turned to him, the sound fraying her already strained nerves.

"That necessary?"

He cracked his neck, then eased his elbows up and cracked his back.

"I guess so," she muttered.

The van had stopped at a red light. They were seven cars

back. She watched as the van indicated a right turn.

Without warning, the van shot across traffic against the red light, hung a sharp left, and disappeared under the bridge that held U.S. 75 traffic.

"Fuck," Sullivan yelled.

The van was gone.

She honked her horn, slammed on the siren, and lost precious time waiting for cars to ease off to the side and get out of her way.

The light ahead changed to green. Cars started forward at an agonizing pace.

She drove up on the curb, careened off a red Mustang, then raced into the intersection, sliding left and hitting the gas.

The van was nowhere in sight.

"Fuck," she yelled again.

Alex moaned deep in his throat somewhere. A wounded animal moan. Or maybe it was an angry bear moan. Either one, it scared the shit out of Sullivan, and she was not scared easily.

She pushed the gas to the floor, driving blind now, with no idea where the van had gone.

Chapter 35

Sarah still couldn't see the gray van. She had passed a couple of vans, none of them gray. According to the GPS on the iPad, the red dot of the van heading north was still about half a mile ahead.

The red dot of the van heading south—Aaron's van, her beloved—had disappeared from the iPad's small screen as she sped out of the city heading north.

When Aaron's red dot disappeared from her iPad screen, she felt more alone for some reason.

She increased her speed, passing vehicles at an alarming rate. Alex and Sullivan were after Aaron. They would all die in the ensuing explosion if what the email said was true. Her selfishness had condemned Alex, and quite possibly Sullivan, to a horrible death.

"Why did you even call Sullivan?" she asked herself.

"Better yet, where are you, Vivian?"

She had called Sullivan because she couldn't allow Aaron to die without some kind of effort. How could she live with herself then? It was getting increasingly harder and harder to live with herself ever since February. This was only exacerbating things.

"I could sure use some help, sis."

She pushed on, knowing she had a finite amount of time to catch the van and save those kids.

The traffic on U.S. 75 thinned out as the land flattened north of Dallas. A concrete median separated the north and south lanes, with a grassy shoulder to her right. She would force it off the road when she caught up to the van by getting in front of it and slowing down. She'd find a way to signal the driver.

Car after car, truck after truck, she raced by them all, watching up ahead but still not seeing the van.

The speedometer said she was nearing a hundred miles an hour. Something caught her eye in the rearview mirror. Red lights flashing. She snuck a quick look, saw a state trooper following her a couple of hundred yards back, and pushed the Buick harder.

The red dot was near an area on the map called Howe. Moments ago, she passed a sign that said Van Alstyne or something similar. Another glance in the rearview confirmed it. The trooper was closer and trying to catch up.

The first sign for Howe zipped by on her right. She was close. It was almost over.

Two cruisers passed her, going the other way, lights flashing.

"No, no, no," she whispered. "Don't try to stop me now. I'm too close."

Then, upon the distant horizon, she thought she saw what looked like a van. And it was gray.

The Buick shook with the violence of the road and the speed, but she was able to keep it under control. Minutes now, maybe less, and she'd be right beside the van, forcing it off the road with state troopers nearby to help. Maybe it was a blessing she had attracted their presence.

"Vivian, you brought me to Texas. Help me out."

Sarah felt her sister before she heard her words.

"There you are. Any advice?"

No judgment for her absence. No questions. She just wanted help.

Stop the Buick, Vivian said.

"What? No fucking way."

You want my help?

"Yes, but I'm not stopping. I have a van to catch."

Sarah, pull to the shoulder, stop the car, and get out. Then run.

"Fuck you."

She watched the mirror. The sound of the siren was much louder as the cruiser was nearing her rear bumper. There weren't many vehicles in this section of the highway. Maybe he was going to attempt to force her off the road.

She needed more speed, but the Buick wouldn't go faster.

"Vivian," she shouted. "Tell me what to do, but do not tell me to stop the car. I did not come all this way to let those kids die."

In Sherman, minutes ahead of you, the area is too

populated for a bomb. Stop this. Get out of the car.

She tightened her grip on the wheel and changed lanes to be behind the van, which was less than a hundred yards ahead now.

"One more time. Any help on getting the van's driver to pull over would be appreciated."

There is no bomb in that van.

Then Vivian was gone. The feeling of her easing away was like a fading dream upon waking.

"The bomb is not in the van," Sarah said to herself, her foot easing up on the pedal. "Then there's only one bomb? In Aaron's van?"

The Buick slowed.

"Where's the explosives, Vivian?" She checked her mirror. "*Is* there a bomb?"

Was this a ploy to get her out of Dallas, possibly arrested? To go speeding after phantoms? If so, and they knew she'd choose the van with the children, then what about Aaron? Where were they taking him?

Every piece fell into place in an instant.

Vivian had told her to stop the Buick. She'd said *get out.* Vivian had said, *Then run.*

Vivian had rules on the other side. She couldn't directly reveal Sarah's immediate future. Some quirky rules of fate that Sarah didn't truly understand because Vivian told Sarah shit all the time, and it had to do with what was coming and what she had to do to stop it, and Sarah did those things. So, indirectly, she spoke of Sarah's future.

But not directly.

Wasn't 187 a code for something?

Why would Vivian mention Sherman and its population if the bomb wasn't in the van?

When she realized where the bomb was, a cold sweat covered Sarah.

She was going fifty miles an hour now.

Multiple cruisers were lining up behind her, all their sirens and lights flashing.

The iPad on the dash blinked off. Whoever monitored her progress saw she was easing off her pursuit of the gray van.

They knew.

Her right hand numbed. She stared at it as the numbness ran up her arm.

"Vivian? What are you doing?"

Sarah hit the brakes and jerked the Buick toward the shoulder and the grassy area beyond.

She got the car on a straight path in the middle of the grass, hopefully far enough from the highway to not involve other vehicles.

Vivian's presence slammed into her, knocking Sarah sideways into the car door.

"Vivian!"

Her numb hand wasn't responding to her anymore, just like at the beginning when Vivian took over to make her write out notes. But this time, she wasn't writing notes. Her deviant hand unlocked and opened her car door.

"Vivian. No! I'm still going too fast."

Sarah was shoved sideways once more and out the open door at around thirty miles per hour.

The earth shook when she hit the ground. She tried to land with her shoulder and roll into a tuck, but from that speed and that angle upon exiting the Buick, all bets were off. Rolling that fast, her arms shot out, and her legs splayed wildly.

The earth shook again, but this time for a different reason.

The Buick exploded twenty feet away as it rolled to a stop.

The heat from the Buick's total destruction swept over her as she stopped spinning, her body wracked with pain everywhere. Unable to breathe after having the wind knocked out of her upon impact, she gasped for air like a landed fish.

She turned onto her side and covered her head as debris fell around her while silently begging the advancing police cruisers not to run her over.

Chapter 36

"IT'S BEEN FIVE MILES and fifteen minutes," Sullivan said. "We've lost them."

Beside her, Alex rubbed back and forth along the tops of his thighs in obvious agitation.

"We have to do something."

She checked a street sign, then another, before pulling over. "I think I know where they may have gone."

Alex jerked toward her, his gaze hard. "Where?"

"True Legacy's head office is about ten blocks from here on Commerce Street."

"We go," Alex said.

"We can't storm their building. It's a thirty-story tower. Their offices occupy the top two floors."

"Drive."

"Hey, I don't take orders from you. You were supposed

to have been arrested yesterday."

He adjusted himself in the seat to turn bodily toward her, lifting his left leg and folding it under him. "Get me there. I will find a way in and get my friends out. Everything you have seen so far points to them being kidnapped. This isn't law and order, good guys versus the bad guys like on TV. This is you doing the right thing before something bad happens to them."

"Yeah, and losing my badge. No way."

"Then leave your gun and get out."

"Fuck you."

"This is not a road you want to take." He pointed out the windshield. "That's the road." He shrugged. "We all have choices. Make yours."

She studied him a moment, watching his eyes, his body language. He suddenly made her think of an underfed coyote, feral and dangerous, with a hunger for violence in his eyes. "Are you threatening a federal agent? I could arrest you."

He pointed at the clock on the dashboard. "That is simply another choice. Please make one because my decision has been made."

"What's that supposed to mean?"

"You are out of time."

"Cocky much?"

Could they really storm True Legacy's corporate offices? And if so, what would they gain? No one would confess to anything simply because they showed up. And if they had Aaron, Daniel, and Benjamin, they'd have them locked somewhere. Only a search warrant would gain access.

"This is crazy." She started the car forward, merging into

the first lane. "I'll drive us there. If, and that's a big if, we see the van, and if we think they've been kidnapped, that *might* garner enough probable cause for me to call Walentiny back and get her moving on a search warrant." She looked at Alex, then back at the road. "But I don't want to do that."

"Why?"

"Things are going on behind the scenes you aren't aware of. None of you are."

"Tell us then."

She changed lanes to set up for the one-way that Commerce was. She'd have to double back if she turned on it too early.

"We've been investigating them for a couple of years at least."

"Any charges yet?"

"None."

"That's expensive."

"You sound like my boss."

"Long investigation, no results. There are budgets. I understand this as I take part in the dojo business. No one to teach, no money, no dojo. So we make sure value is added. People love us."

She turned her attention back to him again. "You always like this? Short sentences? Say whatever you want? Seem dangerous, yet calculated?"

He shrugged.

She slowed at a red light.

"Look, it's more involved than, say, investigating a homicide. There are financial records, deaths around the state, and deaths country-wide. True Legacy has satellite offices in Los Angeles, New York, Boston, and a dozen other states. They're huge. Multiple people are involved, but that means more people know, and in this business, the more they know about a secret investigation, the faster the company being investigated learns of it and changes their operating procedures."

"You mean they become more stealthy in their activities."

"And they have. We were close to nailing them twice, but one coroner was killed in an accident, and the other one backed off."

"Looks to me like Sarah's handing them to you on a platter."

She scowled and turned to frown at him. "Not the way I see it as a federal officer who believes in due diligence and our court process."

"Courts don't work for companies like this."

They drove in silence as Sullivan navigated downtown Dallas. After ten more minutes, she turned onto Commerce Street.

"There it is. That tall brown building. It's sandwiched between those two glass towers."

She found parking a block away, eased into a spot, and cut the engine.

"Now what?" she asked. "You going to storm inside and demand they release your friends or else?"

"Something like that." He gave her that steel gaze again. "Patronizing me, making light of this situation, will only get you hurt."

She threw up her hands. "There he goes again with the

threats."

"To me, to Sarah, to everyone I know, you're a human being first, federal agent second. If you were to get in our way, we see only an obstacle. We don't see rank. In our world, you earn rank through honor, not a badge or an epaulet on your shoulder. Understood?"

"I've earned the right to be Special Agent Melanie Sullivan. I'm not a fucking obstacle."

"I didn't say you were." He opened the door. "But try and stop—"

Her phone rang. She went to hit the button on the dash, but the car was off, so she had to pick it up.

"Agent Sullivan."

Alex sat half in and half out of the car.

"It's Walentiny. Sarah Roberts just got arrested. State troopers have her."

"State troopers just arrested Roberts?" She stared at Alex, who was easing back inside the car. "Where?" she asked.

"Near Sherman."

"Sherman?"

"Yeah, and she's banged up pretty bad."

"How bad?"

Alex was stretching now. She could tell he was listening even as he pulled one arm over his head, then the other, pushing at the elbow to stretch his triceps.

"All I've got so far is she jumped from a car that exploded."

"She called us and said there was a bomb on a van she was following."

"What?"

"That's why I was following the van that picked up the three Canadians," she said, which was a half-truth.

"Did it explode?" Walentiny asked.

"Wouldn't I have told you that already?"

"Hey, just asking."

"Call it in, Walentiny. Pull jurisdiction on the troopers. Get Sarah in our custody. Once you have her, meet me downtown."

"Downtown? Why there?"

"Because that's where I am at the moment."

"Shouldn't we process her first and then interview her—"

"Walentiny, go get Sarah. Bring her to me downtown. Can you do that?"

"Sure, Sullivan, but it depends on how bad she's banged up. I didn't get all of it from them."

"She'll be fine. Just do it. I'll tell you where I am once you have her with you." She tapped her phone's screen.

"Sarah will be here in about an hour, maybe more."

"She'll know what to do next." Alex got out of the car and started toward the True Legacy building.

Sullivan hopped out and ran after him. "Wait up. You can't just walk in the front door and demand—"

"I'm not using doors."

She gawked at him. "What? Then how are you going to get inside?"

"There are other ways."

He left her side, sprinting toward the building. She kept up at her own pace to see what his plan was.

In under a minute, Alex had made the base of the building. He continued until he'd gotten to the side door access, where he jumped.

Above the side door was a concrete landing. One handhold, one swing, and like a monkey, Alex defied gravity and landed on top of the concrete above the door.

Rising away from the ground all the way to the roof were two concrete wall-like structures that bookmarked the access door. Through small windows to the thirtieth floor, she glimpsed the stairs.

Alex planted his feet against one side of the wall, leaned down, and placed his open hands on the other. Then he started to climb, one hand, one foot, the other hand, the other foot. In seconds, he was one floor up, then two.

Fascinated at his agility and his Spiderman-like abilities, Sullivan was transfixed by the sight. The man was dead if one hand or foot slipped. Soon, he was passing the tenth floor.

She raised a hand to her forehead to shield her eyes and looked at the roof. On the thirtieth floor, there was another concrete roof similar to the one above the access door. How would he get past that with both hands and feet occupied in keeping him from falling? And don't muscles lock up?

Her phone rang. Glad she'd grabbed it when she ran from the car, she brought it to her ear.

"Yeah?"

"On my way to pick up Sarah now."

"How is she? Did they say?"

"The trooper I spoke with said she had no broken bones, but she had a splitting headache and was burned in several places where debris from the explosion hit her."

"Is she good to go, though?"

"Yeah, they salved her wounds. She wants to be taken into our custody."

Sullivan looked away from Alex, who was nearing the twentieth floor on the outside of the building.

"Did you say he *wants* to be in our custody?"

"Yeah, she told the troopers she had to get downtown. When I called to tell them I was on my way to take her downtown, they said I could have her. Apparently, she's being quite the pain in the ass."

"Okay, that makes sense. I've met her friends. Canadians, eh?"

"Was that a joke? The *eh* part?"

Ignoring her, Sullivan asked, "How long before you're downtown?"

"Not sure. The trooper I spoke with said he'd meet me halfway to speed up the process."

"They really want to get rid of her." She turned back to Alex. He was two floors away from the roof. "Look, just hurry. Call me back when you're downtown."

She hung up and stared at Alex.

On the thirtieth floor, when the concrete roof bumped into his back, he let go of the side wall with one hand. Holding the wall's outer edge with his hand backward, she watched in horror as he released his other hand and both feet.

"No," she whispered as Alex swung out and away from the wall, dangling with one hand over thirty stories above the concrete below without a rope. "Fuckin' insane. Absolutely nuts."

Then his other hand clamped onto the outcropping, and he started to swing his legs. After three wide swings, he did what he did on the first floor above the access door. A wide arc, legs rising upward, over his head, and onto the concrete platform above his hands.

A second later, Alex lay prone on the roof. He rolled once to be supine, then got up and disappeared from sight.

"Well, I'll be damned. Fucker made it to the roof."

Sullivan turned around and ran back to her car to wait for Sarah and her partner.

Chapter 37

“WHY ARE WE STOPPING?” Sarah asked.

The cop driving the cruiser didn't answer. Once stopped, he exited the car, walked around to her door, opened it, and pulled her out. Due to the small burns on her arms, they'd cuffed at the front so her arms weren't twisted backward.

“What's this?” she asked, standing beside the cruiser while the cop stared down the length of the highway.

“Shut up,” the cop said. “No more talking.”

She took in the area. “You've pulled over and taken your prisoner out of your cruiser on the shoulder of U.S. 75, nowhere near a police station. This is not procedure, and you know it. So, what the fuck is this?”

He moved back from her as if moving away would limit his hearing.

A car whooshed by, shaking the cruiser slightly. Then

another car. The low growl of a rig approaching got louder, and then it passed them, buffeting Sarah's hair.

Something was going to happen. He didn't pull over to take a piss.

Vivian?

The trooper was checking his phone, holding it over his head and spinning around.

"No signal?" she said.

A car slowed and approached them on the shoulder. The trooper started toward it.

He wasn't watching her. She considered running for it but figured it was a bad idea. She was cuffed, in an all-body dull pain from several of the burn wounds and bruises, and would only have to run another twenty miles or so before getting back into Dallas. Dumb idea.

The female driver of the new car pointed at Sarah. The woman looked official. A paper pusher in that suit, for sure. Maybe an FBI agent.

They exchanged a few words by the roadside, and then the cop who drove her here started toward her, a key in his hand. She raised her wrists, knowing what the key was for. A moment later, the cuffs off, she massaged her wrists as the trooper made his way to the cruiser without saying a word.

The woman who had just arrived strode toward her. "Sarah Roberts," she said. "Please, come with me."

Sarah didn't move. "Where are we going?"

The cop dropped in his cruiser and hit the gas, spitting up dirt and grass as he raced back onto U.S. 75 heading south.

The suited woman placed a hand on her arm.

"I'm Special Agent Walentiny." She started back toward

his car, pulling Sarah along. "I'm supposed to take you to meet Agent Sullivan downtown."

Reluctantly, Sarah trudged along behind her. One cop, another cop. One car, another car. What did she care? She was no closer to stopping True Legacy by herself, a major corporate enemy, than she was stopping a nuclear war. Sarah was better one on one with street thugs, individual murderers, or human trafficking assholes. Fighting an entire company wasn't working out for her. At least not one with True Legacy's resources.

"What's downtown?" Sarah asked as they got in Walentiny's car.

"My partner, Agent Sullivan."

"You said that. What else is downtown?"

"I have no idea." She started the car and gunned the engine. "I'm sure she'll tell us when we get there."

"Your field office isn't there?"

"No, our field office is not downtown."

"I spoke with her before my accident back there. She was following a van."

"She was."

"And?"

"Then she wasn't."

"You're full of riddles. Tell me something else."

"Like what?" She looked at her, looked away.

"Like where we're going."

Walentiny glanced at her again. "I can see why the troopers were happy to hand you off. You are annoying."

"I'm more than that. Now, fuck off with the bullshit and tell me what you know."

"All I know is Sullivan got called off the tail, and now she—"

"Called off the tail?" Sarah shouted, startling Walentiny.

The car jerked in its lane. "Don't fucking yell at me when I'm trying to drive."

"Who called it off?"

"I have no idea," she said, her voice raised to match Sarah's. "Our boss, maybe. Your friends were released, and a van picked them up, and for some reason, Sullivan followed that van even though she wasn't supposed to."

"And? What happened?"

"All I know is what I just said. And now she wants to meet us downtown."

Sarah thought hard about downtown. There was no field office, yet Sullivan was following the van and now wanted to meet there. What was downtown? The Glenmarks?

She massaged her wrists while she considered her options. When the trooper gave her to Walentiny, she had to assume she wasn't under arrest. The second the car stopped anywhere, she could bolt. Find Parkman and Darwin, regroup, and determine what to do next.

"Wait, does a company called True Legacy have an office downtown?"

Walentiny's phone rang. "That's Sullivan right now."

She connected it to the car. "Walentiny here."

"You got Sarah?"

"Yes, I'm here," Sarah said.

"Good. How close are you?"

Walentiny turned up the volume. "Fifteen minutes, depending on traffic. Where am I heading?"

“Commerce Street.”

“That’s right downtown.”

“That’s where I am,” Sullivan said.

“What are we going to do?”

“You’ll see. Just get here.”

“Sullivan, if it has anything to do with that van,” Walentiny looked at Sarah, “then you can forget about it. We were called off.”

“Walentiny, bring Sarah Roberts to me at the True Legacy building on Commerce. We have crimes in progress. This is above board.”

“Drive faster,” Sarah said.

“This better be legit, Sullivan, or it’s both our jobs.”

The line died. Sullivan had already hung up.

“Shit,” Walentiny said.

“Drive faster,” Sarah repeated, this time louder.

“I am, I am.” Walentiny looked at her once, then again.

“You want me to drive?” Sarah asked.

“No, we’ll be there in ten minutes.”

“Good.” She crossed her arms gingerly. “Make it eight.”

“Fuck sakes …”

Chapter 38

Sullivan stood at the side of a large parking area by Commerce Street, watching for her partner's car. She checked her phone for the time, then scanned the street again.

Alex had disappeared on the roof over fifteen minutes ago.

"Where are you, Walentiny?" she mumbled under her breath.

Three Dallas police cruisers turned onto Commerce a block down, their lights flashing.

"They'd better not be coming here," she whispered.

All three cruisers passed her, turned into the True Legacy's parking lot, and stopped in front of the building.

"Shit, what did you do, Alex?"

Five members of DPD exited the three cruisers, left the lights flashing, and ran inside the building.

She lifted her phone to call Walentiny, then hesitated. Her partner wouldn't get there any faster. She assured herself that the FBI could take over the case as soon as she entered the building.

Two men slowed as they were about to walk by her position.

"Wow, I wonder what's going on inside there?" the man with the toothpick in his mouth said.

"Did you see those cops race in there?" the other, shorter man said.

"Yeah." Sullivan shrugged. "They sure seemed in a hurry."

The men watched the cruisers from beside her. Something about them made her feel they were watching her.

What the hell is going on here?

With the toothpick in his mouth, the man swished it to one side, nodded at her, and then they were gone.

Had she seen them before? The toothpick indicated he'd just eaten a late lunch. Or was he the kind of man who always had a toothpick in his mouth?

She watched them as they strolled toward the front of the building, walked around the parked cruisers, and entered the foyer.

"Shit, everybody's going to True Legacy today."

She couldn't recall which companies occupied the other twenty-eight floors, but she thought a law firm had several of them. Maybe an insurance company, too.

Walentiny's car was a block away at a red light when she checked Commerce again. She waved and saw her partner's hand in the windshield waving back.

Sarah Roberts sat stone-faced in the passenger seat. It felt like she was glaring at her, but Sullivan couldn't tell at that distance.

She stepped back into the parking area and waited. When Walentiny pulled in, she parked beside Sullivan's vehicle and hopped out. Sarah got out, too.

"What's going on?" Walentiny asked.

Sarah ran around the trunk of the car. Sullivan saw the frazzled dark hair, the cuts and bruises, the red blisters where the burns would leave scars.

"Holy shit, you okay?"

"Where's Aaron and the others?" Sarah asked, ignoring her concern.

"I don't know." She turned to Walentiny with a look of dismay. "I was called off the tail."

"Then why are we here?" Sarah asked, glaring at the Dallas police cruisers. She refocused back on Sullivan. "Are we going in, confronting the bastards? They tried to kill me."

"What happened with the bomb in the van you were chasing?" Sullivan asked.

Sarah shook her head. "The bomb wasn't in the vans. It was in the car I was driving."

"How did they get a bomb into your car?"

"It wasn't my car."

"So you stole a car, and they bombed it?" Sullivan was thoroughly confused now.

"Don't worry about it. Long story." Sarah stepped away. "Come on, we need to go inside and see what's going on."

"Wait a second," Walentiny said. "We can't storm their offices without a search warrant or some serious reason." She leaned in close to Sullivan. "It could jeopardize everything we've been working on for years."

"Walentiny, if we can connect them to that truck Sarah stopped by Laredo and get them on Luke Roland's murder, as well as several other—"

"How about my attempted murder? I've got an email from them that'll help."

Sullivan met her gaze. "They emailed you?"

She nodded.

"Seems reckless."

"They're above the law. Can do whatever they want. The money backing these kinds of people can hire a team of lawyers. Deflect, deflect, deflect. Years in court." Sarah stepped farther away again. "I'm going in. You coming?"

"Sarah, wait," Sullivan said. "What's your plan?"

She shrugged. "I have no idea. But what I do know is inside that building is probably one man, or many more, who are pulling the strings. You can't arrest the entire corporation for murder, but there's someone inside there who's responsible, and I'm going to have a word with him." She turned away and started toward the front doors.

"Sarah," Sullivan said. She looked at Walentiny, then shrugged. "Well, we better go in, too. Make sure she isn't killed."

Walentiny started walking. "Or make sure she doesn't kill someone herself. She's a bit unruly."

"This might get bad," Sullivan said from beside her partner.

"Isn't it already?"

Chapter 39

Sarah entered the lobby and stopped. Two cops stood on either side of the bank of three elevators. A security desk shaped like a half-moon sat in the center of the lobby, with two security officers stationed behind it. Half a dozen men and women strolled by, dressed in business attire. She was out of place, dressed in jeans and a ruined shirt. Her hair, bruises and dried blood wouldn't get her far in this building.

Both security officers were watching her now.

"Can we help you?" one of them said, stepping out from behind the counter and advancing toward her.

"She's with us," Sullivan said, displaying her ID.

The guard slowed and stopped, reading her ID. "Got it, Agent Sullivan. No problem with us, then."

"What's going on here?" she asked, gesturing at the two officers by the elevators.

"Got a complaint on the twenty-ninth floor. Something about an intruder coming in from the roof." He shrugged. "Not sure why they didn't call us. We would've gone up and escorted the man off the property."

"And that makes sense, how?" Sullivan asked.

"What? Calling us? That's procedure, ma'am. We're security here."

"No, the other thing. An intruder from the roof. How's that possible?"

The guard scratched his head. "No idea, really. Gee, never thought about that."

"Excuse us," she said, pulling Sarah and Walentiny aside. "They've got Alex now, too."

"Alex?" Sarah said, surprised. "How?"

"He came in from the roof."

"How'd he get up there?"

Sullivan rolled her eyes. "He climbed the outside of the building."

Walentiny leaned back. "No way."

Sullivan glared at her. Something was going on between them. Only partners understood.

"We have to get up there," Sarah said.

"And do what?" Walentiny asked. "There are officers on site. DPD can handle this." She pulled Sullivan's shoulder until she looked at her. "We've made a mistake coming here. People are climbing buildings, and Dallas police are on site. Come on, Sullivan. You know this isn't how we work. This investigation has been going on far too long to approach the end game this way."

In an even voice, Sullivan said, "The only thing you said

that I agree with is this investigation has gone on far too long." She turned to Sarah. "Let's go."

"Wait," Walentiny said. "Where are you going?"

Sarah jerked her head toward the elevators. "To the head offices of True Legacy. It seems they're going out of business today."

"You want to help, Walentiny?" Sullivan added as they walked away. "Call for more agents."

"You want backup?" her partner asked.

Sullivan didn't answer her.

At the elevators, one of the DPD officers raised a hand. "Elevators are closed until the matter upstairs can be sorted out."

Sullivan pulled out her ID. "FBI. I'm Special Agent Melanie Sullivan. Elevators just opened up again."

He blocked her way. "I'm sorry ma'am. Strict orders."

"Well, I'm changing your orders. Step aside."

"Can't do it, ma'am. No one is allowed upstairs at this time."

"Step aside, Officer"—she stopped to read his tag— "Patrick, or I will have you arrested for obstruction. The FBI is taking over this building. We now have jurisdiction."

The other officer by the elevators moved closer. "Everything okay, Pat?"

"Yeah, this FBI woman and her friend were just leaving."

Sarah turned back to Walentiny. She was watching the whole thing, already tapping on her cell phone.

"Agent Walentiny is calling for backup, Sullivan."

She turned to her partner and raised her voice. "When more agents arrive, Walentiny, please take this officer into custody for obstruction." She looked at the security guards. "Until then, he doesn't leave the building. Got it."

They nodded.

"That won't be necessary, ma'am. This'll be over in minutes, and you can go up then."

"Officer, I'm going up now."

The man stepped back and put his hands up. "Afraid I can't let you."

Sarah had had enough of the power struggle.

"Don't touch me," she told him.

"Excuse me?" he said.

"Don't touch me. I'll consider it assault."

"I'm not going to touch you, but you can't—"

Sarah started by him on his left. The officer grabbed her arm right where she wanted him to. She'd even moved that part of her arm toward him, tempting him to grab her.

She spun around, wrenching his wrist back until he released her, and then she dropped and kicked the backs of his knees in one fluid motion. The cop dropped forward into Sullivan. She grabbed him and yelled as if he was attacking her, then kneed him in the balls.

The other officer was on the move. Sarah anticipated him coming in fast, so she stayed low and lunged upward, her head launching into his stomach, her fists pumping three fast jabs into his groin.

Both cops guarding the elevators were rolling on the floor, grabbing their crotches, when the elevator doors opened. Sarah and Sullivan stepped on. Not a single weapon had been pulled. Sarah hit the button for the twenty-ninth floor, proud she didn't hurt them more. Something deep down inside made her want to.

"What did you do to the cop who fell into you?" she asked.

"I defended myself. I kneed him in the balls."

Sarah smiled. It felt good to smile. It had been a long time.

The elevator was fast. The twenty-ninth floor came up within fifteen seconds.

Sullivan gently pushed Sarah back from the doorway, then eased to the right and placed a hand on her holstered weapon.

The doors opened.

No one was there.

Sullivan eased off the elevator while Sarah placed a hand on the doors to keep them open. Then Sullivan jerked her head, telling Sarah to follow her.

Sarah moved into the vast foyer of True Legacy's head office. Voices emanated from somewhere to the right. Sullivan was already moving that way. Sarah let the elevator door go and followed her, watching their back.

Her right arm was stinging anew from the scuffle downstairs. Blood dripped from one cut she'd reopened, and pain seemed to be getting worse from behind her right shoulder. That was where she landed on the ground when her sister helped toss her from a moving vehicle. Jumping from cars wasn't as easy anymore. She would be thirty soon.

Are we walking into anything here, sis?

A large office area with a reception desk was walled off with thick glass. The ornate desks, plush-looking leather chairs, and artwork spoke of serious money. This company had to be the richest human procurement company on the planet, and Sarah knew exactly how they made that money.

They *created* their own supply for the immense demand.

But today, that stopped. It had to stop.

Sullivan eased back until she was close enough to whisper in Sarah's ear.

"Those cops downstairs probably called up to tell them we were coming."

Sarah nodded.

"There are three DPD officers up here already," Sullivan added.

"Got another gun on you?"

Sullivan frowned. "Even if I did, I couldn't give it to you. I wouldn't just lose my job. I'd be up on charges as well."

Sarah shrugged. "I'll have to take my chances without one, then."

They got to another door, but it was locked.

"All accesses are locked," Sarah said. "But someone's talking inside somewhere."

"I know. Let's try the stairs. We'll go one floor up."

When they entered the stairs, Sarah checked the knob. It wasn't locked. They'd be able to get back inside.

On the next level, one short of the roof, Sullivan twisted the knob, but nothing happened.

"Shit," she said. "It's locked."

"They're here then. We have to get inside. Can you pick the lock?"

Sullivan shook her head. "Don't know how."

"Back to the elevators then."

Sullivan nodded, and they retreated one floor. When they

got there, the door to twenty-nine was locked.

"I checked the door," Sarah said. "It turned."

"They're watching us, then."

Sarah grabbed the railing and started back up to thirty. "C'mon," she said.

"We can't get in up there."

"I know. Hurry."

Sullivan chased after her. "What are you going to do?"

At the door to the thirtieth floor, Sarah held out her hand. "Gun."

"No way."

Impatient, Sarah jerked her fingers several times in a come-on gesture. "There's no time. Give me the gun. I will shoot through the lock and force the door open."

"What if there's someone on the other side? What if you hurt someone, or worse, kill them? No way, Sarah. That's not how it works."

"It's either willing or unwilling. I don't mind either way, but you have to choose because I'm getting inside there somehow."

She stared at Sarah. "Do all you people come from the same school of combat in Canada or something?"

Sarah nodded, jerking her hand once more. "Something like that. Now, gun."

Sullivan huffed out her defiance and handed it to Sarah. Then she stepped down a couple of stairs.

Sarah flicked off the safety, carefully aimed, and applied her finger to the trigger.

The door lock clicked in front of her. The door popped open a few inches.

Sarah lowered the weapon without firing it.

They were watching.

"Sarah. Wait." Sullivan said.

She kept the gun by her thigh as she stepped onto the thirtieth floor. Sullivan bounded up the couple of steps she'd descended, then came through the door behind her.

"Sarah Roberts." A man's voice. It was the same man who called the Glenmarks' house. She would recognize that tone anywhere. "Glad you could join us. Please, the third door on your left."

Sarah started forward.

"Sarah," Sullivan whispered. "We should wait. Backup is coming."

Sarah kept moving. She wasn't waiting. This was it. Final straw. Game ender. Sudden death playoffs.

If it was over, she was leaving with her man and friends. Otherwise, it wasn't over.

She opened the third door on her left and carefully stepped inside.

The area was set up like a comfortable living room, decked out with three couches, coffee tables, and trays on wheels that held multiple bottles of alcohol. Near the back was a huge cherry oak banker's desk. A man sat at the desk, a glass of amber liquid in one hand. To his right were three large monitors. From where she was standing, she could see the stairwell on the far one.

She raised Sullivan's weapon.

"I wouldn't do that if I were you." The man with that horrid voice said. "You'd never see Aaron again. Or Alex and those other two Aaron arrived with."

"Where. Are. They?" Sarah asked, pronouncing each word. The weapon remained steady as she walked toward him.

The man had the confidence of a male lion at the center of his coalition. He took another slow sip from the glass, appearing to savor the taste, staring at it.

"You know, I wasn't so sure about gold grappa, but I'm enjoying this bottle." He looked up at her. "Where are my manners? Take a seat on any couch you prefer. We have much to talk about."

"I'm not here to talk."

He set his glass down on the desk and leaned over it. "You're here to shoot me, is that it, Sarah?" He spoke childishly, raising his voice a notch. "Let's all kill the bad guy."

"We're not here to shoot anyone," Sullivan said. "Isn't that right, Sarah?"

The pain in her arms made her hands waver. She lowered the gun, knowing it would take a mere second to point and shoot if necessary.

"That's more like it," he said, his voice back to that monotonous drone. "Have a seat."

A door to their right slid open. Sarah brought the weapon up, then slowly lowered it.

A pretty middle-aged woman entered the large office.

"Maura Eskenas is my personal assistant. Please refrain from shooting her."

Maura entered slowly, keeping a watchful eye on Sarah. She sidled over to the man at the desk, picked up his glass, and started back to where she'd entered.

"Maura, bring the rest of them in to join us, will you."

"Yes, sir." Maura slipped out of the room.

"She has impressed me since I hired her in my accounting department. She used to live in Phoenix, where she was hired. Got her to move to the head office here in Dallas. Loves the New England Patriots and the Boston Red Sox. Great woman. Doesn't much care for the entire job, but she does what she's told. Loyal. Which is something I admire in a person, Sarah. Loyalty."

Two other doors opened. Three lifters entered the room. All three men were larger than Dwayne Johnson but not as big as Arnold in his prime.

Sarah watched the large men step into position as sentries by the doors, hands clasped together, staring blankly.

"This meant to intimidate us?"

Sullivan had moved up beside Sarah. They now stood shoulder to shoulder.

"Not at all," the man said. "They're part of my personal security team. Since you have a member of the FBI with you, I just want a little security myself, seeing as you have a weapon, and we are all unarmed."

"Who are you?" Sarah asked. "What do you want? Let's just get this over with."

"In time, Sarah, in time. Have patience."

She was about to respond when another door opened. Two uniformed police officers dragged Aaron and Daniel into the room. A third cop pulled Benjamin behind them.

Sarah gasped, and a well of emotion flooded through her at the sight of Aaron. He was cuffed but otherwise appeared unharmed. His eyes were half-lidded, as were the others.

"You drugged them," she said.

The man shrugged. "They are all prone to sudden violence. We needed assurances they would perform in a more docile manner. It'll wear off in time."

Sarah moved toward the man, but Sullivan blocked her.

"Wait," she whispered.

The police dropped all three men on the couches in the center of the room. Each officer was armed. The unarmed ratio just changed.

"Please, Sarah, join your friends." The man pointed at the couches. "Sullivan, you might as well join them, too."

"Look, whoever you are," Sullivan said. "I'm Special Agent Melanie Sullivan with the FBI. These men were recently freed from our custody. I'm going to escort these men and Sarah off the property, and you and I can set up a meeting at our field office to discuss things further."

While Sullivan was talking, the man behind the desk was shaking his head.

"I don't think so, Sullivan. The time for talking is over."

The man tapped his keyboard on the desk. A large screen lowered behind him. As it lowered, Maura reentered with the glass full of grappa again. She set it on the desk, then stepped back to stand beside the lowered screen.

Two of the weightlifters moved behind Sarah and Sullivan.

"Boss said sit," Beefy One said.

"I'd rather stand," Sarah said.

They advanced. Sarah shoved the weapon under the chin of the lifter closest. He froze a moment, staring at her, then lowered his head, pushing down on the barrel.

"Sarah," the man behind the desk said. "There's no need for that."

Something clicked beside her.

"Sarah," Sullivan said, her voice a pitch higher.

She looked to the left. The other lifters had weapons out aimed at her. The cops who escorted Aaron and the others inside the room had pulled their weapons.

"Sarah," the man with the grappa said. "Don't die like this. Lower your weapon." Then, as an afterthought, he added, "And what a waste that would be. You haven't even heard my proposal."

Sarah eased her weapon away from the lifter. He snatched it from her grip, twisting her hand. Pain flared from the burn marks. The gun was torn from her grip.

"So much for the *we are unarmed* shit," she said.

"Please," Grappa Man said. "Sit."

She moved around the couch and sat by Aaron, Daniel to her right. Benjamin was on the other couch. Sullivan sat by him.

With the uniformed cops and the lifters evenly surrounding them all on the couches, the man with the grappa got out of his seat and walked over to stand by Sarah.

"I don't know why you chose to come to Dallas. I still can't figure out how you knew about that truck in Laredo or the Glenmarks." He leaned down close to her. "But I was truly saddened when you stopped that plane. I needed that business. I already had a couple of people in prep, waiting for new organs. And now Luke Roland is dead." He stood back up to his full height. "That's on you, Sarah."

She glanced at Sullivan to make sure she was listening.

She wanted all charges against her, and her men dropped if they made it out of this alive.

Sullivan was listening. She stared at Sarah, her expression one of sorrow.

Maybe hope resides inside her somewhere, after all. To be thinking about getting the charges dropped when their situation was so bleak astounded her. The dead calm inside her did, too. For some reason, she was back. Fully back. She felt it, and it felt good.

Sarah Roberts had returned after all. And she was ready to finish this.

"Witness on the screen behind my desk your partial payment for fucking with my business."

The screen lit up with a security camera view of the outside of the building, an angle that showed the expanse of the city from the roof.

The man pushed a button, and the camera swiveled to the right. It stopped on two hooded men holding another man.

Alex.

Aaron had let his head fall back, and it appeared Daniel was asleep. All three men had their eyes closed. None of them saw what was on the screen but Sarah and Sullivan.

"What is this?" Sarah asked, anticipating exactly what it was.

"Your partial payment, Sarah. Weren't you listening?"

He nodded at one of the lifters, who then spoke into a cell phone. "Go ahead."

"No!" Sarah shouted, jumping up from the couch.

Hands grabbed her shoulders, forcing her down. A thick arm slipped around her throat and heaved her backward over the couch. Gasping, unable to breathe, another hand snatched a clump of her hair and wrenched her head up to watch the screen.

There was nothing she could do. The hooded men on the roof had a firm grip on Alex as they marched him to the edge. Alex tried to fight them, kicking and spinning his body, dropping to the gravel on the roof, then pushing upward, but nothing worked as his hands were locked inside their firm grip.

They held Alex suspended over the roof's edge, then, as if counting to three, the hooded men pushed out over the edge and let go of Alex.

Resilient to the end, Sarah watched as young Alex spun in the air, clasped onto the forearm of the man on the right, and swung back toward the building as he was already falling over the edge.

Alex's grip what it was, the man was pulled bodily to the surface of the roof. His head and arms dipped over the edge, but his hooded partner landed on his back in time before the man was yanked off the roof.

The arm around Sarah's throat eased enough for her to inhale. She gasped a breath, her eyes rooted to the screen. One hooded man got to his feet. The other man, whose arm Alex had clung to, rolled onto his back and then sat up. He seemed shaken by the fact that he almost fell off, too.

Both men nodded at the camera, then walked off to the left, their job done.

Alex had disappeared over the edge of the thirty-story building, his scream heard through the window to their right.

The screen on the wall went blank.

Chapter 40

SARAH WRIGGLED UNDER THE power of the arms that subdued her, but all they did was tighten again. With no air to breathe, her strength diminished quickly, the fight in her quelled.

A lightness overcame her. Alex was gone now, and she would join him soon. Their world would never be the same without Alex. His name resonated in her head, and each time she heard it, a feeling of utter devastation enveloped her soul.

Her body relaxed, and her eyes were closed. Someone shouted something to her right, but it felt like it was coming through a tunnel. Just before her eyes closed, she saw that FBI woman, her mouth gaping, closing, gaping, like she was speaking in slow motion. There was a fierceness in her eyes. A fire Sarah hadn't seen before.

Then she was falling. And oxygen, rich and full of life, filled her lungs, and the horrible evil world spun back into reality. The nightmare was still in full swing as she gasped, lying half on Aaron's legs and half on the floor.

Her hearing returned.

"You could've killed her," Sullivan was saying.

Then Sullivan was beside her, pulling hair out of her eyes.

"Sarah, are you okay? Can you breathe?"

Sarah tried to nod, grabbing at her neck.

"They almost strangled you to death."

"They … should have." Her voice was raspy, gravelly. "Because …"

"What? No …"

"I will kill them all now."

"Sarah, don't try to talk," Sullivan said, lowering her voice. "You'll only piss them off further. We'll find a way out of this."

The stars were retreating from her vision. Alex falling was vividly imprinted on her brain. She looked at Aaron's blank face, his chest moving up and down slowly. Who were these people? How could they do this? Vivian?

She refocused on Sullivan. "Piss *them* off?" She shook her head to dispel the lingering fuzziness. "I'm the one who is pissed."

Sullivan helped her onto the couch. Grappa Man was back behind his desk.

"Now, where were we?" he said. "Ahh, yes, discussing your payment for hurting my organization." He turned his attention to Sullivan. "It's a shame an FBI agent went missing today."

"Missing?" she said.

Sarah watched her face as the realization of what the man had said set in.

"Clever, but it won't stick. My partner knows I'm here."

"Without a body?" Grappa Man shrugged and raised his hands in a who-knows gesture. "Even if she saw you enter the building, you might have left through another door."

"GPS. My cell phone. She'd know."

Grappa Man shook his head. "Cell jammers."

"Yours worked when you called to the roof."

"We have our own communications up here." He waved a hand at them. "I'm bored with this debate. Discussing if I'll be in trouble after you're all dead and gone doesn't matter, now does it? I know how the law works." He pointed at the three officers in the room. "I have several who work for me. Lawyers, too."

Sarah placed her hand on Aaron's wrist. The pulse was weak but still there.

Vivian, tell me what to do.

"I don't know how you survived that Buick," Grappa Man said, his attention back on Sarah. "That will mystify me to no end. My driver in the van said you slowed before trying to overtake him. Then drove onto the grass and dove from the car. I couldn't activate the device fast enough."

Sarah bided her time, holding Aaron's hand, letting his pulse remind her he was still with them.

"What are you waiting for?" she asked. "Let's move to the next stage."

"Impatience isn't attractive."

"I'm not here to be attractive."

"Well, if you must know, I'm waiting for the phone call

—on the landline—that the body of your friend was discovered on the concrete below. I have witnesses that we tried to stop him from his suicidal jump." Grappa Man pointed around the room. "The authorities will arrive in minutes. Many of them will come to the roof. Some will ask me questions. I want to know when they're coming so they will be witness to the actions of self-defense my men had to take when you attacked us."

"Seems like a stupid plan. No way it works."

"It isn't a plan. We aren't the A-Team. This is your future."

"And how will you get me to attack you, Mr. John Hannibal Smith?"

He smiled at her. "I'm no George Peppard, but I'll take that as a compliment." He sipped more grappa. "I'm going to give you a gun. Then I will shoot and kill your boyfriend, Aaron Stevens." He paused. "Naturally, you will try to kill me."

Sarah clutched Aaron's wrist tighter. Vivian's prophecy.

Alex was already dead. Aaron would be as soon as that phone rang. And there were six cops and six bodybuilders in the room, all armed.

In the seconds she had left, she needed to talk it out, think it through.

"Wait, if they come up to this suite to talk to you about the jumper—the man you killed—and witness your team killing us—"

Grappa Man was shaking his head. "I only need them on their way." He pointed at the three uniformed officers, one of whom wouldn't stop staring at Sarah. "I already have three decorated Dallas police officers who will testify that we all acted in self-defense when that crazy Sarah Roberts, the one reputed to be armed and dangerous by the FBI, attacked me in my office. She killed Luke Roland, tried to kidnap a pilot, then came after me." He clapped twice, making Sarah jump. "Isn't it lovely?"

"It's a plan. You're still in the 80s."

He frowned. "What?"

"You said it wasn't a plan." She nodded once. "You were wrong. It's a plan."

A scowl replaced the frown. "Wow, aren't you annoying?"

"You know what God does when a man makes a plan, right?"

Maura Eskenas had moved toward the only door that wasn't being guarded. It had to lead to a kitchen or bar because it was the door she'd gone through to get the man's grappa refill.

Sarah wondered where she was going. No one seemed to notice her preparing to leave. She probably didn't want to see people shot.

Grappa Man pushed back his chair and got to his feet. "Enough of this. My phone will ring any second. I have two officers stationed downstairs. They should've called by now." He walked over to the closest lifter. "Give me your weapon."

The man handed him a gun.

"Empty Sarah's gun into my wall and desk, then hand it to her."

Sullivan stood. "You can't do this."

Grappa Man pivoted with surprising speed, his gun arm

up. Then he shot her.

Blood spurted from the wound upon impact. Sullivan jerked backward, lost her balance, and fell to the floor, where she clung to her wounded shoulder, gasping and moaning. Blood pooled on the tiles.

Sarah was on her feet, but before she could lunge at the man, huge, thick fingers grabbed her and yanked her back onto the couch.

She screamed like an animal in a bear trap, all pain and fury.

Another weapon fired close to her head. Instinctively, she ducked, covering her head. The weapon fired several more times, and Sarah ended up sprawling across Aaron's lap before she realized they were just emptying her weapon.

Her arm was yanked backward, and her fingers were splayed open, the empty gun forced into her hand. If only it had one bullet left in it.

During all the gunfire, Aaron, Daniel, and Benjamin hadn't stirred at all. Whatever it was they shot them up with, Sarah wondered if it would kill them.

She raised the weapon and aimed it at Grappa Man.

"That better be empty," he said, looking over Sarah's shoulder.

She pulled the trigger. It clicked empty. She did it again and again. Empty each time.

She hauled back and threw it at him. One of the lifters anticipated the move and stepped in front of Grappa Man, taking the brunt of the gun on a pectoral.

"Come now, Sarah. It'll all be over in moments."

Her head spun as she inhaled rapidly. She shot a glance

at Sullivan. The FBI agent was bleeding out onto the floor. If it wasn't staunched soon, she could be in trouble.

But weren't they all in trouble? It certainly looked like the end was near.

She glanced around the room, realizing there was no escape.

Something was different, though. They were one less. She snuck a glance at the door she thought led to a kitchen.

The assistant, Maura Eskenas, was gone.

The phone on Grappa Man's desk rang.

"That's it," he said. "It's over. Payment in full complete. This whore bitch, Sarah Roberts, and her pig friends from Canada, fucking nuisance that they are, will be gone."

He aimed his weapon at Aaron's chest from about ten feet away.

"Watch how easily death can happen, Sarah. I do it all the time."

He pulled the trigger twice.

Sarah wailed and lurched sideways to get in front of Aaron, but the shooter was too fast.

Aaron's body jerked with each bullet's impact, and then Sarah landed on the floor at his feet, her world over, her mind locked into a hell of its own.

Chapter 41

ONE OF THE MEN yanked her off the floor as her arms struggled to grab Aaron, to hold him one more time. She heard her own voice and knew she was screaming the word *No!* but couldn't bring herself to fight. Aaron was dead. Alex was dead. They would all be dead, and then what? What was this all for? More pain, more suffering—all so someone could make more money?

She breathed in, quelling the scream for a second, those stars back at the corners of her eyes.

The man placed her in the spot by the couch where he'd emptied the weapon they'd forced into her hand. She'd dropped the empty gun somewhere. Another man was shouting orders to find it.

She was as good as dead. Even if she walked away from this, why keep going?

All the pent-up pain, the rage, oozed through her, and she screamed again. This time, it was more of a caterwaul.

The man behind her held her arms tight, his chest brushing her shoulder blades.

A door slid open somewhere.

Another man shouted. Then another. A gun fired. Another weapon discharged.

The end had come.

She closed her eyes, placed a foot flat on the floor, leaned forward, and then jerked her head backward. The man behind her was close enough that the back of her head connected with his nose. While chaos erupted around them, she could still feel the cartilage crumble under the impact. Sarah continued her backward launch, climbing the side of the couch with her feet while the man still miraculously held her arms and shoved backward, twisting, dislodging his grip. She landed behind the couch on her stomach.

Another weapon was fired. Then several all at once. Three distinct weapons were firing in quick succession. With bullets flying overhead, she stayed down.

Shouting replaced the sound of weapons fire as they ceased.

"Are they all down?" a man asked.

"Affirmative. We have seven down."

Seven? Sarah thought. Aaron, Daniel, Benjamin, Sullivan, and Sarah made five, not seven. Maybe they got Grappa Man.

"Sarah?" a familiar voice called out.

Parkman?

She lifted her head, not wanting to speak yet. She had to

find a gun.

"Sarah, it's over." Darwin this time.

Where the hell did they come from?

She rose higher.

"It's okay," Parkman said. "Ambulances are here. They're coming in any moment."

Sarah got up higher and looked over the couch. Darwin and Parkman stood side by side near the door Maura Eskenas had left through. They both held large weapons, hung limply by their thighs.

Parkman offered her a smile. "We'll explain later, but Alex is okay." He turned around and pointed. "He's right here."

Alex stepped into the room and nodded at her.

She hoped she wouldn't faint. "What the hell …?" was all that she could say.

To her left were three other men and Sullivan's partner, Walentiny, all dressed in suits. They, too, held weapons.

She leaned over the couch and grabbed Aaron. His wounds hadn't started to bleed yet. She frowned and ran a hand over the holes in his chest. There was a soft leather-like material under his shirt.

"He asked for a favor before he got on that van," Sullivan said from the floor. She was still holding a hand over her shoulder wound, but now she had a balled-up piece of shirt in it. "So I gave him a super-thin vest to wear under his shirt. Said you told him he was supposed to die. Wanted protection." She coughed, then laid her head back down and stared up at the ceiling, breathing evenly.

"Oh, Aaron …" Sarah whispered as she cried.

She clung to his wrist. The pulse was still there but weaker.

"They gave them a drug of some kind." She turned to everyone, frantic. "They need help."

Maura eased out behind Parkman and Darwin. "It's a neurotoxin mix from something called a puffer fish and a toad. My boss uses it often to take parts from victims while they're still alive. They only appear dead. In certain countries, it's called a zombie drug because it makes someone look dead, but then they wake up. I'll advise the paramedics accordingly, and these men will be watched closely at the hospital, but I assure you they aren't dead or dying. It's okay, Sarah, they'll bring them back."

The door opened, and paramedics ran in, followed by other officers. Sarah moved out of the way so they could collect Aaron and his two teachers. She stared a moment at Daniel, who seemed untouched. Benjamin was bleeding from his forearm.

"What happened?" she said, pointing at Benjamin.

Parkman moved a step closer. "Grazed by a bullet. It's nothing."

Their eyes met. "He's going to be pissed."

Parkman nodded. "Royally."

Something about that made Darwin smile. Then Parkman smiled.

"Poor Benji," Darwin whispered, shaking his head.

"He hates that name," Sarah said.

"Can he hear me right now?" Darwin retorted good-naturedly.

Parkman punched him in the arm.

The mood was lightening, the stress and anxiety lifting.

She watched as they were loaded onto stretchers, and Maura explained to the paramedics what the drug was that they were dealing with. She said she would accompany them to the hospital.

Sarah moved closer. "I'm coming, too." She pointed at Aaron. "I go with him." Then she turned back to Parkman and Darwin. "I'm staying with Aaron. Will you meet me at the hospital?"

Parkman nodded. "As soon as we're done here."

"I need to understand what just happened before I lose my mind."

"We'll explain. Just take care of Aaron."

Agent Walentiny was now standing over Sullivan as paramedics tended to her shoulder.

"We're just going to let Sarah Roberts leave?" the woman asked.

Sullivan tried to smile. "We're all going to the hospital, aren't we?"

The men lifted the stretcher Sullivan was on and started for the door, stepping over the fallen bodies of two uniformed officers.

As Sarah followed Aaron's paramedics to the elevator, more men in suits entered the suite.

She glanced back and saw Darwin and Parkman surrendering their weapons.

The last thing she saw before the elevator doors slid closed was the caved-in face of Grappa Man.

She never did get his name.

Chapter 42

FBI AGENTS CAME AND went. Statement after statement was written up. It had been two days since the deaths in the suite on the top floor of the building that housed True Legacy.

Rose Marie Van Dee, the investigative journalist Sarah met at the Glenmarks' home, got the first story from the people inside the suite and ran with it. She was the natural choice since she'd already published an exposé on True Legacy the day before the shooting.

Special Agent Melanie Sullivan was recovering well. Sarah had taken time away from Aaron's bedside to visit her and hear everything she'd been up to behind the scenes in attempting to help Sarah, even arrest her to keep her safe. Sullivan had learned quickly that catching Sarah had been another thing entirely.

Sarah thanked her for bringing Detective Marina Diner to

Texas. It meant a lot to her. She also thanked her for giving Aaron the Kevlar vest. Without it, he would've died. They hugged—gingerly, as Sullivan's shoulder was still sore—and promised to see each other again before Sarah left Texas.

Having interviewed with Sullivan's partner, Special Agent Gigi Walentiny, several times, Sarah was allowed to spend her remaining time with Aaron as long as she stuck around another couple of weeks as they would want to speak with her again.

Aaron, Daniel, and Benjamin had all woken up from the drug concoction Grappa Man had given them. They were all fine as the drug wore off completely, but Aaron had huge welts where the bullets had hit him. They had trouble getting Benjamin to keep his voice down as he ranted about being shot again, claiming he could see the future and had actually predicted it would happen. When Daniel told him, 'What you think about, you bring about,' Benjamin lost his shit, screaming a blue streak up and down his best friends as they watched and laughed.

Sarah was sure the entire floor of the hospital heard him.

They'd finally told her Grappa Man's name was Eugene Wallson. Apparently, those close to him just called him Wally. He was the CEO of True Legacy, now deceased. A lot of the company was being dismantled as the FBI had taken over dozens of their offices country-wide.

Daniel and Benjamin had recently been released and had left the hospital hours ago to join Alex at the hotel. Sarah was staying one more night with Aaron as his chest ached too much to leave yet—bruised ribs ached like a bitch, he'd said—and they wanted to keep him one more night to make sure he was okay.

She was reading Rose Dee's article when Darwin and Parkman entered the room, a tray of Starbucks in Parkman's hand.

Sarah set the book down. "You must be psychic," she said. "You knew I needed coffee."

Parkman eased the grande out of the tray and handed it to her. They pulled up chairs close enough to talk in hushed whispers so as not to wake Aaron. Both men held cups in their hands now as well.

Sarah took her first sip. "Thank you."

Darwin nodded. His doing.

"So, you guys want to fill me in on the rest of it."

They looked at each other, then back at Sarah. "I think our part started when we went for lunch that day back at the motel just out of the city," Darwin said.

"When we came back to the room," Parkman jumped in. "You were gone, and there was a police car parked at the front lobby area. Darwin slipped in to look at brochures and try to listen to what was happening. He gathered you stole the clerk's car."

Sarah nodded. She pulled her phone out, opened the email, and handed it to Parkman. "They sent me this."

They read the short email together while Sarah drank more and held Aaron's hand. She loved the sound of his breathing, even and steady. It resembled the sound he made the last night they slept together in the motel the FBI raided.

Parkman handed back the phone. "That must've been a hard email to read."

Sarah nodded. "You guys weren't there, and I needed to

get back to the Glenmarks' house, so I grabbed that woman's Nissan."

"Well, we had no idea where you'd gone, and without raising attention to us, we were stuck. Darwin here called Rosina, and within an hour or so, we all decided that since True Legacy was to blame for everything, we'd just head over to their offices and see what we could learn."

Darwin cut in, "Funny thing was, we walked right by Agent Sullivan as she was watching the front of the building. We had no idea Alex had just finished scaling the exterior."

"Wait, what?" Sarah said. "How did I miss that? He scaled the building?"

Parkman was nodding. "Yeah, he climbed the outside of the building to get to the roof."

"So that's what he was doing up there?"

"Let's not get ahead of ourselves," Parkman said, raising a finger. "We saw the two cops guarding the elevators and thought you were upstairs, so Darwin found an unsuspecting woman in the lobby and snatched her keycard from the side of her purse. Then, we used the stairs to get to the thirtieth floor. Unfortunately for us, that keycard wouldn't give us access to the top two floors, so we walked out onto the roof to see if there was another way in."

"And you found Alex?" Sarah asked.

"Actually, he jumped us."

Sarah almost spit out her coffee. "What?"

"Yeah, he'd already knocked out two guys on the roof, splayed out with black hoods beside their bodies."

"Then how did Eugene get that video of Alex ..." she drifted off as Darwin was nodding now, appearing eager to explain.

"When Alex swung onto the roof, they were waiting. They'd seen his ascent with cameras. The place was wired well."

Sarah snickered at her own stupidity. "They watched Sullivan and me trying to gain access to their floors. We should've been more careful."

"Well, Alex listened as they radioed down that they had him and heard their boss tell them to put on hoods and wait in front of the camera for his signal. Once they heard from him, the camera would turn on, and they were to throw Alex from the roof."

"Let me guess," Sarah said, holding up a hand. "Not something he was interested in, so he knocked those assholes out, and when you guys came through the access to the roof, he thought more men were coming."

"Exactly. When he saw it was us, we put on the hoods and did as their boss asked."

"But if you threw Alex from the roof, how is he alive?"

They exchanged a knowing glance, then turned back to Sarah. "Were you watching the camera?"

Sarah nodded.

"Did you see one of us fall and get pulled toward the edge?"

She nodded again. "That whole thing fucked me up. Those images are implanted on my brain."

"Alex instructed us to throw him off by these two concrete walls, the ones he'd used to climb onto the roof. By using my arm," Darwin held it up to show a large reddish-purple bruise, "he was able to suspend in the air for a few seconds, but it was long enough to plant his feet and his other free arm. When he released me, he planted his other hand and waited. Parkman saw the red light on the camera go off, and we helped him back onto the roof."

"Holy fuck, that guy is insane. My stomach just flipped thinking about such a crazy move."

Parkman shook his head. "When he first told us what he wanted to do, I refused, certain that we were participating in the death of our friend. But Alex knows his shit and said it wasn't just possible, it was easy."

"Okay, everyone's saved now. So how did you get inside?"

Darwin smiled wide. "That's where luck came in."

"Luck?"

Parkman was smiling, too. "Yeah, luck. The assistant, Maura Eskenas, not only hated her job, but she'd tried to quit several times. Eugene Wallson threatened her family, he threatened her, and over the past several months, he was hitting her. The violence was getting worse. The guy was becoming unhinged. She admitted to us that she was going to kill him the next time he laid a hand on her."

Sarah held up a hand, drank more coffee, and then said, "I'm confused. When did you meet Maura?"

"That's the best part, the *luck* part. She came onto the roof as we were donning the hoods."

"And she saw Eugene's men knocked out."

Darwin leaned back and crossed his legs. "Yup, and you know what she did?"

Sarah eased forward as if they were telling campfire stories, and the scariest part was coming. "No, what? Tell me, what did she do?"

"She clapped. Apparently, one of the guys Alex knocked out had tried to have his way with her last week after a few drinks. Eugene didn't seem to mind. She was lucky and got away from him. We told her she couldn't go back inside. She explained she had no choice and how she would help us. She gave us an extra access card for the entire thirtieth floor and explained who was in the room, who were our enemies, and what to expect, namely, if that phone rang, Eugene would kill you and Aaron."

"Oh shit, so Maura saved us all."

Parkman shrugged. "Well, technically, she played a part. We all saved us all."

"Right." It was Sarah's turn to nod. "Of course. Sorry, didn't mean to lessen the effort by everyone else."

"From the roof, we were able to watch the FBI mobilizing on the ground as they prepared to storm the building. Once the camera thing was finished, the three of us came down and stood just outside the door, waiting for the phone, watching Eugene."

"Okay, I think we missed something. Why would that phone ring if there was no body on the concrete thirty floors below? Building security wouldn't be calling, and they certainly wouldn't be allowed to call up once the FBI took over the building down there."

Parkman pointed at Darwin. "That was Maura and Darwin's doing."

Darwin uncrossed his legs and sat forward. "Actually, Rosina too. Maura told us that Eugene would receive a phone call because of the body. All that was set in place. Since there was no body, I offered to call when we were ready to enter the suite. Maura said it wouldn't work because of a cell jammer. So I called Rosina, told her the number, and had her call it at a set time. As soon as that phone rang, we were in the room, and it just so happened the FBI came in the other doors at the same time."

"Damn, you guys had it all sewn up, and no one knew. Lucky the FBI didn't shoot you, too."

"Rosina called them as well. Explained everything Maura had told us. Cell jammers, number of hostiles, all of it. She was able to get a direct line to Agent Walentiny, Sullivan's partner."

"I'm blown away. None of this would've happened without your help, their help, Alex's help. Everyone is still alive, and it's all over." She sighed, and a tear crept from her eye. "I was pretty freaked out there for a moment. Thought I'd lost Alex, then Aaron."

"We know. But we could do nothing to reassure you until it was all done. We wouldn't have waited for that phone to ring, but the FBI took precious minutes to organize and get in place. So, we waited. In the end, it was their gig. But it all turned out okay."

She looked at Aaron, sleeping peacefully. "What confuses me is I had a vision of Aaron's death." She turned back to Parkman and Darwin. "Vivian showed it to me."

"Makes sense to me," Darwin said. "He was determined to come here. We tried to stop him, but he came anyway. Once here, he wouldn't listen, and he would've died if you didn't tell Sullivan where he was in that motel."

"But that led him to getting bail and being placed right

into their hands."

"Exactly, and you scared him enough that he asked Sullivan for a vest. You saved his life several times."

"But a vision is a vision. I just felt it would come true."

"Sarah," Parkman said. "Since you started listening to Vivian, she's always shown you shit that was supposed to happen, and then you stopped it. That's what you do."

She looked at Aaron again. "I'm rusty. I felt it over the past few days. Just not myself after what happened last February." After a moment, she set her coffee cup down and looked at Darwin, then Parkman. "I've been more emotional lately. I don't mind, but sometimes it sucks, muddies my thinking. Anyway, after everything that's happened, I feel more myself now."

"Good."

"Although, I still can't figure out why Vivian had me fill in an organ donor form for Texas online before I came here."

"When you stopped that truck of people by Laredo, did you know why you were here?" Parkman asked.

She shook her head. "No, I didn't know until after the kidnapping thing at the airport. Vivian's been strangely absent."

"Then it makes sense to me. She was trying to tell you who True Legacy was by getting you to fill out the organ donor form online. That's it. You weren't supposed to die here, especially not donate your organs. Maybe one day, but not this time."

"That's probably all it was."

"Have you heard from her since this all ended?"

Sarah stared at them, studying their faces. "Once," she

said.

"And?" Darwin said. "Anything you can tell us?"

She looked down at the hand that held Aaron's and waited a moment.

"She said that I was needed again."

"So soon?"

Sarah shook her head slowly and turned to them. "In about a month. Something about planes and airports."

"More kidnappings?"

"Not sure. All she said was that I would be on *The Hunt*, whatever that means."

"*The Hunt*?"

Sarah nodded. "But it's not until next month. Something happens at the airport. She said she would tell me more when we get home in a week or two."

"You going to listen to her or hang up your psychic shoes?" Parkman asked.

Sarah waited a full minute before answering. "I've decided to do it," she said finally. She tightened her free hand into a fist when she turned their way. "I can't sit idly by or even *think* about bringing a child into this world if I have a chance to deal with people like Grappa Man, and I don't do it. Going forward, I've decided to work with Vivian as much as possible, and I will need all the help I can get."

Parkman smiled wide and withdrew a toothpick from his back pocket. He shoved it in his mouth, tossed it around with his tongue, and then said, "Sarah, if there's anything we can take away from Texas, it would be how everyone helped. Without one of us doing what we did, lives would have been lost. We only wish we could've gotten in that suite before

Agent Sullivan was shot."

"She's tough. That woman has been in and out of the hospital before. She'll survive for many more years to come. I have faith, and so does Vivian."

"Good, because you may need her again."

"Yeah, you never know. It sure adds meaning to that saying about it taking a village."

"What's that about a village?" Aaron asked.

Sarah started at his voice and got to her feet. "Honey, you're awake." She planted a couple of fast kisses on his lips.

"Sarah, my chest. Take it easy."

"Baby, you can take a little pain. Don't whine. It's unbecoming." She shot Parkman and Darwin a look. They both got up and stepped from the room.

Sarah climbed onto the bed and snuggled up beside him as he moaned when the bed moved.

"That prophecy of me dying," Aaron said.

"Yeah."

"Stop moving. You're fucking … killing me."

Sarah laughed with a devious snarl at the end of it, then moved her leg an inch.

"Fuck's sake," he whispered.

"Love you, honey."

How would she tell him that *The Hunt* was on in a few weeks and there was no going back?

She wiped a tear as Aaron's breathing returned to a regular rhythm. Would they ever settle down, have a baby, or raise a family?

It was something she wanted to talk to Vivian about.

As soon as she could.

Afterword

DEAR READER,

In my opinion, there are two kinds of writers. Some authors outline a novel, and authors who don't. We call them plotters (outliners who prepare the plot) and pantsers (non-outliners who don't prepare the plot and often have no idea where the story is going until it gets there, thereby writing from the seat of their pants—pantsers).

I'm a pantser.

I make it up as I go because I don't have an outline. They are sometimes called "free writers" because we just write freely.

Let me explain a little more, but I'm issuing a spoiler alert before you read further.

Below are plot points you probably shouldn't keep

reading if you haven't finished this novel.

When I first thought about this novel, I had an image of Sarah showing up to stop the truck smuggling people across the border. That was where it started for me. Since Sarah had been away for almost two years, I wanted her to return on the scene (think on camera as that's how I see a lot of what I write in my head) in style, showing up out of the dark, fighting, moving fast, dealing with the issue, then disappearing. Even while I thought about that scene, I was already mentally cheering her on when she rose from the dirt to attack Alejandro.

So, at that point, I had my first scene.

And I started writing—no outline, nothing prepared. Just a man driving a truck. Somehow, I had to get José to drive onto the dirt so Sarah could jump up and attack Alejandro, and there you have it. Scene one happened for me as it happened for you. Sarah *freaked* me out, too! When Alejandro's arm broke, I had chills. In my head, I could hear the snap of the elbow. Damn!

This is because I don't plot anything, I don't have an outline, and I have no idea what's coming next—Sarah's novels always play out while I write them. I've often felt like I'm the first reader because I'm reading the novel while typing it.

When I'd reached the 25,000-word mark in the novel, I had no idea how to save Aaron's life. One of my writing rules is asking myself, "How can I make it worse?" With that in mind, I wanted Sarah to have a vision that Aaron would be killed. I knew I would avoid his death (I can't kill Aaron … well, not yet anyway—cue devilish author laugh), but I had no idea how to save his life yet, nor did I even know how he was supposed to be killed.

While writing the novel, I don't often worry too much about that stuff because opportunities to kill characters always come up when I'm thinking about how to make things worse.

By 35,000 words, the idea of the two vans going in opposite directions came to me. One held Aaron, and one held the preschoolers. Making Sarah choose after what happened in February would definitely make things worse for her. I thought how great it would be to have Aaron's life as her responsibility, yet she would have to save the kids. There, I was done, prophecy fulfilled.

But I couldn't kill Aaron.

So, I had a dilemma. How do I stop the bomb that's in Aaron's van? Well, make it so there isn't a bomb in his van. Place it in Sarah's Buick. Perfect! And on and on, it goes when you don't write from an outline. I just make shit up all day long and type, type, type.

Back when Sarah told Parkman about her plan to save Aaron, I had no idea what that plan was. I just knew someone had to have a plan because I certainly didn't have one.

Then I got it.

She would call in a tip about the motel and get Aaron taken into police custody, where he would be safe.

At one point, I thought the scene with the two vans would end the book, but then I saw an image of a high-rise building and thought it would be great to have Alex scale it.

Finally, you have a novel.

I write five days per week, Monday to Friday, taking

weekends off to ruminate on the plot, where it's going, where it's been, and what else I can do. Often, on Monday mornings, I fix things that aren't sitting well with me and rewrite a few scenes to get my head in the game. But then I'm at it, and I have a word count each day that I refuse to miss. I don't beat myself up if I cannot hit my daily word count. I just pick it up the next day. If it's a Friday, then I end up writing on the weekend because I refuse to start a new week of writing already down words. While writing this novel, there was only one day where I came in short of my word count, but it was picked up the next day. I was short by two hundred words, mentally exhausted, and found myself staring at the ceiling of my office, saying out loud, "Now what?"

Yes, there are days I have no idea what's coming next as I don't have a plan or an outline. I've been found to wander the house, nap, eat, drink, and wait for something to come. Fingers hovering over the keyboard, blank screen in front of me, aching for inspiration. And guess what? It always comes. Always.

And the novel gets written every time. Writing this way has a natural, organic feeling—yet every writer is different.

Author Andrew Gross has been known to create up to eighty pages of outline before he begins his actual novel writing. He credits this outlining technique to James Patterson, a famous outliner. James Patterson says, "I always know what I need to write on any given day. I want to control the plot. I don't want the plot controlling me."

Whereas author Lee Child is famous for not outlining anything. He says, "I don't even know what I'm going to write in the next paragraph."

I've been there, staring at the screen, wondering what the hell my characters are doing, and having no idea what's coming.

With all that said, I find it quite thrilling to write the way I do. As it happened for you while reading it, it happened for me while I wrote it. When Sarah turned left and chased after the van with the kids and tried to make peace with her decision, I cried. That was so hard to write after all she'd been through. It was so hard for me to watch Alex being tossed from the roof, even though, by that point, I'd decided to have Parkman and Darwin in those hoods. (I wasn't exactly sure how it was them yet, but I knew it had to be)

You're probably getting a firm grip on how I write a novel. Good, because damn it all to Hell, I still have no idea!

Ultimately, it feels like the novel is already written, and I'm just the fingers that type as the novel channels through me. Sure, it all comes from me, and sure, I'm the author, but I'll be damned if I'm not surprised every other chapter by something happening that I had no idea was coming. This leaves me feeling as if it wasn't my doing, yet obviously, it was like someone from the other side is channeling novels through me.

Could my dead brother be to me what Vivian is to Sarah?

No, he couldn't. My brother wasn't a reader, nor was he a writer.

Speaking of the dead, let's discuss the novel itself. As you are all aware, this is a work of fiction. That said, organ donation is wonderful and has helped hundreds of thousands of people worldwide lead better lives. I do not know any single company perverting human procurement to the level of True Legacy. That was all made up after I'd read an article on organ donation. While reading that piece, I said to myself, "Hey, wouldn't it be great if a human procurement company got greedy and began *creating* its own supply?"

Allow me to qualify that sentence. When I say "great," I mean, "wouldn't it be a great story" for a novel, a thriller? Not great in the sense of how wonderful it really would be.

Off-topic: this brings to mind a debate I once had in the eleventh grade with the principal of my school. We argued in her office (I can't recall her name) about the use of the "Great" when calling World War I the "Great War." I asked how it could be so great after all the lives lost. She tried to explain that the definition of *great* in this sense was more about how large and intense it was. Well, I wasn't listening to that and explained that others weren't reading it that way. Eventually, I recall being given two options: return to class and let it go or head home for a three-day break to cool my jets. I headed back to class. To this day, I still don't like calling it the Great War.

Back on topic: I've dedicated this novel to "Old Friends," and I want to mention who they are. I met Patrick Besteman in the eighth grade, who would become one of my best friends. I had many friends growing up, as we all do, and I'm still in touch with dozens of them—some are even new authors like David Darling, and others are terrific writers like Chris Luttrell and Ryan Burdett.

During the writing of this novel, my friend Patrick Besteman died.

He had been on dialysis for approximately eight years

after being diagnosed with kidney issues. Patrick died eleven days before he turned fifty years old on November 14, 2019.

Organ donation works. Patrick would still be here if a match had been found in time.

One last thing to say about my friend. Patrick's father passed away two months before he did. I don't recall his father's age exactly, but I'm sure he was around ninety-six. Patrick had been caring for his father at home for over a decade.

He remained honorable until the end.

With all my traveling, I was fortunate to see Patrick in Toronto during the summer of 2014. We had lunch, chatted, and caught up on each other's lives. I didn't know that was the last time I would see him.

We messaged several times over the years since then, and he sent me a heartwarming message in August 2017, when my mother died. He remembered her well.

Goodbye, Patrick. Rest well, my friend. We'll hang out again one day, I'm sure.

The eleventh grade was important for me because it was when I registered my first business. John Gazior, another dear friend, started a window cleaning company with me. It was called "Windows Plus" because we did more than just clean windows.

Free estimates, business cards, and flyers were all done on John's home computer, and distribution of those flyers was handed out to houses in dozens of city blocks by the two of us.

Man, we made a lot of money that first summer. We even did our business class teacher's house up near an area called

Port Perry.

I randomly bumped into John in Mexico in 2009. Hadn't seen him since the nineties. He was looking good.

It was the last time I would see John Gazior alive. His body was found in a creek in the city he lived in about a year ago.

We all lose people close to us. The older we get, it seems, the more people we lose.

Much of what I included in this novel was true and fact-based. Laws protect human procurement companies except in cases of extreme wrongdoing, but good luck trying to prove that. And yes, human procurement companies have indeed made mistakes. Sometimes, the cause of death cannot be determined due to a procurement company's negligence, even though the person had been murdered. Sometimes, a procurement company comes in and causes changes to bodies that medical examiners mistake as injuries or abuse. Other times, these changes are the reason murder charges are dropped.

Human skin really does sell for the amount mentioned by Brian Glenmark in this novel. There are many cases before the courts regarding procurement companies, and there most likely always will be. But in the end, the lives they've saved outweigh the errors, according to the laws of our nations.

That's why procurement companies have contracts with hospitals and morgues and access government websites searching for cadavers to feed the ongoing need for tissues, ligaments, skin, hearts, and kidneys.

Research it yourself, look into it, and decide to donate. Or don't.

But consider this: what will you do with it once you're gone?

I need to thank the people who contributed their names to this project.

Firstly, I want to thank Melanie Hallford Sullivan. Great job trying to keep Sarah and Aaron safe! I loved what you did. Thanks to Gigi Walentiny for being Sullivan's partner and coming in at the end to clean up the mess in True Legacy's thirtieth-floor suite.

Thank you to Rose Marie Van Dee for being an investigative journalist. And Nancy Bibb for being a great flight attendant. And finally, thanks to Maura Eskenas Meats for helping Parkman and Darwin save everyone. When you got Eugene Wallson that glass of gold grappa, I yearned for one, too, but had to fulfill my word count for the day before any of that kind of drinking could occur.

Oh, and, of course, a huge thank you goes to Detective Marina Diner, who has shown up again to help Sarah just when she needed a friend at the airport. Marina was in book thirteen, *The Unlucky*. Sometimes, it's necessary to bring characters from previous books forward to pitch in when needed. Isn't that right, Buck Tuell?

Lastly, I have to thank Courtney Warnecke. She emailed me to explain that her mother was born in Kansas City, Kansas, and had grown up in Texas. Her mother's car is described as ice blue, but because of her mother's southern drawl, she pronounces it "ass blue."

The things Courtney's mother did for her kids to give them a life and to find success in their lives were remarkable. I wanted to honor her with a surprise sighting in this novel.

Courtney's mother had no idea she was a guest character until she read the novel.

So thank you, Suzann Scott, for helping Sarah at the airport when she needed to stop that plane. Calling out a bomb threat in an airport is dangerous business, but you proved you were a badass, and I love you for it. Thank you, Suzann Scott, for all that you are. We need more people like you in this world.

A special thanks have to go out to all of my proofreaders and editors as well. Without them, this novel would have many more mistakes than it has. Wait, what? Are there errors? Well, they say almost no book is error-free. So, if you see any, they're my fault, and I apologize for them.

Until next time, check out *The Hunt*, Sarah Roberts book 22. As mentioned above, I'm a pantser, so I have no idea what it's going to be about other than Sarah is "hunting" the people responsible for what happens at the Toronto International Airport. So far, just like the scene with José's truck in this novel, all I can see right now is that image of what's about to happen. I know nothing else. But yet, that novel will be written.

I'll have to wait and see what Vivian tells me. Or perhaps it's my brother …

Until then, take care of yourself and your loved ones.

Get caught reading.

I'm eternally grateful to you, my dear reader.

Jonas Saul

About Jonas Saul

Jonas Saul is the bestselling author of the Sarah Roberts Series—more than two million sold!—and has written and published over sixty thrillers. After acquiring an agent, he signed several deals in Los Angeles, with MadRiver Pictures optioning his Sarah Roberts Series— over forty books!—(currently in development).

Jonas has often outranked Stephen King and Dean

Koontz on Amazon over the past decade. He's regularly invited to be a guest speaker, teacher, or workshop presenter at international writing conferences and film festivals worldwide. He hosts an annual writer's retreat in Greece, where he currently lives. He focuses his teaching on how to get tension and emotion in every scene, on every page, how he made it as a creator/writer, the path to success in this business, and the pitfalls to avoid. He also hosts a reading retreat in Greece with guest authors, yoga retreats, and hiking retreats. Visit the Imagine Greece Retreats website at www.imaginegreeceretreats.com, or email him directly to discuss an opportunity to join one of the retreats at jonas@imaginegreeceretreats.com.

Jonas is also a professional freelance editor. He works for several publishers and does private editing for clients, with many testimonials on his website at www.imaginepress.org, which details each author's response to Jonas's editing skills. Email Jonas directly for an editing quote at editor@imaginepress.org.

To book Jonas for a speaking engagement at a writer's conference/festival, to have him on your jury at a film festival, or even to say hello, email Jonas directly at jonassaul@icloud.com.

For updates on releases, hit the "Follow" button on Amazon or Bookbub, and join Jonas on Facebook, where he's most active.

Contact Jonas Saul

Linktree: Find me here

Email: jonassaul@icloud.com